damaged
DOLL

Jennifer Bene

The Beth Series

Breaking Beth

Damaged Doll

Scarred Siren

DAMAGED DOLL

JENNIFER BENE

ISBN (e-book): 978-1-946722-64-5

ISBN (paperback): 978-1-946722-65-2

Cover design by Laura Hidalgo,
https://www.spellbindingdesign.com/.

ONE

Beth

___

She felt like she was underwater. Floating in emptiness, with no ground to stretch her toes out for and no air to swim toward.

It was endless… but not in a peaceful way. Someone had told her once that drowning was peaceful, that the brain gave a sense of euphoria as the lungs filled up with water, but Beth had never felt anything like that.

No calm. No peace.

Just a flickering memory of panic, and an absolute fear of the surface.

Survival was supposed to be an instinct, and she knew she should *want* to reach the surface. To breathe air again, to stop suffocating in the dark… but all she ever did was dive deeper. The deeper she went, the easier it was to block out the flickering glimpses of things happening above. All the sounds, the textures, the sensations. The things that were so much worse than drowning.

But it got exhausting to stay down when her body wanted to be buoyant, wanted air, wanted freedom. A constant fight, a battle for depth whenever the water got rough, and the waves turned the distant surface into chaos.

It was happening again.

That steady rise to the surface that brought back the panic, heart pounding in her ears as she became aware of the world outside the water. She wanted to dive down, to hide from the pull, but she was so fucking tired — and then there were the voices.

Muffled, blurred by the water for a while... until she got closer. As the light grew brighter, and she started to feel, she could hear them. Too many.

And him.

His voice always stood out the strongest, even though it was always calm. Cold and calm. Just like the water farther down, where she was safer... but she wasn't safe up here.

Surfacing was always bad. Always.

If she reacted, if she made a sound, then they'd know she *could*. Then the storm on the surface would just get worse, it would be harder to swim down with the water too rough. Harder to hide.

Despite her best efforts to avoid it, the light got stronger, the world coming toward her, and she clenched her teeth tight to stay silent, to avoid the urge to scream or fight.

And then she broke the surface, instinctively pulling at the cable around her wrist, tethering her to the bed —

but it was better to be connected to the bed. Out of the bed was always worse. Out of the bed meant there might be someone new, somewhere new, which always meant pain.

Although the surface was always painful, and she did her best to brace for it as her mind joined her body, as her eyes focused on the light, and she felt the texture of sheets against her back and thick plastic around her wrist and—

Curtains. Pale purple.

A poster of a boy band.

She was home.

She kept forgetting she was home, that she didn't have to stay under anymore, didn't have to fight the surface or feel the panic. Of course, knowing it didn't keep her heart from racing, or her nails from digging into her palms as she pulled at the zip-tie around her wrist.

Shuffling back to the headboard, Beth ignored the wad of sheets she'd kicked to the bottom of the bed during her nightmares and leaned over to turn on the lamp with her free hand. Flinching against the light, she pulled out the drawer of the bedside table and dug around blindly until she found what she needed.

Taking out the scissors, she focused on the sharp edge of them for a moment, distracted by the way the light glinted off the angles. She wasn't suicidal, not really, but the thought still crept in sometimes. Especially when the nightmares were still fresh. Taking a breath, she pushed away the dark thoughts and slid the scissors under the thick plastic of the zip-tie. One snip and she was out, but her wrist was red, and her heart was still pounding. It always took a while to readjust when she woke up. To get over the constant underlying panic that felt like ants crawling under her skin on the better days, and like glass in her veins on the worst.

"You're home. You're safe. You're free," she whispered as she put the scissors and the broken zip-tie in the drawer and shoved it closed. Pulling her knees to her chest, Beth wrapped her arms around them and repeated it. "You're home. You're safe. You're free."

Ailsa kept telling her that the daily mantra would help her, but she wasn't convinced. Sure, the other girls had posted that they were improving, doing better. Some of them had jobs, were living on their own again, a few had even started relationships.

And she couldn't even go to sleep without her wrist tethered to the fucking bed.

Not that the other girls didn't have problems. They were all screwed up in their own ways, but Beth still felt different. More broken. Where the others talked about waking up screaming, fighting monsters from their memories, Beth never did that. She couldn't relate to it. Sure, she woke up panicked, felt like someone was crushing her lungs, like her heart was trying to bust through her ribcage… but she was always quiet.

Mostly still. As soon as the sheets were off her anyway.

Ailsa wanted her to believe she was free, but she didn't feel free. She couldn't handle anything on her while she slept, not even clothes. So, even though she was home, even though she was safe, she still slept naked, still slept restrained. But it was the only way she *could* sleep, so… how was that free?

But Thalia had managed it. She'd somehow moved past the damaged parts of herself, figured out how to actually *live*. She'd gotten married, she was happy, she was *functional*. Other girls were getting closer to it too, making real progress… while Beth was still at step one.

Or less.

Grabbing the iPad from the charging cable, she put it on the bed in front of her and logged into the forum. It was secure, only accessible with one of the tablets Thalia and James had provided, and that was the only reason that Beth continued to use it. Because even though every one of their stories was different, at least the other women behind those usernames understood. Some of them had only known Anthony, some had known Marcus too, but all of them had suffered. They knew the pain, the shame.

They knew the rules the bastards had tried to make her learn. Obey.

Their little forum was a safe place. A place without judgment, without awkward glances or uncomfortable pauses, where everyone could be honest because the others understood in a way no one else could. Ailsa was the only one with access who hadn't been taken, and it had taken time to trust the woman. But Thalia had explained her presence and who she was to everyone. A close friend, a family friend, and a therapist who knew everything that Thalia had gone through and was helping her deal with the PTSD — *without* judgment.

In the almost two years since Beth had first logged in, Ailsa had been the only therapist she'd actually spoken to about her experiences. Her parents kept trying new ones, but she would only sit in their offices. Silent. Waiting for the time to end so she could go back home. She didn't want to talk about what happened with strangers, and she definitely didn't want to tell her parents, no matter how many times her mom offered to listen. It was bad enough they had a broad understanding of what happened to her... details wouldn't help anyone. Not her, not a therapist, and definitely not her parents.

Still, Beth held out hope that they'd eventually give up and leave her to work with Ailsa on the tiny amounts of progress she'd made. *Maybe.*

Skimming the recent posts, the photos, the comments, Beth liked seeing the other women sharing their accomplishments. The 'small wins' that Ailsa told them they had to celebrate together, but it left an empty feeling in Beth's stomach. She never had anything to share. Not since they'd let her go home from the hospital, and it felt like the more time that passed, the further ahead everyone was getting from her. Not that it was a race, or that any of them were even heading toward the same place, but if she could just have *something* get better. Anything.

Maybe she wouldn't feel so... *empty*.

Beth locked the iPad without posting and plugged it back in before she stood to get dressed. It was only a little after six o'clock in the morning, but she knew both of her parents would be downstairs, and it took a deep breath and a conscious effort to unlock the deadbolts on her bedroom door.

Heading for the bathroom, she left the light off as she brushed her teeth, washed her face, and then put her hair up in a ponytail.

Even when she'd run out of things to do in the bathroom, she hesitated to go downstairs. Her parents loved her, she knew that down to her core, and she was incredibly lucky to have them, to have her entire family there for her, wanting to help, wanting to show her how much they loved her. But most days it was just... too much.

Glancing at the mirror in the dim light from the hall, she tried to smile, but she couldn't look at herself for very long. The girl in the mirror didn't feel like *her* anymore. Ailsa called it depersonalization, another side effect of the trauma, but having names for things didn't make them any better.

Beth clenched her jaw tight, eyes closed as she tried to let go of the lingering emotions from whatever nightmare she'd had. She didn't want to remember it. She just wanted the feeling of panic to go away, to feel like she could go downstairs without one, or both, of her parents asking her if she was okay.

Fuck it.

Heading downstairs, she could hear her parents talking in the kitchen and she tried to make enough noise that they would stop talking about her and effectively change the subject before she walked into the kitchen. Not that she could hear them yet, but she was almost always the topic of their early morning conversations. *Would Beth have a bad day today? Should they try a new therapist? Should they change her medications? Were they doing what they were supposed to?*

What happened? What happened? What happened?

They never asked the last question anymore, but it was a constant undercurrent in every awkward talk, every overly intense look. She cleared her throat as she rounded the corner from the stairs, and they fell quiet just before she passed through the doorway where both of them were waiting for her.

"Good morning, honey!" The cheery tone of her mom's voice was clearly forced, but it was how her mom handled the stress of having a broken daughter in the house, and Beth had given up months ago on getting her to act 'normal.'

Apparently, no one got to be normal ever again because of what had happened.

"Morning, Mom." Walking over, Beth hugged her first so her mom would know it was okay today. They still avoided touching her without asking, even though constantly having to give them permission was more exhausting than dealing with the surprise panic on the bad days.

"Did you sleep well?" her mom asked, squeezing her tight and patting her back lightly before she let go.

"Yep," Beth lied, holding onto the edges of her sleeves so that the redness on her wrist could fade without them noticing it.

"Good. I was going to make pancakes. How does that sound? Or we could have—"

"Pancakes sound good, Mom. Thanks." Beth forced a smile and moved toward the coffee maker, but her dad made it there first, refilling his cup as her mom looked between them.

"Did you want coffee, honey?" she asked, and her dad turned to look at her.

"Yeah, I—"

"Bill, why don't you make a cup for Beth too, okay?" Her mom was already rifling through the fridge for breakfast supplies when Beth looked at her, frustrated, but she wasn't willing to disturb the morning by arguing that she could do it herself.

"You like the sweet cream, right, pumpkin?" Dad gave her an apologetic smile as he handed her the cup of coffee with plenty of room for cream, just how she liked it.

"Yeah. Thanks, Dad." She offered a small smile to him before her mom stepped close with the creamer in hand.

"Just tell me when." Pouring the creamer *for* her, Beth had to wait until her mom added enough before raising her hand.

"That's good. Thanks." She blew over the top of the coffee, cooling it down as she took her normal seat at the kitchen table. Her mom continued bustling around making breakfast, but her dad eventually joined her.

"You've got that appointment with Dr. Hernandez this afternoon. You liked her last time, right?" He was trying to be positive, smiling at her, and she knew the answer he wanted, but all she really wanted to do was climb back into bed.

"Can we reschedule?" she asked softly.

Her dad sighed, glancing back over his shoulder at her mom before he faced forward again. "I don't know, pumpkin. We can see what your mom thinks."

That means no.

It was pointless to try and argue. If she pushed too hard, they'd just push back, wanting answers about how she was feeling and what was wrong and why she didn't like Dr. Hernandez... and she just didn't have the energy for that.

Instead, they just sat in awkward silence for too long, both of them sipping from their mugs, and *this* was exactly why Beth wanted to hide in her room all the time.

She'd been back home for over a year and a half now, and they still treated her like the wrong word, or the wrong movement, could send her spiraling back into catatonic land.

Which was possible.

That was the most frustrating thing for her. She hated being treated like she was fragile... but she was. She'd survived and, according to everyone else on the planet, that was supposed to feel like some grand accomplishment — but it never did.

Having a pulse and managing to breathe consistently wasn't an achievement, it was an accident. A fluke. A statistical anomaly. That's all she was... an unlikely outcome to a horrible situation, and she'd never felt like that was worth celebrating.

No matter how many times her mom called it a 'miracle.'

Ailsa understood better than most people, and she always said that struggling with coming home was normal, but even she kept telling her and the other survivors that they had to figure out how to truly live.

But Beth had no idea where to begin.

Sure, she was alive, but she felt like a ghost in her own life. Haunting her parents' house, her sister, and the rest of her family.

Hell, she was haunting *herself*.

Most days she didn't even feel real. She couldn't recognize the reflection in the mirror, couldn't remember how she got any of the new scars on her skin, and even though she kept a band-aid over the tattoo Anthony had put on her hip — because she hated looking at it — at least she knew who'd put it there.

Everything else from those four years was just... buried. All the memories so waterlogged that even the random scraps that managed to surface had no context, just fear, panic, and rage, usually quickly followed by her getting sick. There was no progress to be made in the mess of her head, and without progress she'd never get 'better.' She'd never be one of the girls to find a way to live, or get a job, or a place of her own, or fall in love.

No, there was no chance of that. She was too broken for love.

She was probably too broken to ever do more than survive.

TWO

Jake

_____

The asshole actually tried to run, but Mike had caught him easily and Jake could hear him dragging the cursing, panicked motherfucker back through the house. A high-pitched yelp came from behind him, and he turned to see Benny holding the girl, Ashley, against his chest. Protecting her.

With a single tilt of his head, Benny relayed his unspoken question. _Want me to take her outside?_

Jake shook his head once, turning back just in time to see Mike throw the trash at his feet. The asshole tried to get up, but Mike landed his combat boot in the small of his back and pushed him down. Crouching slowly, Jake stared at him like he had all the time in the world. Which, he did.

Another squeak of pure terror from behind him, and if he hadn't gone so cold on the inside just to be able to focus — he knew he would have turned to comfort her.

Help her. Show the girl she was safe. But that was Benny's job right now. His job was *proving* she was safe.

"Darren Pierce. Age thirty-six."

"Fuck you," the man spat, wheezing when Mike dug his heel in.

Chuckling low, Jake shook his head. "So, did you hurt her?"

"I want a fucking lawyer!" Darren yelled, earning a rough kick to the spine.

"Maybe it's hard to hear me with your face in the floor. Get him on his knees." As soon as the order was spoken, Jake stood up. Mike hauled the fucker upright, and Charlie grabbed his arm when he attempted a pathetic swing. For a moment, Jake couldn't take his eyes off the girl. She had bruises around her throat, reddened wrists that one look from Benny confirmed what he'd already guessed.

"I said I want a fucking law—"

A hard right to the asshole's jaw cut him off, and Jake smirked as the man groaned and spat onto the dirty linoleum. "Fresh out of lawyers."

"You can't do this!" Darren argued, as if he had any rights in this place, with Jake or his team.

"I think you're confused, asshole. Do we look like cops to you?" The question lingered in the air for a moment as the son of a bitch finally looked at them — *really* looked at them — and Jake saw the moment he realized that it hadn't been the police who showed up at his secret house. His face fell, all of that useless rage disappearing because he was facing six well-armed men and not a petite, nineteen-year-old girl.

"I-I-I—"

"I asked you a question. Did you hurt her?" A moot point, really, but he wanted him to admit it. Not for them, but for Ashley. Everything that was about to happen was for Ashley.

"Fuck you," Darren growled.

"Get the tarp, Brendan." His tone was calm because *he* wasn't the one about to get shot in the head.

"HELP!" Darren had the balls to actually shout for someone to save him. And then he did it again, at the top of his lungs.

Charlie raised an eyebrow from behind him, asking for permission, and Jake gave it with a flick of his wrist. The thick *crack* of a semi-automatic slamming into the back of Darren's skull was satisfying for everyone in the room — except for the stalker, turned kidnapper, turned *probably* rapist. Clenching his jaw, Jake looked over at Ashley, at the wide-eyed, trembling fear as she squeezed her thighs together, covered only in a tank top and pale underwear, clinging to Benny's vest.

Definitely a rapist.

"Lift him up," Jake snapped. Mike already had the asshole by the hair when he deigned to look at him again. Rolling his shoulder, Jake hit him again, and again, and again, until the bastard could only spit blood and groan, the first pathetic sound of a sob leaving him. Flexing his fingers, Jake stood tall and turned his back on the monster, blocking Ashley's view of him as he took one careful step closer to her. "Hey, Ashley. I just need to know one thing, and you don't have to say it out loud. Just nod or shake your head, okay?"

She nodded, but she also slid back from him. *Understandable.* He probably looked like he was about to kill someone... because he was.

"No matter what, when you walk out that door, I swear to you, you'll never see this bastard again. You won't ever have to worry about him. He's gonna be gone." A choked sound came from behind him, and he was sure it was one of the guys making sure Darren didn't ruin this moment with his retching or crying. "But you can stay, watch, if you need to see. So that you *know* he's gone. Or, my friend Benny here can walk you outside, get you tucked into the car, and you can wait for us to take you back home."

Wide-eyed, still not breathing right, only taking little sips of air into lungs that whined from the effort, Ashley watched him, her gaze flicking across his face and then to his men behind him.

"There's no wrong answer here, Ashley. This is about what you need. So, do you want to stay?" He waited, watched her for a hint of an answer. "Do you want to go outside and wait with Benny?"

No answer. Her eyes were glued past him.

Trying to soften his tone, he took a half step closer, and her eyes snapped back to him so fast he froze. Hands lifted, showing her his palms, he focused on sounding gentle when he was anything but. "It's okay. You're safe now. I promise."

Ashley nodded, and Benny gave him the same look he always did. Protective, borderline mutinous. But in the last year or two, Jake had learned something very, *very* important about women in these situations. Sometimes the knowledge that their nightmare was over wasn't enough, sometimes they needed to see it end... or it never really went away.

"Do you wanna stay?" he asked again, quietly, and this time he got a stiff nod. Just a quick tuck of her chin to her chest, and he gave her a small smile in return. Reassuring, accepting, judgment free.

Hell, he was the one about to torture what someone might loosely call a human being.

The rustling sound of plastic heralded Brendan's return, and Charlie and Mike immediately hauled Darren to his feet, dragging him out of the way so that Brendan and Ollie could lay it out. "No! No, no... I have money, I have—" Darren's pleading was cut off by Charlie's hand around his throat, choking without mercy because the asshole didn't deserve it.

One more look at Ashley as he rolled his shoulders. "Two things. You decide when it's over, and you decide when you want to go. Just tug twice on Benny's sleeve and he'll take you outside."

A nod.

"One more question. Does he deserve to suffer?"

"Yes," she whispered without hesitation, the word trailing into a hiss that pulled her lips back from her teeth as she stared at the monster who had ruined her world for a while. Turned it into a nightmare. They hadn't got to her fast enough to prevent all of it, he couldn't erase her four and a half days with Darren Pierce, but Jake could give her *something* back. He could give her this.

"Done." He nodded at the plastic and his men dragged Darren onto it, the edges kicked flat by Charlie and Ollie as Mike locked cuffs around the asshole's wrists.

Jake didn't say another word to the trash in front of him, he just hit him until his hand started to burn, his knuckles aching in warning that he needed to back off, and then Charlie stepped in. He started off with a hard kick straight between the asshole's legs, and the guttural groan was still less than the monster deserved. Charlie took his time between punches, shaking his fingers out before lining up again to make each one count. Mike clocked him with a knee to the back of the head when the asshole had the balls to lean back against him.

This was the part of the job that made them all feel a bit better, and he knew the guys needed it.

Lifting his chin toward Charlie, the man stepped back, and Brendan tapped in, delivering a series of lefts that *almost* balanced out the muddled bone structure of the bastard's face. But then, just as Ollie popped open his knife to have some real fun, Benny cleared his throat. Turning to look at him, Jake saw that Ashley was hiding her face.

She hadn't tugged, or Benny would have already walked her out, or carried her if she was past it.

Still, it was done.

Bracing a hand on Ollie's shoulder, he eased the disappointed man back and took out his gun. "Your choice, Ashley. You don't have to look, but you can."

Flicking the safety off, he waited. He looked at Benny who was whispering to her, but she stayed curled into his bulletproof vest, clinging to the edges with a white-knuckle grip. Benny nodded once, and Jake tilted his head to make Mike move. Small caliber meant it may not go all the way through, but it was never smart to risk it.

This was where he took over.

Unless it was unavoidable, he always pulled the trigger. Each of the guys had blood on their hands, but he was their leader. The one who'd pulled them into this work, and it was dark on the best of days, and fucking hell on the worst. Carrying as many bodies on his conscience as he could — even if the bodies belonged to subhuman bastards like Darren Pierce — was the least he could offer them.

To his right, Ashley was still standing, but he'd given her more than enough time to make the choice. Raising the gun, he aimed, checked the angle, and fired.

One more dead asshole.

Even with the silencer, the shot was too loud in the quiet space. Ashley yelped, buckled, but Benny was there to catch her. Lifting her, he swung her around slowly, and Jake caught her reddened eyes as she saw the body that *had* been Darren Pierce. It was only a glance before she closed her eyes, but at least she'd seen.

She knew, and that was all that mattered.

Walking out of Ashley Hendricks' house, Jake couldn't decide how he felt.

The way her mother had sobbed and held onto her, cradling her on the couch like Ashley was still a little girl... that shit just never left his head. Her father, Patrick, had shaken his hand with tears in his eyes, thanking him and the guys over and over, but all Jake could think about was what they could have done better.

What mistakes did we make?

Where could we have moved faster?

How can we improve so that the next girl doesn't have to spend four days in hell?

Unfortunately, the world was full of enough monsters Jake never had to wonder *if* there would be a next girl. Sometimes he had to refer people to other teams because they were already working on a job when another desperate request came in. He never knew when the calls or emails would come, but they always did. In another week or two they'd be hunting down another monster, looking for another girl, and crossing all their fingers and toes they found her still breathing.

In the almost five years they'd been doing these kinds of jobs they'd returned eighteen women and five kids... but they'd failed nine victims. Nine people they hadn't found in time, and one of those they'd never found at all. Lisa Cantrell's picture was still tacked to the wall in the house, and whenever Jake found Brendan up late at night, the man was almost always looking for new information on her — unless they were on a job. But at least they'd been able to give the other eight families answers. The Cantrell family only had nightmares.

"What's up, Jake?" Charlie stopped beside him, glancing at him before he looked over at the guys getting back in the van.

"Nothing."

"Don't pull that shit with me, man." Charlie grabbed his shoulder, squeezing it. "We found her. She's back home. The bastard that took her is dead. What more could you hope to get out of a job?"

Shaking his head, Jake dropped his gaze to the stone walkway under his feet and Charlie gave him some space, removing his hand, but he knew the man wouldn't drop it. They all worried about him. "You saw her, Charlie. That's what four and a half days did to her." He wiped a hand over his face before he continued. "And why did it take us so long? His goddamn name was on the property."

"Brendan said the guy had a bunch of properties like that. Rundown shit he bought for cheap, scattered all around. There was no way to know that was the specific one he was using, or that we needed to focus on that area for cameras and shit."

He knew Charlie was right, and as much as he wanted there to be a simple answer, a clear way to fix this, to be faster next time… he knew Brendan had done everything he could. Every man on his team had done their best, like they always did. And he should probably just accept today as a win and move on, but the weight on his soul wouldn't shift. Every girl they found reminded him of Thalia, the one that had pushed him and his team into the more specialized field of abduction recovery. Not just kidnappings, but the even darker shit, the ones where there weren't any ransoms and the people who disappeared weren't ever supposed to come back home.

A whole world filled with psychopaths and sociopaths whose only goal was to ruin lives.

And Jake had shoved his team right in their path.

"You need a drink, boss," Charlie said, slapping him on the back before he tilted his head toward the van. "Come on."

"Tell me the truth, Charlie. Is this what the guys wanna keep doing?" he asked, meeting the man's gaze, but he only saw confusion, so he tried to explain. "There are other jobs we can take. You guys know that. Plenty of freelance shit we could be doing for money if—"

"Fuck off, Jake." Charlie grabbed a strap on his vest and hauled him toward the open side of the van where the rest of the team was busy talking. Slapping the side of the van shut them all up, everyone looking at Charlie as he finally let go and crossed his arms. "Apparently Jake's thinking about broadening the kind of jobs we take. Cutting down on *these* jobs and going for other freelance shit."

"Why?" Ollie asked, looking and sounding irritated by the suggestion… and then everyone exploded.

"You want us to start running black ops shit again?"

"Did something happen?"

"We just found this girl, why the fuck would we stop?"

The other guys' comments got caught up in the mix of voices and Jake groaned, running a hand through his hair before he held both hands up. "Okay, okay! Hey! Everybody shut up for a minute."

"Ready to explain yourself?" Charlie prompted him, leaning against the passenger door with a cocked eyebrow, and Jake grumbled.

"Look, I know we kind of stumbled our asses into this shit, and no matter what you guys say... these jobs are dark." Huffing, he tried to find the words he wanted to say, scratching at the back of his neck as the spring sun beat down on all the heavy, black gear he was still wearing. "Even when we find them, it's still dark. It's still shitty, and I know I got this team together, but I'm not a fucking dictator. We don't have to keep going down this road if you guys want a break."

"And go back to... what?" Mike looked around at everyone as he spread his arms. "Killing people for money? How is that any better?"

"Yeah, we're called mercenaries for a fucking reason, Jake. That shit is dark too," Ollie added on. "Not that I've got a problem if you want us on that again, but there's nothing easy about that shit either."

"That's why people pay us the way they do." Brendan chuckled, shrugging a shoulder. "We deal with the dark shit. At least with these girls we're trying to do something good."

Asaf reached over and rested a hand on Brendan's shoulder, nodding. "I think we've all got enough blood on our hands — right or wrong. These jobs mean something. Even when we fail, it still means more than running dark in some random country."

"The other guys might be okay with going back to the other shit, but…" Benny trailed off, shaking his head as he stared at the floor of the van with his arms braced on his knees. "I can't. *Won't.*"

"I'm with him," Charlie said, jerking a thumb toward Benny. "What about you, boss?"

Jake had let each of the guys speak, and he'd been prepared for at least one of them — like Ollie — to admit that they wanted to go back to the way things were four or five years back. Brendan hadn't been a part of the team back then, but things were simpler. Name and a photo and some random data that told the team who needed to die, and they made it happen.

Death was so much simpler than life. Less stressful.

But the guys didn't want simple, they didn't want to take the easy way out in this fucked-up job, and he couldn't deny the pride he felt that each of them were just as committed as he was.

"I think you guys already know how I feel about these jobs, and why I'm such an obsessive asshole when it comes to them." Looking around at the team, he couldn't help the way his mouth twitched up at the edge. "And I know we've all got blood on our hands, and each of you fucks may be twisted in your own ways, but you're good men and… I'm glad you're at my side — and that's all I'm saying about that shit! Let's swing by the liquor store to get some stuff to celebrate with tonight."

"Hell yeah!" Brendan shouted, and the other guys added their own approvals as they got comfortable while Jake walked around the van to get in the driver's side. Charlie climbed in the passenger side, grinning at him as he buckled up.

Jake glanced over, studying the shit-eating grin on Charlie's face as he cranked the engine. "What?"

"I just like reminding you that you can be wrong."

"Asshole," Jake muttered, but he couldn't bite back a chuckle when Charlie busted out laughing.

Yeah, they were a group of misfits with their own issues, but at the core they were the best men he'd ever worked with, and if they were still on board with the dark shit... then he'd stand beside them for as long as they wanted to do it.

THREE

Beth

"How have things been, Beth?" Dr. Hernandez asked, rephrasing the question for the third time since they'd sat down in her office seventeen minutes before.

Beth just offered a shrug, and the woman sighed.

"I want to help you, and I don't have an opinion about what that looks like. We both know that you're still dealing with the things that happened to you, but if you don't want to talk about those things with me yet, then we don't have to."

Glancing up at her, Beth studied the woman's face. She looked sincere with all that concern wrinkling her forehead, and she even sounded sincere, but the woman didn't want to know about what she'd eaten for breakfast, or what movie she'd watched with her parents earlier in the week. Everything about this room, this situation, had one goal — figure out why she was so fucking broken and try to fix it.

Well, *why* wasn't really the issue. It was more like *how* she'd been broken so that the woman could create some bullshit plan to put her back together again.

But it wouldn't work.

Nothing ever worked, and she was tired of trying. She didn't want to jump through any more hoops for therapists… or her parents. But saying *that* would only hurt their feelings more than she already did just by existing every day.

"Come on. Tell me one thing you did this week," Dr. Hernandez pressed. "Anything."

"I don't want to come here anymore," Beth whispered, and the woman sat up straighter in her seat, nodding.

"Okay, let's talk about why you feel that way. Is there something about the office that bothers you? Would you like to work with a different therapist?"

Beth shook her head, tracing patterns in the pillow she'd wedged onto her lap.

"What is it then?"

All she could do was sigh, because her parents already knew what she wanted, they just wouldn't listen to her. Her mom was convinced that the forum was only making her worse, that 'focusing on the trauma' was only slowing down her recovery, which was why she didn't want Beth to work with Ailsa. At least, not *only* Ailsa.

Her mom believed there was some magical cure for how damaged she was somewhere out there in the universe, that if they could just find the right therapist that Beth would be normal again.

Even though neither of her parents had ever said those words out loud… she knew it was the truth.

They'd been so happy to get her back, but they didn't actually get their daughter back. They got a damaged doll. A hollow, drowned, broken version of the girl she'd been before the Williams brothers had taken her, and there was no reversing the clock. She couldn't be that person, she barely remembered what it felt like to be Elizabeth Doherty. Fresh out of college, so excited to have her first job. That girl had a life. She'd had friends. She'd played volleyball on the weekends and went shopping with her mom and her older sister.

There wasn't anything left of that girl.

There were no pieces to patch back together, so talking to this woman wouldn't solve anything. It was a waste of both her and the therapist's time, a waste of her parents' money.

"Beth… please talk to me," Dr. Hernandez pleaded, leaning forward in her chair with an even more intense look of concern.

It wasn't like she didn't feel bad about being silent. The woman was just trying to do her job… but Beth was tired. She was tired of the pity, the concern, the constant attention focused on the worst things that had ever happened to her, and she didn't want to do it anymore.

Taking a breath, she made herself say the only thing that mattered right now. "I'd like to go home."

"Okay." Closing the notepad in her lap, Dr. Hernandez set it on her desk before looking at Beth again. "All I want is for you to find a path to whatever happiness looks like for you. If I can't help you get there, then I'm okay with that, but I don't want you to give up on yourself."

Nodding, Beth rose from the couch and put the pillow back. She debated telling the woman about Ailsa, about how the forum was the only thing that had been able to pull her out of the depths when she hadn't been able to function at all — but then Dr. Hernandez would ask what the forum was, and who Ailsa was, and she'd make her talk about the Williams brothers and the other girls and... *no.*

The woman opened her office door, holding it to the side so that she could leave, and Beth glanced at her as she walked into the waiting room, quietly adding, "Thanks."

When Beth turned around, her mom's face made her sick to her stomach. She looked like she was about to cry, her chin wobbling as she forced a smile and stood up from the chair.

"Did you finish early?" she asked, and although her mom tried to sound positive and happy, the way her voice cracked told the truth.

I'm horrible.

"I don't think I'm the right person for Beth, Mrs. Doherty." Dr. Hernandez looked between the two of them before smiling kindly at her mom. "I think that Beth might benefit from some time to herself, without any of me or my fellow psychologists meddling with her thought processes."

Beth jerked her head up, surprised by what the woman was saying, and there was a small flicker of hope in her chest that her mom might actually listen.

"The doctors at Greenwood said that getting her into therapy was a necessary next step for her recovery, and we've already tried—"

Dr. Hernandez raised a hand, and her mom went silent. "I understand, and I think for many patients that finding a good therapist post-treatment is important. However, I think that the most important thing for Beth right now is to spend some time discovering herself, which can be hard to do when other people are involved."

Maybe she actually gets it.

"Well… if-if that's what you suggest, then we'll absolutely talk about it at home. Thank you, Dr. Hernandez." Her mom nodded stiffly and then forced an uncomfortable smile as she looked at Beth, waving toward the door. "Come on, honey. Let's go."

"I'll be happy to talk on the phone if any of you have questions or would like some suggestions," Dr. Hernandez added as she followed them to the exit. Beth's mom just nodded at the woman, holding the door open, but Beth paused at the doorway and turned to face her.

"Thank you for understanding." Her voice was quiet but judging by the sudden sadness in the woman's face and the sound of a stifled sob from her mom, Beth knew they'd both heard her.

The conversation at home was going to be miserable, and her mom would definitely cry, which would probably end up with her parents arguing in their room after Beth went to bed.

All she did was cause trouble, tainting everything around her, *everyone* around her. Some days it was hard to believe that coming home from the facility had been the right decision. She hadn't wanted to live at the hospital, and they'd wanted her to come home, begged her to come home... but now her parents were miserable.

They'd probably be happy right now if she'd never been found. Sure, there would have been sadness when they had to declare her dead, but at least they could have mourned, they could have moved on. They could have lived their lives.

Now? They were trapped with her. She weighed everyone down like an anchor, dragging them to the bottom of the ocean where they couldn't live any more than she could.

If she'd never come back at all, the world would be a better place.

Everything would be better if she hadn't survived.

"I think we need something good for dinner tonight. Oh, pizza! We haven't had pizza in a while." Her mom wore that brittle smile like a shield as she pulled out of the parking garage and headed toward the highway. She was already trying to change the subject, to avoid all the things Dr. Hernandez had said just because they didn't fit in with what she wanted to happen.

Sliding down lower in the seat, Beth crossed her arms over her stomach and leaned her forehead against the window. The sun was bright, and it was another beautiful day in Carmel-by-the-Sea. Before all this, she probably would have been out playing volleyball somewhere, enjoying the day.

"Beth?" her mom prompted, still forcing that cheery tone into her voice. "Does pizza sound good?"

"Sure," she answered, speaking to the window. A moment later, her mom turned on the radio, but she still heard the hushed sniffle. Closing her eyes, she tried to give her mom space, to not look at her so that they could maintain the illusion that the pop song was covering up the sound of her crying.

It wasn't. Not even when her mom reached over and turned up the volume again.

The traffic was slow, and Beth pinched the inside of her arm as she tried to block out the sniffling coming from the driver's seat. She deserved to feel the pain, because she was causing her mom pain, and the zing as she twisted the delicate skin helped her hold her tongue. Bringing up Dr. Hernandez's suggestion would only make her mom feel worse, and she shouldn't do it.

She knew it was a bad idea, but the words kept pressing against the back of her teeth, and even when she dug her nails into her arm, she found her lips parting. "The doctor agreed with me."

"What, sweetheart?" Her mom sniffled, and Beth took a deep breath and turned to face her. Her mom's nose was red, a flush in her cheeks, and she was gripping the steering wheel too tight... but if she was going to try and get her mom to agree, this was her chance.

"Dr. Hernandez. She agreed with me, with what I've been saying about—"

"That's just her opinion, honey. There are plenty of doctors who take their jobs seriously." Wiping a hand under her nose, her mom glanced at her with that fragile smile. "We'll find someone who can help you, who *wants* to help you."

No. Beth clenched her jaw, digging her nails into her arm as she tried to contain the rush of frustration and anger at being ignored for the millionth time, but it just wasn't working today. "I don't want to see any more doctors. I just want to work with Ailsa on the forum and—"

"That forum isn't helping you, Elizabeth. You need outside perspective, and we can—"

"Forcing me to go to all these doctors isn't helping me!" she snapped and immediately regretted raising her voice as her mom's chin wobbled, another sniffle following that made her feel even worse. Shaking her head, Beth slumped against the window again, tears burning at the edges of her eyes.

After a minute or two, her mom reached over and turned down the radio. "If... if you don't want to see another doctor right now, we can maybe take a break for a while."

Glancing up at her mom, she was surprised to hear her finally giving in, but there was so much tension in her shoulders and her grip on the wheel as she stared straight ahead. Still, she was about to thank her when her mom took a deep breath.

"But you're going to have to talk about everything, Beth. Eventually." She wiped tears off her cheeks, her voice shaking. "You can always talk to me if you don't want to talk to a doctor right now… I just want to help you, honey. All I want is to help you get better."

Listening to her mom's voice break was torture, but there was no way she could talk to her about any of it. They could barely look at each other right now, and if she let her see just how broken she was — it would hurt her mom too much.

"You were making progress at Greenwood, maybe we could…" The words trailed off, but Beth's stomach tightened anyway. She didn't want to be locked in there again. She didn't want to have to jump through all the hoops to get back out again. Hours of therapy, hours of group. Even more drugs, sedatives on the nights she got upset, and no zip-ties to help her sleep. She'd had to use a pair of underwear to feel connected to the bed, to feel secure enough to sleep, and even that much was too risky there.

"I can't go back there," she whispered, and her mom sighed.

"I don't want you to go back there, honey, but I don't know what you want me to do. I can't just stand by and let you suffer like this." Her mom's voice wavered, and then she was crying again. "Your dad and I love you so much, Beth, and we know you. We've known you your entire life, and you can't hide how much you're suffering from us. I just wish you'd let us in, let us help you… th-that's all we want."

"I know, Mom." Sitting up straight, Beth reached over to squeeze her mom's shoulder, and with contact made, her mom reached up to take her hand.

"Just let me in, sweetheart." Pausing in the traffic again, her mom looked over, and she could see the concern, the panic, the fear. "Tell me what you're thinking about. Tell me what happened. Maybe if you talk about it… maybe it could help?"

"Mom…" Beth felt sick to her stomach. Just the idea of saying anything to her mom made her want to lean out the window and throw up whatever was left in her stomach from lunch.

Other girls had talked to their family about parts of it. Not everything, not every horrible detail, but they'd found words for it. The training, the men that had bought them, where they'd been taken… but all the other girls had more memories than she did, which wasn't a good thing. Remembering had to be worse than only having flickers and flashes of what she'd endured overseas.

But then why are you still such a fucking mess?

Dammit. She wasn't supposed to compare herself. Ailsa always said that comparing herself to the others wasn't reasonable. The Williams brothers hadn't sold her to a master. She'd been too broken for an auction after what he'd done to her on that table. Anthony leaning over her, backlit by those bright lights, the camera high above them, watching everything… that was the last clear memory she had before the strange memory of gunfire. Being ripped back to the surface when they took the cuff off her wrist just before someone wrapped her in a blanket, and then she was carried out of hell by a man in black.

What would telling her mom about that do? What would talking about the torture Anthony and his brother had put her through provide other than more pain?

There weren't any answers in her fractured memories or her fucked-up nightmares.

"Beth, please. I want to help you. I'll do anything to help you, sweetheart." Her mom let go of her hand to wipe her face, and Beth took the opportunity to fold her arms over her stomach again. "Just talk to me. If you don't want to talk to the doctors anymore, I won't make you go, but you can't carry this alone. You don't *have* to carry this alone. I'm here. Your dad is here."

"I know," she whispered, swiping at the tears on her own cheeks.

"Will you please just let me in?"

It was such a simple question, and Beth wished she could say yes. She wished it was as easy as her mom made it sound… but it wasn't. Letting someone in was a good thing for most people, but Beth wouldn't wish her mind on anyone. It would be a curse, not a gift, and her mom definitely didn't deserve that.

Even if she just talked about the flickering memories she had of the helicopter taking her away from that horrible place, it wouldn't be a happy conversation because she'd sunk right back under the surface. She could remember the fleeting hope that the blanket and the gunfire and the helicopter meant she was really safe, but she hadn't managed to hold onto the world — and the time after it was just as hazy.

Her doctors, and her parents, knew more about that time than she did.

They'd told her that a group had pulled her out of Thailand and taken her to Germany for medical care. Supposedly, she'd spent three weeks there while things were arranged to verify her identity and transfer her to the mental hospital in California.

Yet even after she was back in the United States, so close to home, with her family visiting her — she hadn't been able to break the surface. Her mind wouldn't let her, or she'd pushed herself so far down that even when she knew it should be safe, she just couldn't make it before she was too tired to keep trying.

Five months of being a walking zombie. Five months of silence. Five months of watching her mom and dad cry as they sat with her, held her hand, showed her pictures of the nephews she didn't know — but she couldn't make herself talk. Couldn't rebuild the connections in her brain that allowed those things to happen because she'd torn them apart out of desperation.

"Beth?" Her mom reached across the car, barely touching her arm, but she flinched involuntarily, and her mom yanked her hand back fast. "I'm sorry. I…"

"It's okay." Leaning forward, Beth buried her face in her hands, trying to figure out why she was still so fucking broken. She'd been out of hell for over two years now, she'd been back home for a year and a half. Everyone else was rebuilding their lives, they were figuring out how to be real people, and Beth just… couldn't. "I want to be better, Mom. I promise I'm trying."

"Oh, honey… I know that. We all know that." More sniffling as her mom's voice wobbled, but this time she couldn't look at her. Couldn't watch her cry anymore because she was hurting her. Again. Just by existing.

"I'm sorry I'm not better," she mumbled into her hands, and her mom reached over to rub her back.

"You don't need to be sorry, Beth. You never need to be sorry. We'll get through this together." Soothing circles looped again and again on her back, and she hoped her mom wasn't thinking about the scars under her shirt, but since she was still crying there was no way to know. "I'll tell your dad that we're taking a break from therapy for a while. We'll figure out something that works for you. I promise."

"Thanks," she whispered, swallowing down another surge of nausea. Her mom promised her things like that all the time. That she'd feel better, that the terrible things would fade away… but how could something fade away when she couldn't even remember it?

How could she get better when it was her existence that was causing everyone so much pain?

FOUR

Jake

"Keep your fucking hands up, idiot!" Ollie shouted.

"He's waiting for an opening," Asaf replied, and Ollie waved a hand dismissively before tipping his whiskey up.

Jake chuckled, shaking his head as the other guys shouted over the UFC fight. He wasn't as big a fan as some of the others, but he was still trying to pay attention while he sorted through all the emails he'd ignored the last few days.

He just hadn't expected there to be so many.

The alerts Brendan had set up *did* need to be looked through, and even though it was just a bunch of bad news… this was part of the job.

Missing girls.

Abductions.

Tips from people who mined data from the dark web.

None of it was 'fun' to read, but it was a necessary evil, and he had the tequila they'd picked up to help him.

He flagged a few of the alerts, forwarding them over to Brendan so he could do some research. Brendan would look into news reports, police reports, and see if the families might be the kind of people they could help — because they couldn't help everyone.

As much as he'd like to take on the whole list of tragic cases, they couldn't be in two places at once... and they still had bills to pay. Sure, they were trying to do some good, but at the end of the day they were still mercenaries. Plus, money greased wheels faster than anything else when they were hunting down leads and information. Not everyone had that kind of cash to hand over, however, which meant there was always a list of names that just never had a chance.

More shit to carry on my conscience.

"Fuck yeah!" Charlie shouted from beside him, and Jake raised an eyebrow at him as his friend started laughing before reaching over to nudge the lid of his laptop, threatening to close it. "Come on, boss, you're missing the whole fucking fight."

"Yeah, yeah," he replied, rubbing at the back of his neck as he skimmed through the other unread emails. He was about to shut it down and finish in the morning when an alert caught his eye because of one name.

Williams.

Clenching his jaw, he clicked on the email, and it only took a few seconds to realize why it had shown up connected to the fucking Williams brothers... and it definitely wasn't good news. "Fuck."

"What's up?" Charlie asked, glancing over at him with a grin, but it disappeared instantly. "Jake, what is it?"

He kept re-reading it, navigating to the page the alert referenced as the other guys turned toward him. They gradually went quiet, which told him everything he needed to know about the expression on his face... but he'd never been good at hiding his rage. Grinding his teeth, he kept trying to get the shit to load, but it wouldn't. "Son of a bitch! Brendan, I need you to—"

"On it. Send it over." Brendan was off the couch and heading over to the big ass table where they ate most of their meals. The end by the hall was definitely Brendan's space. His laptop was always set up, shit spread out around it, and he settled in just as Jake clicked forward and rubbed a hand over his face.

"Going to fill us in?" Mike asked before taking a swig from his beer.

Asaf reached over and paused the fight because none of the guys were looking at it anymore, but Jake didn't want to get everyone wound up until Brendan confirmed it. Slamming his laptop shut, he put it on the coffee table and walked around the couch to stand over Brendan's shoulder.

"Tell me someone didn't take this job." Jake's grip on the back of the chair was too hard, his hand ached from the pressure, his stomach twisting into knots, but he was grateful none of the guys pushed him. They knew he'd fill them in once he had an actual fucking answer, and all he could do was hope it was a false alarm.

Watching Brendan clicking around the screen, typing shit in as fast as he could, Jake bit down on his tongue because he was already doing the math in his head... and it wasn't good.

Two fucking days.

He'd gotten the alert in his inbox two days before, but they'd been so wrapped up in tracking Ashley down that he hadn't even skimmed through it on his phone, and Brendan obviously hadn't been looking either.

A goddamn mistake he'd never make again.

Hell, he'd make Brendan connect any alert related to 'Williams' to some kind of alarm on his fucking phone.

It felt like it took forever, but it was probably only ten or fifteen minutes before Brendan sat back and looked up at him with an expression that was way too fucking grim. "I'm sorry, Jake. I—"

"Fuck!" he shouted, pacing away from Brendan as he rubbed at the back of his neck. There was a headache focused at the base of his skull and it was only getting worse as he tried to think through what the right next steps were.

Get it together.

"Okay, I need you to see if you can find out who the fuck took the job," he said, pointing at Brendan as he paced back toward the table. "Then I need you to track her down. Get whatever info you can, whatever surveillance is in the area. Those video doorbell things, check if there's one at her house or nearby."

"On it," Brendan answered.

Jake turned to look at the other guys. Asaf and Benny were standing up, the others still in their seats, but everyone was tense and looking at him. Ready and waiting.

"Okay. I'll cut straight to it. Someone is looking for one of the Williams brothers' slaves. *Ex*-slaves," he corrected himself, muttering curses as he tried to crack his neck to relieve the tension. "They were looking to hire a team to take her, and I fucking missed it. I— *goddammit!*"

"Was it Badass?" Ollie asked.

"No, it's not Thalia." Jake shook his head, not remembering the girl's full name from the email. "It's Elizabeth… something. Brendan?"

"Doherty," he filled in.

"Elizabeth Doherty. She's here in California, so we should be able to get there fast if…" *she's still there.* Jake couldn't finish the sentence out loud. Just thinking about missing something this fucking important had his stomach churning. They had alerts on every fucking name James and Thalia had provided him. They'd added the data James tracked down on the bastards to their files, and Brendan had worked his magic expanding on the data as much as possible.

The entire point of setting up the alerts was to get ahead of shit like this, to try and keep those women safe, to keep them from going through what had happened to Thalia.

She'd earned the name Badass when she'd killed the psychotic bastard that took her for a second time, but she'd never really accepted the nickname. Thalia had always said it was luck — and she was right — but luck wasn't something any of them could rely on. If luck gave a shit about any of these girls, they never would have been brutalized by the Williams brothers in the first place or sold off to whatever hell they got yanked out of when James got INTERPOL involved.

He was pacing again because his head wouldn't stop pounding, and other than the rapid clatter of Brendan's fingers across the keyboard, everyone was quiet.

If I fucked this up, I'll never forgive myself.

"Where is she supposed to go?" Mike asked.

"It wasn't in the original notice. Just one of those details provided upon hire things," Brendan answered absentmindedly. "And I can't fucking find who posted it originally, or who responded. Fuck… Jake, I'm sorry, man. I should have been watching, I should have—"

"I'm not blaming you, Brendan. You were pulling out all your tricks getting Ashley home to her parents. I should have stayed on top of the fucking alerts." He met the man's gaze. "This is on me, no one else."

Brendan jerked his chin in a stiff nod before he turned back to the computer, and Jake caught a photo just before he scrolled past it.

"Hold up, is that her file?"

"Yeah, it's on the drive. BD0211."

"Got it." Heading back to his spot on the couch, he left his laptop on the table so the guys could lean in and read over his shoulder as he pulled her file up. The first photo of the girl was old, probably one of the photos her parents had provided the police when she went missing in 2011. It was her smile in the picture that had caught his eye. She'd only been twenty-two years old, and she looked so young, so fucking *happy* with her dirty blonde hair pulled into a ponytail and that big smile on her face as she posed with a cup of coffee on some street.

He made himself scroll past it and skimmed the original missing person reports before stopping when he got to another photo.

If it wasn't in the same file, he would never have guessed it was the same girl. Her hair was down, and it looked stringy, greasy. She wasn't looking at the camera in this one, her eyes unfocused, and there was no smile. It was obvious she'd lost a ton of weight from the earlier picture. Her cheekbones were too sharp, her shoulders bony underneath the institutional clothes that hung off her.

"Oh fuck," Charlie mumbled. "She was sold to a brothel."

"Where?" Asaf asked.

"Thailand." Jake shook his head, rubbing at his eyes for a moment before he reached forward and snagged his tequila, finishing off the last of it in one gulp. Mike reached for the glass, and he handed it to him wordlessly.

He definitely needed another.

Staring at the information on the screen was making him sick, but he knew he needed to talk. The other guys weren't close enough to read this shit. "Three years and seven months in Thailand in a fucking brothel. Anthony Williams sold her there, apparently *after* he broke her."

"Broke her?" Benny echoed, a deep crease forming between his brows as he took a step closer to look at the haunting photo on the screen.

"It's why he didn't sell her to some master," Jake answered.

"Says she was catatonic when they found her," Charlie added.

"No fucking shit." Ollie huffed. He was playing with one of his knives, weaving it between his fingers, but Jake knew it was just a nervous tic. The guy could be unstable at times, but they'd all learned to deal with him constantly carrying a blade around like a security blanket.

"Fuck." Jake got up from the couch again, almost running directly into Mike who held out the tequila like a peace offering. Taking a breath, he accepted the glass with a nod. "Thanks."

"We'll figure it out." Resting a hand on his shoulder, Mike tightened his grip for a second, forcing Jake to meet his eyes. "You gotta believe that, 'kay?"

"Yeah." He clapped the man on the back before moving over to Brendan, yanking out a chair to sit next to him. Jake took another swallow of the tequila, feeling it burn on the way down as he watched him work for a minute. Lowering his voice, he tried not to let his panic show. "Tell me she's still at home, man."

"They have a security system and I've already got a backdoor into that company's online storage, I'm just going through the last few days of footage from the front cameras." Brendan was hunched forward, face close to the screen as the video moved at high-speed. Cars and people and dogs flew across the road and sidewalks in front of the Doherty house, back and forth, day and then night, and then day again.

When it finally stopped, it showed night and a quiet street. The timestamp was ticking steadily which meant it was live now, but he hadn't been watching the whole time. "Any gaps?"

"None," Brendan answered, and Jake glanced over at the guys who'd crowded around his laptop. Their mumbles and grumbles told him all he needed to know about whether or not they'd take the job — *if* there was a job.

"Okay, so that means she's either still safely at home, or she's not safe and they snagged her somewhere else... but that's not likely. We'd have seen police or detectives or someone come to the house." Rolling his neck again, Jake pushed away the initial guilt and panic and shut down all that shit so he could think straight. "That means we're working within a narrow window where we can still intercept these assholes."

"We need to confirm she's there," Brendan said, and he nodded.

"You're right." Looking back at the guys, he focused on handing out orders. "Charlie, I need you to call Luke and tell him we need a plane to Carmel ASAP. Tonight, if possible."

"Got it." Charlie stepped over Mike, taking out his phone to make the call.

"I'll get transportation for us," Asaf said, peeling off from the group as well to stand near Charlie so they could coordinate shit. The rest of the guys were still huddled around his laptop, and when he caught Benny's eyes, he knew he needed to read more about her situation before they showed up at her door.

Fuck.

Looking around at his team, he knew that wasn't an option. He couldn't do that to her. She was already fucking traumatized, and he didn't need to read the rest of her file to know that. Almost four fucking years in a brothel, and that was *after* that sick fuck had his hands on her.

But she'd survived. She'd made it home against all the fucking odds, and there was no way in hell he was going to ruin that if he could avoid it.

Jake checked the time, relieved that it was still before ten o'clock, which meant they might be able to get shit organized tonight. If they could be on the ground before morning, they had a better chance of protecting her. Shielding her from ever knowing a single fucking thing about this.

"What's the plan?" Ollie asked from beside him. The man wasn't toying with his knife anymore, instead he had it gripped in his fist, white-knuckle tight.

When Jake looked up at him, he saw the lines etched into his expression, revealing the intensity in the man's face, that darkness that had tainted all of them to one degree or another — but he also saw the man's raw commitment. They didn't even know who this girl was beyond a photo and a name on a page, but every member of his team was ready to move right now if it meant they could stop this.

Ollie flipped the knife in his hand and caught the blade like he was planning to throw it. "Are we moving her to a safe house?"

"No." Jake shook his head.

"Why not?" Mike asked as he got up from the couch, glancing over at Benny before they both faced him.

"Good question," Benny added.

"Because I'm not upending this girl's life unless we absolutely have to," Jake explained, raising his voice so the whole team could hear him. "If we're still ahead of this, we have plenty of opportunity to intercept whatever fucking team took that job. We'll get there, verify she's at home, and then we'll keep a few of us on her house twenty-four-seven while we try and track down who's gunning for her."

"And if we can't?" Ollie asked, staring down at him, and Jake met his friend's gaze with a sigh.

"We'll cross that bridge if we come to it. Until then, we're all on." Lifting his glass, he stood up and tossed the last of the tequila back. "Finish your drinks and then put the bottles up, boys. If we run into trouble, I don't want anyone off their game, got it?"

Everyone mumbled their agreements, except Charlie who gave him a thumbs up because he was on the phone.

Nodding, he set his glass down. "Let's get it done then. Clock is ticking."

FIVE

Beth

Dinner the night before hadn't been as dramatic as she'd feared. Her dad had even seemed a little relieved her mom wasn't going to make her keep seeing doctors, but it was still a tough conversation.

The one they'd had today was just as uncomfortable. Her mom and dad had set her down in the living room to talk through the 'deal' they were willing to make. There were more tears, and no one had enjoyed it, but they'd come to an agreement. If Beth wanted to manage her own mental healthcare, then she couldn't hide in her room all day, every day. She still had to get up, still had to try and talk to them, and she had to show *some* improvement while working with Ailsa.

Although neither of them had been able to explain what they meant by 'improvement.'

An awkwardness had lingered since then, but she'd stayed in the family room with them all evening just to prove she was trying. Watching TV helped to fill the silence, but every roll of the sitcom's laugh track felt like nails on a chalkboard and — even though it meant she was breaking their new deal — Beth needed to escape.

"I'm going to go take a shower," she mumbled, standing stiffly as she fought the prickly, skin-crawling sensation running up and down her arms.

"Oh, okay," her mom said, the forced cheerfulness returning to her voice. "Sleep well, honey."

"Night, pumpkin," her dad added.

"Night." Beth couldn't even look at them because guilt was roiling inside her as she bolted for the stairs like a coward.

You're a horrible daughter.

What the hell is wrong with you?

You don't deserve them.

Her inner thoughts chased her as she practically ran for her bathroom. Shutting the door and flipping the water on didn't stop them, though, which was fine. She needed to face the truth. She had amazing parents. Loving, wonderful parents who would do anything for her... and she couldn't even sit in the same room with them for a few hours and stare at a television. Even though she'd *just* told her mom and dad she'd do better.

Pathetic.

The shower was probably too hot, but she didn't reach to adjust it, she just sat under the stream and tried to get her heart to stop racing. A slow, deep breath in... and out. Then another as she worked shampoo into her hair and rinsed it. Repeating it with the conditioner.

Eventually she opened her eyes and grabbed for the soap, but her hands froze as soon as she lathered it. The fucking band-aid on her hip had fallen off in the water, and the sight of the damn tattoo brought another wave of tears.

Stop it.

She hated crying over it almost as much as she hated looking at it, but it was like a gravestone permanently inked into her skin. An inescapable marker that showed the death of who she used to be before the Williams brothers had ruined her life. Beth knew her mom could be lurking in the hallway outside but, luckily, she'd never made much noise when she cried.

Just close your eyes and finish.

When she dried off, she put a fresh band-aid over the top, covering up the dark 'W' with its crown that may as well have been a skull and crossbones. She knew she should have it covered up, just like she knew her parents would happily pay for it if she asked — even though they'd always threatened her and her sister to never get tattoos.

Not like Beth had chosen to get this one.

But even knowing they'd do it for her, she hadn't asked them. She wasn't ready.

It felt like she *couldn't* get rid of it yet. Not when she was still so broken. She needed to erase it when all those nightmares were actually behind her, when she was someone new.

Then it would have meaning.

It would be like Thalia's branding ceremony. Destroying the tattoo before she got married had been symbolic, and that's what Beth wanted. She didn't want to wake up the next morning to a different tattoo on her hip but have everything else be the same.

It wouldn't mean anything like that.

She needed to get better, to make real progress, to figure out how the hell to actually *live* her life… then she'd be ready for a clean slate.

Which is exactly what you promised Mom and Dad earlier today.

With a heavy sigh, Beth finished brushing out her hair and wrapped herself in a towel. Slipping out of the bathroom quietly, she'd only made it a few steps down the hall when she froze. The living room had high ceilings, and she could hear her parents' voices floating up to the section of the hall that overlooked it.

"I understand that," her mom said, clearly frustrated and emotional. "But what if she never gets better, Bill? I know she wants us to trust that group she's a part of, but they've been talking to her for two years and she still hasn't come back to us!"

"We have to be patient." Her dad's voice was calm, soothing, but the sound of her mom crying again was like a knife in her heart, twisting as she slid down the wall to stay out of view from the railing.

"I just wish I knew…"

"You said that you opened that door again. Beth knows we're here if she wants to talk, but she's always been a stubborn girl, Tanya. If we push her too hard, it'll just take longer." There was a pause, and Beth wished she could see them, but she didn't want to interrupt.

It was the first time she'd heard anything honest out of either of them, and even if it hurt… it was better than the false smiles and the forced cheerful conversations that were so painfully fake. Her father's chuckle brought her attention back to them, and she leaned toward the railing to listen harder.

"You remember when she was little, and she went through that phase where all she wanted to wear was dresses?"

"Yeah," her mom replied, clearly still crying.

"Well, what happened when we tried to tell her she couldn't go on that Girl Scout hike in a dress?"

"She put that Easter dress I bought in her backpack and changed out in the woods." A quiet, sad laugh came from her mom. "She totally ruined that dress."

"Exactly. That's what I'm trying to say." He sighed heavily. "She's not going to talk at all if we push her. It's why I've been telling you for months that we had to stop dragging her to all those therapists."

"I was trying to help!" her mom snapped, and then the sound of her sobbing floated up, twisting the knife in her chest a little deeper.

"I know, I know. But we have to remember that Beth survived whatever she went through because she's strong. We have her back because she's strong. Eventually that strength will guide her back to us… but not if we try to force it."

"I just want to know what happened. If I knew, maybe I could... I don't know. *Do* something." The sound of liquid being poured into a glass told Beth her mom had opened the wine, and she wondered how much she'd already had while she'd been in the bathroom. "Maybe I — maybe it would make a difference if she wasn't carrying it all by herself."

"We're her parents, Tanya. If anything, we're the last people she'd want to know the details."

"Why!" There was shock and pain in her mom's voice, but Beth just leaned her head back against the wall because it seemed her dad at least understood.

"She wants to protect us from it, honey. Come here... You remember what the doctors at Greenwood said, right? The best thing we can do is provide a normal environment for her. Let her adjust to life again."

"She's not adjusting though. She's not getting better."

"I know, but we have to be patient," her dad replied, and Beth clenched her jaw tight, fighting the tears that leaked out anyway as she quietly pushed herself up from the floor and slipped into her bedroom.

Closing the door as softly as possible, she lay down on her bed and stared at the ceiling. There were still a few glow-in-the-dark stars up there that had lost their ability to glow years before, but she'd never brought the ladder upstairs to pry them off, and her parents hadn't touched her room at all when she was missing.

It looked exactly like it had when she graduated high school. The lilac accent wall behind her bed that she'd begged for, that they'd finally let her paint for her thirteenth birthday. She'd got the matching purple curtains for that same birthday, and they'd left all of it. Even the outdated posters of bands she'd liked were still hanging on the walls.

The whole room was a monument to who she used to be. Volleyball trophies on the shelves beside her dresser. Her high school diploma framed with the tassel from her cap. Everything frozen in time from before she'd left for Berkeley.

Beth hadn't asked about the stuff from her shitty little apartment in Santa Rosa, but she was sure her parents had cleaned out everything there. They probably had it in the attic, or a storage unit, which was where all that stuff belonged.

She wasn't that girl anymore, and as much as her parents wanted her to get better... she knew she'd never be the daughter they remembered.

Sniffling, Beth hung the towel up on the back of her door and flipped each of the locks as gently as possible, trying not to make too much noise. As soon as the door was secure, she felt like she could breathe a little easier. The world was locked out, which meant she didn't have to pretend to be sane, or stable, or functional. She yanked the sheets down to the foot of the bed and grabbed the tablet from the charging cord, laying it down in front of her as she typed in her code.

She'd missed several posts from that day and the day before, and she skimmed through each one, replying to them with encouragement and cheers and comfort where it was needed. Two of the other girls were sharing wins — working at a coffee shop and hitting ninety days without a nightmare. Another of the girls with the username LA0813 talked about the guy she'd been dating and how she'd finally slept over at his house... and they'd had sex.

It hurt to type out how excited she was for her, because although Beth *was* happy for her, she was also jealous. There wasn't a nicer word for it, and she knew it was petty, but she was twenty-eight. So many of the people she used to know were already married, some of them had kids, and she'd stalked their Facebook profiles just to see what their lives were like.

But her old friends from school didn't make her feel like a failure.

LA0813 made her feel like more than a failure. It highlighted just how broken she was, how far away she was from any kind of 'normal' or ever making her parents feel better. She couldn't even touch *herself*, and the idea of being with anyone else wasn't remotely realistic. She never even went anywhere, so how could she meet someone?

And who would want to put up with her shit anyway?

Rolling her eyes, Beth opened a new post and wrote a short paragraph about how her latest psychologist had actually suggested she take a break from therapy for a while. She talked about how much of a relief it was, and how she was looking forward to continuing to work with Ailsa so she could make progress too.

She didn't mention the conversation with her mom, or the one she'd overheard downstairs, or the fact that reading everyone else's successes was sometimes torture. All the negative stuff wasn't worth posting about, because it wasn't new, but this was finally a small win she could share. Plus, it would let Thalia know she was doing okay, and the others might stop tagging her so often asking her to check in.

Almost as soon as she posted it, a comment showed up from one of the other girls wishing her luck. Then another comment appeared saying how great it was that they'd finally listened to her.

It was the kind of understanding she'd never get from her parents, which was why the forum was so important. Her mom might hate it — hate that she didn't have access to it and hate that she never got a report from Ailsa like she might from another therapist — but without the forum Beth wouldn't have anyone to talk to.

She wouldn't be talking at all.

Dropping back against her pillows, Beth looked up at the ceiling and tried to focus on the relief she felt that she wouldn't have to face off with a new therapist anytime soon. That was a win, no matter how tiny, and it lifted some of the pressure because her mom wouldn't be getting the constant negative updates from therapists.

Which might help her mom, too.

And if she kept talking to Ailsa, if she kept following the other girls' successes… then maybe she could be someone else. *Eventually.*

She just didn't know how long that would take.

For now, she didn't have anything comforting to tell her parents. There weren't any words she could say that would make her mom stop crying or her dad stop worrying.

Not yet.

Someday though... someday she'd have to start getting better.

SIX

Jake

The sunrise painted the sky in golds and oranges over the Doherty house, but Jake couldn't tear his gaze away from the tablet in his lap. Everything about this girl just… stunned him.

She shouldn't be alive — every fucking statistic was against her — but *somehow* she was. Ripped out of hell by a team that apparently no government or organization was willing to take credit for, and then she'd appeared at Ramstein Air Base in Germany as if by magic.

Thailand to Germany. Completely off the books. Delivered directly to Americans.

It was insane, and the more he'd read, the more he wondered which was the more miraculous part of Beth's story.

The fact she'd survived at all, or the idea that James and Thalia's data had actually managed to find her, or that some team had pulled her out and got her to safety without a single fucking country taking credit.

Hell, the US hadn't even tried — which was probably the most amazing part of all.

Then again, she hadn't exactly been able to smile for the cameras when they first got her back to the States, and the government probably wasn't looking to advertise what could happen to pretty young women in what was supposed to be one of the safest countries in the world.

Such absolute bullshit.

Grabbing his coffee, he felt how light it was and grumbled when he remembered he'd finished it sometime in the early morning hours. Jake tossed the empty cup into the floorboard, so he'd stop reaching for it, and turned around to check on the guys.

They'd crashed after he'd offered to stay up on watch, and they were still out, but he was still wide awake. Jake had known there was no way he could sleep until he'd seen her with his own eyes, but the other guys didn't have that issue. Ollie was snoring in one of the captain's seats, and Mike was crammed onto the row in the very back. The dude was close to six-foot-five, but they'd all slept in worse situations than a nice SUV with A/C.

He was glad they were sleeping, though. He wanted them to grab as much rest as they could now so they could get to work once the other guys came to relieve them for the next shift.

Then *maybe* he could sleep.

Glancing down at the remaining cup, Jake shrugged, picked up Ollie's coffee, and took a sip that he instantly regretted. "Oh fuck, seriously?"

Cold, black, and bitter as fuck, he forced a few swallows down before he dropped the vile shit back into the cup holder. *Crazy ass*, he thought to himself, glancing at Ollie in the rearview mirror for a second before he turned his eyes back to the tablet and scrolled up to her picture again. Not the pretty one, but the one that gave him an idea of what she might look like now.

Elizabeth 'Beth' Doherty.

A fucking walking miracle.

Shaking his head, he looked out the window again as the early morning light turned the house into a picturesque slice of the suburbs. Pretty green lawn, cute little porch, complete with a goddamn white porch swing and a little colorful flag in the flowerbed that read 'Welcome.' If anything made the old saying 'don't judge a book by its cover' true, it would be that house. She'd grown up in the kind of neighborhood where bad things just weren't supposed to happen. It was supposed to be all barbecues and kids playing and shit... but the monsters of the world never really gave a fuck about that.

They'd taken her outside of work. Barely out of college, first job, and then — *poof*. Gone.

Jake had listened to too many parents crying over missing daughters, so he didn't even need his imagination to picture what the inside of that suburban paradise sounded like six years ago when their youngest disappeared off the fucking map. Nothing but pain and grief and fear.

Part of him wondered if he'd been doing this shit back then if his guys could have found her, could have prevented every nightmarish thing he'd skimmed over in her file… but that was probably just his ego talking. Her parents were doing well for themselves, but not 'hire a team of fucking mercenaries' kind of well. Groaning, he rubbed at his eyes and almost reached for that bullshit excuse for coffee before he stopped himself from removing whatever was left of his stomach lining.

"Ah… fuck." Ollie grunted behind him, stretching.

"Sleep well, princess?" Jake asked, turning to flash a grin at him, and Ollie replied with a middle finger. Chuckling, he shifted in the front seat to see him more easily, watching as Ollie yawned, obviously still tired. "You've gotta start wearing one of those mask things over your eyes or something, man."

"I'm fine. Sleep is for pussies." Snapping his fingers, he held out his hand and pointed at the coffee.

Jake handed it over with a sneer of disgust. "I don't know how you drink that shit, Ollie. It's fucking toxic."

"Cream and sugar is for pussies too," he said, grinning before he tilted the cup back and drained it.

"Guess you didn't mind the piss though."

"What the fuck?" Ollie threw the empty cup at the windshield, and Jake couldn't hold back the laugh as he watched him groan and wipe his mouth. "You're fucking with me. No fucking way you pissed in my coffee."

Jake chuckled for a second more before he shrugged. "Nah, not *this* time, but I doubt you would've noticed. That shit is terrible."

"Dick move, Jake." Grabbing onto the armrests, the blond soldier tried to stretch out his back, but the muttered curses made it clear it wasn't helping. "I'm gonna go for a walk and grab a smoke."

"Okay. Keep an eye out," he cautioned him.

"Yep," Ollie replied, popping open the car door to climb out. When he slammed it behind him, Jake saw Mike twitch in the back row, letting out a low grumble before slowly sitting up.

"That's Ollie's version of 'good morning,'" Jake said, laughing under his breath as he waited for Mike to rearrange himself into a comfortable position.

"Does that crazy asshole ever sleep past dawn?" Mike mumbled, leaning forward to brace his elbows on his thighs.

"Not unless he's in that vampire cave he calls his bedroom."

Rolling his eyes, Mike stretched out his legs and rotated his shoulders before he turned to stare at the house. After a couple of minutes, he jerked his chin toward it. "Any movement?"

"Not yet, but it's only a little after six."

"Figure out what you're gonna say yet?"

Jake sighed heavily, leaning back against the window to stare at the front door like if he imagined knocking on it the words would finally show up in his head. *Any time now would be great…* "Nope. Not a fucking clue."

"Want me to come with?" Mike offered.

"Nah man, but thanks. You're built like a goddamn tank, and I think one of us is going to be more than enough to send their whole fucking day into a tailspin." He shook his head at the visual of Mike standing in their doorway. Jake wasn't short at six feet, but Mike managed to make him look small. Six-foot-five, packed with dense muscle, he was always someone Jake had been glad to have at his back when shit went south. But even though he was probably one of the nicest and most gentle guys on the team, Mike always made one hell of a first impression and they weren't trying to intimidate the family.

"So, you gonna tell them what you know?"

Shit.

"Not yet." Groaning under his breath, Jake smacked his head back against the glass. The last thing she fucking needed this early in the morning was a reminder of what she'd survived, but it felt wrong to hide it. Fuck that, the whole situation felt shitty, and he hated that he didn't have control of it yet. He knew way more than he needed to about the girl, and absolutely fucking nothing about the team coming after her or the motherfucker who hired them. Flying blind was bad under normal circumstances when he was only putting himself and his team at risk — but this lack of information was putting the girl at risk too.

Ten out of ten, an absolute shitshow.

"Then… what the hell are you gonna say, man?" Mike asked, moving into one of the captain chairs, but having him ask again wasn't making Jake's thoughts any clearer. The big man leaned forward, laying a dark hand on his arm to grip it firmly. "Listen, I know you don't want to fuck up their whole day. I get that, you're trying to be a good guy, but we need to know if she's in the house or not." Mike patted his arm a couple of times like he was trying to offer some kind of comfort in the shitty situation before he sat back. "Cause if she's not, then why the fuck are we staking this place out?"

"I know how fucked the situation is, but I can't exactly knock on their door asking if their daughter is home and not expect them to call the fucking cops in a panic. Not after everything that happened to her." Jake looked over at him. "You know how twitchy the parents get."

"Then tell them the truth," he replied, as if *that* was an option either.

"You're not helping, Mike."

"Yeah, well… clock's ticking either way. I can sit here and watch you crank those rusted-out gears in your head for the next thirty minutes and you still won't have a fucking clue when you walk up there, or I can piss you off until you think of something." Mike yanked the recline lever on the side of the chair and angled himself back. "So, stop being an asshole and make a decision."

Clenching his jaw, Jake could feel his teeth grinding together as he crossed his arms and glared out the window at the front door of the Doherty house. He didn't have a thing to say in response to Mike because the motherfucker was right but telling him that would only make him keep talking and Jake needed to think.

Rusted-out gears? Fuck off.

He just needed to focus on the mission parameters. Primary goal? Verify her location and safety. All that required was seeing the girl in person and maybe asking her a few questions. If he could figure out a way to talk to her without her parents around, he *might* be able to avoid bringing down a shitstorm on all of them. But why on earth would any of them let him within a hundred yards of her?

Ollie yanked the car door open, and Jake didn't even need to glance back to know it was him since the scent of cigarette smoke came with him. Jake hadn't smoked since he was enlisted, but at the moment a little boost of nicotine sounded pretty good. Anything to get his nerves settled so he didn't fuck this up before they even got started.

"Light's on inside." Ollie pointed toward the house, and Jake narrowed his gaze at the front windows. There were curtains, but when he focused, he saw what Ollie was looking at. It looked like there was a light on in a room farther back. Probably the kitchen.

"Tick tock, Jake," Mike added, and he had to bite back the urge to rip the guy's head off.

"I get it," he grumbled. Checking the clock, he knew that he couldn't put it off all morning. They might have plans for the day and there was no way they could take Beth out of the house and keep her safe in a public space — not when they still had no idea who was coming for her or how close they might be.

Fuck, fuck, fuck.

"Just tell her parents there's a threat. They'll follow any rules you lay down to avoid what happened to her before," Ollie said.

"No. I only need to talk to Beth about this shit," he said, decisions clicking into place now that he was running out of time. "There's no need to panic her parents when we're here staking the place out, but we need to know she's here and she needs to know something is going on and that we're watching."

"So, how are you going to get her parents to let you talk to her?" Mike asked, looking over at him. "You should have shaved."

"Thanks, man. That's helpful." Jake sighed, rubbing a hand over the stubble on his chin and cheeks before he flipped the visor down to stare at his reflection. His eyes were a little bloodshot from not sleeping, and his hair wasn't as neat as it could be, but Mike was right. Again. If he'd shaved, he'd look a hell of a lot more put together. Pushing a hand through his hair, he tried to smooth it out and get the mess to look at least semi-professional. The only smart decision he'd made was that he wasn't in tactical gear. He'd thought ahead enough to change into jeans and a button-down shirt, which was supposed to help him look more approachable… he just couldn't tell if it was working or not. Smacking the visor back against the roof, he turned to face Mike. "How bad is it?"

"Try not to look like you're ready to murder someone."

"Even if that's the truth," Ollie added with a low laugh.

"How the fuck am I supposed to do that? Smile?" He forced a smile and Mike busted out laughing.

"Well, yeah, but not like *that*. You look like you're imitating the fucking Joker."

Groaning, Jake scrubbed at his face and tried to think happy thoughts that didn't involve murdering the fucks coming after this girl. It took a minute, but he thought back to the last time the team had a free day together and they'd spent it at the firing range before heading to a bar. A few of the guys had brought girls home, but he'd enjoyed just hanging out without some cloud of doom hovering over their heads. Tequila, dancing with a few pretty women, and ending the night watching a movie with the guys who hadn't found a one-night-stand was so much better than how they spent most of their days.

Relax. Be relaxed. If you're tense, they'll sense it and they'll panic.

Beth will panic.

Get your shit together.

"Why don't you just tell them you know Thalia?" Ollie suggested and Jake leaned forward to see him better as he twirled a knife in his fingers. "You know, because they're all on that website together? If the girl knows Thalia, then that's a reasonable way in."

"That's… actually a decent idea, Ollie."

"Don't sound so surprised, asshole. I'm not an idiot." Huffing, Ollie glanced back at the house, and he and Mike followed his gaze. There were more lights on now, which meant people were awake. No more excuses.

"Okay, I'm gonna go," he said, nodding at them.

You're just checking in on Beth. You know Thalia.

Don't fuck this up.

SEVEN

Jake

"You going now, or…?" Mike prompted him and he flipped the man off, which only made Mike laugh again. "Stop being a pussy. Go knock on the damn door."

"Fuck off, I'm going." Jake shoved the door open, slamming it hard to block out the sound of both guys laughing. Taking a deep breath, he ran a hand through his hair again and headed across the street to the Doherty house. Up close it still looked like the picture of suburban life, and he knew he had to chill out before he knocked.

Happy thoughts, happy thoughts…

After a moment, Jake raised a hand and rapped his knuckles on the door. Keeping up with the calm, slow breaths, he was still rehearsing what he'd say when the buzz of voices from inside made him freeze.

They got closer, and then moved farther away again, and he sighed. He was trying to be patient, but after a few minutes he knocked on the door again.

"One minute!" a woman's voice called out, and he shoved his hands into his pockets to wait.

Turning to glance back at the SUV, he couldn't see Mike through the tint, but Ollie was walking down the sidewalk, smoking again as he watched. Then Jake heard the voices get closer again, and he faced the door and tried to look respectable. Calm and relaxed. Friendly.

The door opened a few seconds later, and in the narrow space between the frame and the door, there was an older man in a t-shirt and khaki shorts, his brows pulled together in confusion. "Um, hello."

"Hi, Mr. Doherty, my name is Jake Campbell. I'm, uh, sorry for coming by so early. I just got into town last night and didn't want to miss you guys." Chuckling, he could tell how fucking awkward he sounded but he didn't know how to fix it, especially when Beth's father was still looking at him like he was nuts. "I'm actually a friend of Thalia's. She's friends with Beth and wanted me to check in on her."

The second he said her name, her father's face went blank for a moment and then settled into a serious, tense expression. A woman's voice spoke up from behind the door, and he leaned over to answer her quietly, but neither of them were talking to him.

Shit.

"I work in personal security, and I'm just here to—"

"Did you say Thalia?" The voice was quiet, but definitely female and younger than the woman behind the door. Mr. Doherty turned to look, but he didn't budge from his position.

"Uh, yeah!" Jake called into the house. "I've worked with Thalia and James before and…" He trailed off when she appeared in the gap of the door. Lank blonde hair, brown eyes narrowed, she touched her father's arm, and he finally eased the door open.

"Why are you here?" Beth asked.

Clearing his throat, he realized he was trying to straighten up his clothes and forced his hands to his sides. "Just checking in on you for Thalia, and I had a few things to share if you've got some time to talk. I don't know what your plans are today but—"

"No plans," she interrupted, glancing at her parents. "It's fine, Mom."

The door was suddenly jerked wide, and he saw the older version of Beth glaring at him. Both women were on the short side, although her mom had curves where Beth's clothes hung off her. Holding onto the door like she might slam it in his face any minute, Mrs. Doherty squared off with him. "What do you want to talk to her about?"

"It's um…" *Fuckfuckfuckfuck.*

"Private?" Beth offered, and he smiled at her.

"Yeah."

"Absolutely not," her mom said, raising her voice as she pushed the door forward a little. "There's nothing this man needs to tell you that we shouldn't know too!"

"Tanya, please." Mr. Doherty looked over at Beth and then at him. "Does this involve my daughter's safety?"

"I'm just here to make sure she's okay," he lied and felt terrible about it. Technically it could pass for truth, for now, because they were still standing between her and any kind of danger... but his stomach still twisted as he looked into the worried faces of her parents.

"Fine, you can come in and talk in the living room." Her mom pulled the door wide again, and her father moved out of the way so he could step inside.

"Thank you." Nodding at both of them, Jake looked around the house. There was a large living room to the left, closed French doors on the right that clearly led to an office, and straight ahead he saw the stairs leading up to the second floor where a wrought-iron railing let him see several doors. The click of the door shutting behind him ramped up his nerves, but he tried to keep his body relaxed and his expression casual.

"So... this is about Thalia?" Beth asked and he hated himself for the reassuring smile he offered.

"Yeah." One word, and a total lie. James and Thalia didn't even fucking know about this, which meant he'd need to tell her that or he'd piss the both of them off when she asked Thalia about it on that forum thing.

"Let's talk upstairs." Beth turned toward the stairs, but her mom grabbed her arm to stop her and then immediately let go, raising her hand in the air.

The flash of guilt on her mom's face made it clear Beth didn't like to be touched, but the guilt was quickly wiped away by motherly concern. "No. Honey, you need to stay down here with—"

"It's fine, Mom. I want to know what he has to say and if you guys are eavesdropping then he probably won't be able to tell me everything." Swallowing, Beth flicked her eyes over to him for a second before looking at her mom again. "Please."

"Okay, sweetheart. We'll be down here," her dad said, nodding at Jake as he wrapped an arm around his wife and led her toward the back of the house. Mrs. Doherty definitely wasn't happy about it, but even as he heard her whispering to her husband, the pair disappeared around the edge of the stairs.

"Come on." She was incredibly quiet as she led him to the stairs and started up. He gave her a good lead, not wanting to crowd her, and as uncomfortable as her parents were with the idea of him alone with her in another part of the house… he didn't feel great about it either.

Still, it would be easier to talk about this shit without her parents listening in, so he followed in silence. It was impossible not to notice how thin she was though. The long-sleeved top hung off her shoulders, and the form-fitting yoga pants made it clear she'd never quite regained the weight she'd lost during her ordeal.

When Beth opened the door to her bedroom, he stopped short. "Um, I… we don't have to…"

"They're just going to listen in if we're downstairs, and I'm guessing you don't want that either?"

"Shit," he mumbled under his breath, and she went inside without another word, holding the door open for him. "Okay."

Don't fuck up, Jake.

The inside of her room both surprised and confused him. Beth was in black pants and a dark gray shirt with some band on the front of it, and nothing about how she looked would have made him imagine a room with a purple wall, purple curtains, stuffed animals on top of a chest at the end of the bed, and posters of boy bands on the walls.

"They didn't change anything when I was... gone," she said, as if she was able to read his mind.

"Why haven't you changed it?" he asked and immediately wanted to kick himself. "Sorry, that's none of my fucking business."

Beth just shrugged as she shut the door quietly, and he found himself taking a step back from her to give her more space. The trio of locks on the door told him everything he needed to know about the room. It was hers. Her safe place.

Why on earth are you standing in her bedroom right now? What the fuck are you thinking, Jake?

"What did you want to talk about?" The girl had her arms folded over her stomach, her back pressed to the wall by the door, and the sight made him move deeper into the room just so he wouldn't crowd her. She was five-foot-four according to the files, but she looked smaller than that.

"Well, um..." Jake cleared his throat again, and she tilted her head a bit, those soft brown eyes meeting his. "I want to be honest with you... Thalia didn't exactly send me, but I do know her. My team and I were the ones her boyfriend, *husband*, hired to get her away from Marcus Williams."

Beth tensed when he used the name and he mentally smacked himself.

"Sorry, I shouldn't have just dropped that on you, I—"

"Is it Anthony?" she asked softly, staring at the floor.

"Is *what* Anthony?" Confused, Jake watched her carefully as she seemed to get smaller, her shoulders pulling in.

"Is he..." Her voice got even quieter, the last of her question barely a whisper. "...looking for me?"

"What? No." Shaking his head, he took a step closer to her before he stopped himself. "Beth, he's dead. Anthony is—"

"That's what Thalia said too, but he has money. He knows powerful people. He... he could have faked his death. Paid people off."

"No." Jake had to take a deep breath so that he wouldn't react to the absolute fear in her voice. To think that she, and maybe other girls, had doubted what he'd provided Thalia and James on their wedding day... it made him sick. How long had they been waiting for Anthony to come clawing his way back into their lives? Forcing his fists to unclench, Jake tried to meet her gaze, but she was staring at the floor. "I promise you he's dead. I know it for a fact because my team killed him."

That got her to look at him again.

"He's gone, Beth. I swear. So is Marcus — although Thalia ended his sorry fucking excuse for a life. But my team and I were there. We saw him and disposed of the body."

"He's really dead?" she asked.

He nodded. "Absolutely."

"How did it happen?" Her body relaxed slightly. Arms still crossed over her stomach, but not so tense, not curling in on herself anymore.

"One of my guys gutted him in the prison shower."

"Did it hurt?"

Jake felt his lips tug toward a smile, but he made himself keep a straight face no matter how much he liked seeing her show some spine. "Yes, and it wasn't quick. We didn't know everything he'd done back then, or we would have tortured him first. Castrated the fucker for everything he —" Growling under his breath, Jake closed his eyes and took a breath, rubbing at his forehead. "Sorry."

"He deserved to suffer," Beth whispered.

Looking at her again, he could only nod. She reminded him so much of Thalia. That iron core that made Thalia a badass was inside Beth too. Of course, that was the kind of strength needed to survive the Williams brothers, and Beth had to have plenty of it to survive Anthony *and* the nightmares she went through overseas.

"So, if it's not Anthony… why are you here?" she asked, and his tongue stuck to the roof of his mouth.

Just tell her. She's strong, you can see that, just fucking say it.

"That asshole isn't after you, but… someone is." Jake swallowed in a dry throat when she tensed again. "But my entire team is here, and we're going to keep you safe."

"Who is it?"

"We're still figuring that part out."

Beth shook her head a little, gaze glued to the floor again, and he had the strongest urge to hug her, to try and make her feel safe — but there was no way in hell he'd touch her. Her own mother had pulled back.

"You don't need to worry about it. I just wanted you to know that we're going to keep an eye on you, and my whole team is working on this. I promise you're safe," he said, but he almost bit his tongue with how fast he shut his mouth. Promises were dangerous, and he tried to never make promises he didn't know for a fucking fact he could keep. Sure, they were going to do everything possible to protect her, and he'd put his life on the line to try and keep that promise, but guarantees weren't possible. Life was too fucked up for guarantees.

"Thanks," she whispered, glancing at the door, and he didn't know if that was her way of telling him she wanted him to leave or if she was planning to run herself. Jake was just about to go for the door when she moved, and he froze. "I'm going to get some water, would you…?"

"Sure. Thank you." He nodded, staying completely still as she headed out of the room and closed the door behind her. Groaning under his breath, he scrubbed at his face again. "What the fuck, Jake? What is wrong with you?"

Pacing around the room, he was trying to burn off the excess energy, but he couldn't resist looking at everything. She had trophies from volleyball, some dirty clothes on the floor near her closet, and a laptop on a small table she clearly used as a desk. He was tempted to see if the laptop was unlocked, but he shoved his hands in his pockets and turned away from it. A pair of scissors on her bedside table caught his eye though, and he moved closer.

Is she hurting herself?

Jake was scanning her rumpled sheets for blood, looking for anything she might have used to hide the fact that she was cutting.

Instead, he found a broken zip-tie.

Crouching down, he pulled it from the narrow space between the bed and the table, turning it over in his fingers as things started to click. There were little nicks and scratches in the paint on one of the metal bars that made up her headboard, and he didn't see a single drop of blood anywhere on the scissors or the bedding. The drawer of her bedside table was partially open, but when he tugged it all the way out the pile of broken zip-ties confirmed his suspicions.

Beth was zip-tying herself to the bed at night.

He didn't want to think about *why* she needed to do it but based on the half-empty pack of a hundred zip-ties crammed toward the back of the drawer, the five or six broken ones, and the presence of the scissors, it was pretty clear she was doing it to herself.

The rage swelled inside his chest, and he crushed the zip-tie in his fist, feeling the sharp plastic edges digging into his palm as he tried to calm down. Even though he absolutely wanted to go back in time and castrate Anthony fucking Williams — *after* he skinned the bastard alive and rolled him in rock salt — Jake knew that if Beth came back in her room and saw him like this, it wouldn't be good.

Deep breaths. Don't be an asshole.

It didn't matter why she was doing it, or what had happened to make it necessary for her, all that mattered was she needed it. Like when he got back from being deployed and he kept sleeping on the floor for months because the bed was too soft. Some things made absolutely no sense to anyone else, didn't even make sense to the person doing them, but they still had to be done.

The door creaked when it opened, and Jake froze with his fist still wrapped around the broken zip-tie and the damning drawer wide open beside him.

Fuck.

EIGHT

Beth

"I'm sorry," Jake mumbled, and it took a second for her to understand why he was apologizing, but then she saw the open drawer of her bedside table and the plastic sticking out of his closed fist.

Shit. Why didn't I clean up?

Beth balanced the water cup she'd pinned against her side and shut the door again so that her parents wouldn't hear whatever he was about to say.

She expected him to start lecturing her, but Jake stayed silent, on the other side of the bed, and she moved closer so she could hold out one of the cups in silence. Reaching across her bed, he took the water with his free hand, but Beth couldn't stop staring at the zip-tie in his grip.

White-knuckle tight like he was upset with her, or angry, or… something.

Will he tell my parents?

Is he disgusted?

He knew Thalia so he at least had an idea of what they'd been through. Different, but similar in ways, and terrible no matter what. Still, he probably thought it was completely fucked-up she continued to bind her wrist to the bed after all this time.

Setting the water cup on her small vanity table, Beth risked a glance at him, but his expression was blank. No hints of what was underneath so all she could do was ask, "What are you going to do?"

"Do?" he echoed, tilting his head, and she hated that it somehow made him look more attractive. Maybe it was the way the light from the window highlighted his jaw and the dark shadow of scruff that definitely fed into the whole 'tall, dark, and handsome' thing he had going for him.

Not that any of it mattered since she was just another of the Williams brothers' victims, and the only reason he was in her bedroom was to tell her that all her worst fears were coming true.

"You mean this?" Jake held out the broken zip-tie, rotating it in his fingers as his eyebrows pinched together. "I'm not going to do anything with this."

What?

Beth watched him carefully as he leaned over to set the cup down on her bedside table, his head shaking slowly before he ran a hand through his light brown hair.

"I wasn't snooping through your shit— I mean your stuff. I just saw the scissors on the table and thought you might be... doing *other* stuff. So, I just wanted to see if you were okay, but that's when I saw this on the floor." He held up the broken zip-tie again, the one that she'd cut off in her rush to get to the front door and find out who it was.

So stupid.

She'd been so fucking careful for so long, and the first time she'd made a mistake she'd been caught, because that was her luck. At least it hadn't been her parents. *That* would have resulted in a trip back to Greenwood and it would have destroyed whatever trust she might have built up with either of them.

"Fuck, please say something." Jake definitely sounded upset, but she had no idea what he wanted her to say. She didn't know him at all.

Finally, she looked over at the scissors and decided that was the easiest thing to respond to. "I don't hurt myself."

"That's good to know." He nodded, dropping the hand holding the zip-tie to his side before he looked down at it again. "These help you sleep?"

Beth froze, too stunned to respond and barely able to make herself nod when he looked up at her. Even more surprising was how he reached into the drawer and gathered up the other broken ones, shoving them into his pocket. But when he picked up the pack of unused ties, she tensed.

"Wait… please don't?"

Please don't take them.

"This isn't smart, Beth," he grumbled, shoving the pack of zip-ties in the back of his pants before pulling his shirt over them. "I can tell your parents are all over you, and it's impressive you've been able to hide this from them, but you're going to get caught."

"I need them," she whispered, feeling tears burning at the edges of her eyes as she tried to hold them back.

"They have to be zip-ties? Or is it anything as long you've got that tether?" Jake shoved the scissors into her mostly empty drawer and shut it hard. The clap of it snapping closed made her jump and he winced. "Sorry about that, but I need you to tell me. Does it have to be a zip-tie?"

She shook her head, but it was too hard to explain. She'd tried to explain it to Ailsa, but she'd just told her that it was important to try and move past it, to try and sleep without it... but there was no sleep without it. And whenever she used a shirt, or underwear, or the tie of a robe, it eventually worked loose in the night and then there were just nightmares. Waking up unable to breathe because she was still drowning, only then it was panic instead of water.

"I'll be right back, okay? Don't leave the room." Jake walked around the end of the bed, staying as far away from her as her bedroom allowed. When he stopped at the door, she tried to beg him to leave the package of zip-ties, but the words stuck in her throat, and with one last glance at her — he was gone.

Beth sat down on the bed, her stomach knotting as she tried to think up an alternative. It would take weeks for the girl from the forum, SC1113, to send her another 'care package,' which meant too many sleepless nights. She'd *tried* to go to sleep without something around her wrist that could be attached to the bed. Thick bracelets did nothing, rubber bands didn't help, and if something came loose in the night that wouldn't work either. She had to be tied to it, as fucked up as that was.

Being unrestrained had always meant something worse, something terrible enough to pull her out of the endless dark that Anthony Williams had put her in. When she wasn't tied to a bed, some twisted sense of self-preservation would always make her surface… for a little while anyway. Long enough to remind her why the surface was to be avoided at all costs. She couldn't remember much of her time in that hell overseas. Just flashes, random faces, random feelings, snippets of horror without context — and, of course, the panic.

The panic was always there. Waiting.

And the only thing that gave her any measure of control over the panic was knowing, even when she was asleep, that she was anchored to the bed. That no one would take her from it without waking her up. That she'd have some warning before there was the pain of a whip, or too many hands on her skin. Grabbing, prodding, one after another inside her, keeping her too close to the surface to hide.

Oh God.

Her chest was too tight. Just thinking about it was making the panic rise up, locking like sharp claws around her lungs, squeezing like a vise until there was no air available.

"Shit!" Jake's voice broke through the sudden ringing in her ears, and then he was there, shifting to his knees in front of her as he grabbed her arms and shook her slightly. "You need to breathe, Beth."

She tried to hiccup air, but there was just a strange, pinched sound in her throat and no relief.

"God dammit. Breathe!" he snapped, harsher than anyone had spoken to her since she'd been aware of people talking again, but there was something about it as his fingers dug into her arms that made her lungs let go — and then there was air. It whistled through her throat at first, but his grip slowly relaxed as she continued to breathe. After a few decent lungfuls where she wasn't wheezing anymore, he let out a sigh. "Good. That's it. Keep breathing. Slow and even."

And... Beth did. She pulled air into her lungs, let it out slowly, mimicking his breaths as he showed her exactly what he meant, and when she opened her eyes, she realized just how close he was. Crouched in front of her bed, holding onto her. He was *right there*.

His stare was so intense, so focused, studying her carefully, but she knew it was only because he was worried about her health. That's not why she was staring back though. Jake's eyes were an intriguing mix of green with honey brown closer to the pupil. *Hazel*. That was the word for eyes like that, but she'd never seen anyone's look like this, especially not while looking at her.

"Jesus Christ. Does that happen a lot?" he asked, still holding onto her, but she couldn't figure out how to answer him. "Beth?"

She swallowed, looking over his face, the hair falling over the creases in his forehead formed by the way he stared at her with so much intense concern. He tightened his grip on her arms and she found her voice, even if it was only a whisper. "I need the zip-ties."

Jake chuckled, letting go of her as he leaned back to wipe a hand down his face. "Fuck me. You had a panic attack because I took the zip-ties out of here?"

Beth lifted a shoulder in a slight shrug, embarrassed, but Jake just shook his head and tugged a pair of handcuffs from behind him.

"I went outside to hide your evidence in the car and get you these." The cuffs dangled on his finger, catching the light, the subtle sound of metal on metal making her skin buzz in a weird way. "Infinite uses. No trash to hide. Here."

He pressed them into her hand, and she liked the cold, hard feel of them against her skin, but she couldn't quite believe he was offering them to her when he knew what she'd use them for. "Why?"

"Why what?" he asked, digging in his pocket and taking out a little ring with two tiny keys. When she didn't say anything, Jake pointed at the cuffs in her hand. "Why am I giving you those?"

"Yeah." She nodded a little.

"Because you need them, right?" A mischievous grin lit up his entire face, making him even more attractive, but what really sent her head reeling was that he didn't just understand... he was *helping* her. "Listen, you just can't lose the fucking keys, okay? That would screw us both, I mean— Shit. I keep cussing around you."

"I cuss," she whispered, and he lifted his eyebrows.

"You do?"

Nodding, she chewed on her bottom lip as she turned the cuffs over in her hand. "It doesn't bother me. It's... nice."

"Not sure anyone's ever described my vocabulary as 'nice,' but I'll take it." Chuckling, Jake pushed himself off the floor and she watched him as he stood, holding out the keys for her. When she took them, the grin slowly left his face. "Listen, I'm sorry about... about grabbing you like that. I just—*fuck*. I've been around guys who've got issues with that, and I just kind of reacted. I won't do it again."

Why not?

The question almost made it past her lips, she felt her tongue starting to form it, but she bit it back. She knew why he wouldn't touch her like that. She was damaged, breakable, one wrong move away from another catatonic state... and he was only there to keep her safe.

"Anyway... I think your mom might have a heart attack if I don't leave soon, so I'm gonna head out, but we're going to figure out what's going on and handle it. If everything goes well, you won't even see us. Okay?"

"Okay," she replied, trying to ignore the rush of emptiness inside.

"And don't tell your parents if you can avoid it. Obviously, that's not my decision, but I'm not sure how well your mom would deal with this, and I really just needed to make sure you were still here, and safe, so we could watch the exterior while my team and I handle everything."

"I won't say anything." Keeping secrets from her parents wasn't anything new. There was so much she shielded them from because sharing it just wasn't helpful, and this definitely fell in the 'not helpful' bucket. Beth looked up to meet his gaze again, needing him to be honest with her. "How bad is this?"

"Nothing you need to worry about. Just try and stay home for a few days." Jake reached into a back pocket, pulling out his wallet. He dug through it for a second and then held out a slightly bent business card. "Here. If you have any questions, or see anything weird, just give me a call."

"I don't have a phone."

"House phone?" he asked, and she shook her head. "Well, uh, just hold onto it, okay?"

"Sure." Beth tucked it into her lap with the handcuffs and keys.

"And make sure you put those in the drawer, and just… try not to think about this shit. My team and I are on it." Jake backed up toward the door, shoving his wallet into his jeans, but he hesitated with his hand on the doorknob.

"Thank you." Lifting the cuffs, she tried not to let the emotions overflow with just how grateful she was. "For understanding, and for giving me these."

"No problem. We've all got shit to deal with, right?" Rubbing the back of his neck, Jake mumbled something to himself before he opened the door and stepped into the hall, but he paused again, looking out over the railing into the living room before he turned back to her. "Take care of yourself, Beth. Okay?"

"Okay," she answered, but he didn't move. Instead, his jaw tensed, and his hand landed on her door frame to grip it tight.

"I mean it." Those intense hazel eyes pinned her in place, and that rough edge returned to his voice when he said, "Promise me."

"I promise."

"I don't like it when people break promises to me, Beth, so you better be serious about taking care of yourself. That means eating, sleeping, all that shit." His voice was quiet, but it didn't need to be loud to have her full attention. Something about it sounded vaguely like a threat, even though he was just repeating many of the same things her parents and doctors had told her. All she could do was nod, and he sighed, smacking her door frame before he gave her one last glance. "Good. You hold up your end of the deal, and I'll hold up mine."

Then he walked away.

She heard his big boots thumping on the carpet, then the third step of the stairs that always creaked, and the hollow sound of the landing where the stairs turned. Beth was almost out the door to follow him when she looked down at the cuffs and groaned at herself. Running around the bed, she shoved everything into the drawer and slammed it closed, hurrying back into the hall and over to the stairs, but she froze at the top when she saw Jake talking to her parents.

There was a casual smile on his face as he shook her dad's hand before nodding at her mom. When he looked up at her, she wanted to say something, could feel the urge to speak like a pill too big to swallow, but she couldn't make it happen. Fortunately, he didn't have the same problem as he raised a hand to wave at her. "Have a good one!"

"You too," she answered, but it was way too quiet. He couldn't have heard her, and when he turned and walked out the front door, Beth just sat down on the top stair, leaning her head against the railing.

Her parents turned around to look up at her, and her mom had that look of worry she always wore whenever she forgot to smile. It was permanent, because of her. Because her mom had to deal with her every single day and Beth couldn't figure out how to not be broken anymore.

"What did he want to tell you, honey?" her mom asked, moving closer to the stairs as she called up from the first floor.

"Nothing. He just told Thalia that he'd check on me while he was in town, so he did." It shouldn't have been so easy to lie to her parents. It never used to be that easy. She used to get sick to her stomach, anxious, but now the lies rolled off her tongue smoothly because it was what they needed.

They needed comfort, and she needed handcuffs.

But Jake had given her the cuffs, so the least she could do was make her parents happy for once.

"Want to watch a movie today?" she asked, and both of her parents looked at each other before looking at her again.

"Sure, honey," her mom replied.

"It's Sunday, so what the hell." Her dad smiled and put an arm around her mom's shoulders. "We can put off groceries for a few days."

"Sounds great," she lied again. Too easily. But she owed them this much. If someone really was trying to find her, having her parents home with her, with Jake and his team somewhere outside, was the safest place for all of them.

Even if it was exhausting, she could pretend to be normal for a couple of days. Or, at least *closer* to normal.

And tonight, she wouldn't need to use a zip-tie to get some sleep.

NINE

Jake

His skin itched while he marched down the walkway away from the Doherty house. Every instinct was screaming at him to turn around and park his ass outside Beth's bedroom door. It was ridiculous, and her parents definitely wouldn't be okay with it... but it's what he wanted to do.

Leaving her there, alone, felt wrong.

"Hey fucker!" Charlie called out from across the street, and Jake jerked his head up. The other guys had arrived for their shift, and they were standing around between the two SUVs, all of them looking at him.

"How'd it go?" Benny asked as Jake closed the gap, taking his place in the group that stood out painfully amidst the suburban oasis around them.

"Fine," he answered, a little too short, but he couldn't shake the urge to turn around and check on the house. Giving in, he glanced back over his shoulder, but there wasn't anything to see. It looked like a normal home.

The door was shut once again, the lights inside not as noticeable with the sun rising higher in the sky, and there was no team of mercenaries taking position around the outside.

"Wanna explain the handcuffs?" Ollie grinned at him, and he could see the satisfaction in the other man as the rest of the guys looked between them.

Asshole.

"She needed them. End of story." Jake rubbed the back of his neck, glaring at Ollie and a few of the others who looked like they *might* make a comment about it. "Moving on, here's the update on the situation. She's aware that someone is looking for her, that she needs to stay inside, and that we're out here keeping watch. Her parents think I was here to check in on her on behalf of Thalia. Your turn, tell me what you found out."

"Whoever took the contract is hiding their tracks well. They're still ghosts for now, but I'm going to keep looking, keep reaching out to our contacts. I'll find them," Brendan said, and it sounded like a promise.

The exact same stupid promise Jake had made to Beth upstairs, and he wished he felt more confident in their ability to keep it.

"You need to sleep for a few hours first, Brendan." Benny slapped him on the shoulder before pointing at Jake. "You too. None of you are going to be worth shit if you don't get some rest."

Jake wanted to argue, but one glance at Brendan's bloodshot eyes made him bite his tongue. Sure, he wanted to camp outside the girl's bedroom, to make absolutely sure no one got their hands on her, but he'd be useless without a little sleep.

And if he didn't sleep, he knew Brendan wouldn't either.

"Okay, it's time to change shifts anyway. Asaf, Charlie, Benny, you're up." Jake jerked his chin toward the SUV they'd been camped in overnight, and the guys nodded.

"I can take a shift." Brendan spoke up, but Jake just grabbed his shoulder and turned him back to the other vehicle.

"Not a chance. You're going to sleep for a few hours, then get up and figure out who the fuck is hunting her and who they hired."

"I slept some in the truck last night," Mike said, joining them beside the matching black SUV. "If you'll set me up, I can look through whatever you've found while you rack out."

"I really should—"

"That's great, Mike. Thanks," Jake answered for Brendan, making it clear that it wasn't up for debate. "You drive."

"I can drive," Ollie argued, but everyone just laughed. "What?"

"Fuck no. You always drive like you're in a fucking tank, and that's the last thing we need right now. Mike will drive." Jake snapped his fingers, and everyone climbed in, leaving the front passenger seat for him.

With a wave at the other guys taking their place, they headed out, but even with the exhaustion tugging at him, Jake knew sleep was far off.

Asaf had found them a big house on one of those short-term property rental sites, and it meant that it was a little easier to talk once they were inside. Hotels were a last resort because they were complicated for too many reasons. They had cameras, they had guests in other rooms that might be listening, and they had staff that might pop in — and having civilians walk into a room filled with guns and tactical gear was never a good plan.

Enough conversations with cops in different locations had made that clear.

"Brendan, go lie down before I knock your ass out and carry you there," Mike threatened, and Jake chuckled quietly.

"I just don't want you messing with these windows, I've got programs running and—"

"He's not going to fuck with it, Brendan. Go get some sleep or I'll absolutely let Mike deck you," Jake called over his shoulder, and for a moment the two men on his team just stared at each other.

Finally, Brendan backed down, taking a step toward the stairs, but he pointed at the laptop one more time. "Screw that stuff up and you'll wake up tomorrow with an empty bank account."

"Asshole," Mike replied, but the laugh in his voice showed that neither man was really irritated. They were just busting each other's balls, and they all needed the stress relief that provided right now. Everything was too tense, too uncertain, and Brendan wasn't the only one anxious to get a name so they could keep the girl safe.

Beth.

Knowing the names of the people they were searching for had never bugged him before, but something about her name made him tense. Maybe it was because he usually didn't see them until the job was already over. This time he'd been in the girl's bedroom, given her handcuffs so she could sleep, and he couldn't get the sight of her out of his head.

The pictures didn't do her justice.

She was still too thin, but the photos couldn't capture the way her eyes shined, or the way her nose and cheeks turned pink when she was upset. And there was something about her voice... it was so soft, but there was strength in it too. That iron core that had kept her alive when most people would have given up.

He'd been mesmerized by every word she'd spoken, by the way her lips formed each syllable, and— *fuck*. He shouldn't even be thinking about her lips.

He shouldn't be thinking about her like this at all.

"Sandwich?" Ollie shouted from the kitchen, and for once he was grateful for the asshole's rampant disregard for quiet.

"Yeah, thanks," he called back, just as Mike said something similar. "I'll be right back."

Grabbing his iPad off the coffee table, Jake headed toward the bedroom he was sharing with Asaf and chuckled under his breath when he saw the man had re-made the bed for him. As if he gave a fuck if the room looked nice or not, but Asaf always had been organized to an almost neurotic extent. Crouching down by his duffle bag, Jake pulled out his charging cable and found a spot against the wall by a plug.

He'd forgotten the car charger in their haste to get in front of her house in the middle of the night, but it'd lasted long enough for him to stay awake poring over her file — which was exactly why he didn't need to look at it again, but he couldn't help himself.

It was wrong for too many reasons to list, but he pulled up the photos from the missing person report again and let the one of her holding a coffee cup fill his screen.

That was who she used to be.

Cheeks fuller, rounded from the sincere joy in her grin, and those brown eyes didn't have a shadow of pain cast over them. Beth had been the California version of the girl next door. Tanned and fit from all that volleyball she used to play, and she looked sweet. Happy and enjoying her life.

It just made Jake wish they could kill Anthony all over again. Except this time, he'd do it himself. With his own hands. Slowly. Until the bastard understood just how much pain a human body could take before he finally died.

If only.

Switching out of Beth's file, he pulled up the video of Anthony Williams' death and let it play. The footage was grainy, and the frame rate made it a little jerky, but it was still satisfying to watch it again. It would have been better if the bastard had begged for his life, but he hadn't said a word. He'd just tried to block the first stab of the shiv, failed, and then the next two had ensured his death.

If Beth could see it, she'd know he hadn't lied about Anthony Williams being dead, but he didn't know if showing up with it would help or hurt.

Especially since it was such a short fucking video.

He'd deserved worse, so much worse, but Jake had spent a small fortune making it happen and he didn't regret a bit of it. Well, other than the fact that he hadn't done it himself, but that wouldn't have been possible. Not with all the bribes they'd had to pay to get Ollie in the prison so he could get close enough to take action, he'd needed to stay on top of coordination and keeping the blackmail ready to go if someone balked — and they'd cut it so fucking close to Thalia's wedding day.

Remembering Thalia's wedding brought the ghost of a smile to his lips. When he'd first seen her naked, covered in blood, welted and bruised... he never could have imagined seeing her glowing like a fucking lighthouse with pure joy. James had done that for her though.

Beth just needed to find someone to bring out that light inside her again.

The light he could so clearly see in the photo of her holding that coffee cup, when she was free, without the weight of the world on her shoulders.

And that guy isn't you.

Jake groaned, dropping the iPad into his lap. He didn't even know why he'd thought that. Of course, he wouldn't be that person for her. He was here to keep her safe, to keep anyone from getting their hands on her again, so that someday she could find her happiness again. With someone good.

Closing out of the files, he stared at the ceiling for a minute, unable to wipe away the contrasting pictures of Beth in his head. The bright girl from *before*, and the thin, soft-spoken, traumatized girl he'd faced at her house.

"Fuck it," he muttered, leaving the tablet on the floor to head back into the kitchen. There was already a plate waiting for him with two sandwiches, and he took the seat in front of it silently.

"Someone's extra broody," Mike said around a mouthful of food. "More bad news?"

"No." Jake shook his head and forced down a bite that tasted like ash in his mouth. "I'm just pissed we're flying blind here."

"I know, boss." Ollie nodded, tossing a kitchen knife in the air and catching it repeatedly. "But Brendan will figure it out, he always does."

"Brendan will do everything he can, but he has his limits. We don't even know how the arrangements were made." Dropping the sandwich back on his plate, Jake banged his fist on the table. "We don't know fucking anything. There isn't a single goddamn thread for us to pull in this mess, and we're just dangling her out there like a piece of bait."

"The other guys are there, man. We're not dangling her like bait, we're watching over her and we're trying not to fuck up her life, isn't that what you said?" Mike was using his own words against him, but Jake wasn't in the mood for it.

"I know what I said," he growled, glaring at the plate in front of him like it was the problem. "She's just been through enough already. She doesn't deserve this."

"You're right." Mike shrugged, taking another bite of his sandwich, and Jake almost reminded him to move Brendan's laptop over, but he didn't have the energy to worry about the crumbs that would piss the other man off when he woke up. "But what else are we supposed to do?"

"If I had the answer to that, I wouldn't feel so fucking useless right now," Jake mumbled, forcing another tasteless bite down.

"You should sleep," Ollie said, catching the knife and slapping it down on the table beside his empty plate. "Benny is a fucking pussy most of the time, but he was right that you've been up for over a day, boss. Go sleep and then you'll be as useless as you usually are."

"Fuck off," Jake grumbled, but he still chuckled at the comment. Focusing on the food for a minute, he chowed his way through the first sandwich and was starting on the second when Mike pushed his empty plate away and cleared his throat.

"Want a soda?" he asked, rising from the chair and moving into the kitchen.

"Sure." Jake nodded at him, and Ollie raised his hand, which earned a middle finger from Mike even though they all knew Mike would bring him one.

"So, how was she?" Ollie's voice was surprisingly quiet, his eyes glued to the knife on the table that he was spinning around.

"Doing okay, I think. She's got her baggage, and her parents are suffocating her, but she's strong."

"Just like Badass," Ollie mumbled.

"What are her parents doing?" Mike asked as he came back into the room with three cans of Coke, sliding them across the table as he took his seat again.

"Being parents." Jake shrugged a shoulder, sighing as he popped the top of the soda, and the hiss of the carbonation filled the silence for a moment. "I mean, I get it. I'm sure they thought she was dead. Then she just shows back up on the other side of the world, and she's been through hell, and now they just want her safe."

"Yeah," Mike replied softly, cracking his own soda and taking a sip. "I'd probably be the same way if she was my kid."

"Worse," Ollie added with a grin, and Mike tilted his can toward him in acknowledgement.

"Truth," Mike admitted. "I'd probably never let her out of my sight again."

"Like I said, I get it." Jake turned the can around until he could see the bright red and white of the logo, wiping his thumb through the condensation on the side. "But her room looks like a teenage girl's bedroom, not a twenty-eight-year-old woman's, and she doesn't even have a phone—"

"You went in her fucking bedroom?" Mike sat up straight, leaning forward on the table a little, and Jake raised his hands.

"Hey, she wanted to talk in private. It was her idea, not mine, and I can pretty much guarantee her parents would have eavesdropped anywhere else."

"Who doesn't have a phone these days?" Ollie asked, picking up the knife and using it to point at him. "Doesn't your eleven-year-old niece have a cell phone?"

"Yeah, she does, and she's *twelve* and uses it constantly, which is just one more reason why I don't get it. I'm sure they don't leave her alone, but with everything that's happened to her, wouldn't it be smart for her to have a way to call for help if she needed it?"

"You mean a way to call *you* for help?" As usual, Mike drove a nail straight into the truth, but while there was a slight edge to his voice, he could hear the concern in it too.

"Me, the police, whoever. If something went wrong, she should have—"

"Then we'll order her a phone," Mike said, cutting him off as he pulled the laptop closer. "Easy solution to a stupid problem, and we don't get easy shit very often."

"You think her parents are going to be okay with some strange guy giving her a cell phone?" Jake scoffed, scratching at the scruff on his cheeks as he remembered just how disheveled he'd probably looked showing up on their doorstep at the crack of dawn.

"Who the fuck cares if they're okay with it? The girl needs a phone." Ollie pointed the knife at Mike this time. "Get her one of those nice smartphones, not a shitty burner."

"Yeah, yeah," Mike mumbled, tapping away at the keyboard.

"Tell me where to pick it up and I'll go get it this afternoon while you guys get some sleep," Ollie volunteered, and even though the guy was a crazy bastard most of the time, there was a reason he was on the team. He was a good man underneath it all, even if he was more than a little unstable.

"Just don't wreck the car, okay?" Jake grinned at him, and Ollie flipped the knife in his hand, smiling back like a madman, which only made Jake roll his eyes. "I'm serious."

"Sure thing, boss. Not a scratch." Finally opening his own can of soda, Ollie took a drink and then looked at it, laughing under his breath. "You remember how we gave Badass a case of this for a wedding gift?"

"And that big ass box of Hostess Snoballs," Mike added, chuckling. "I wish I'd been there when they opened it."

"She emailed us that picture of her with all of them," Jake replied, remembering the overjoyed grin on Thalia's face as she sat on the floor with a pile of snowball packages in her lap and all around her.

"We need to take a job in London so we can drop in on her," Ollie said, and both he and Mike stared at the man for a second. "What?"

"Nothing. You just always come up with new ways to shock the shit out of me." Laughing, Jake kicked the leg on Ollie's chair, and the man flipped him off.

"It's not funny, jackass. The rest of us didn't get to see her when she got married," Ollie groused.

"But she *did* give us an open invitation to dinner the next time we were in London," Mike said, and all Jake could do was groan.

"Fine, after we square this shit away with Beth and make sure she's safe, we'll go see the Badass."

"Good. I'll shoot Charlie a text." Setting down the knife, Ollie pulled out his phone and started tapping away at it while Jake just stared. It took a second for Ollie to notice, but then he looked up. "What? He brought it up last week, and I told him to ask you, but he was too much of a pussy. I can't miss this opportunity to bust his balls."

"That makes so much more sense than you texting Charlie about which boy you want to take to prom," Jake snarked, laughing through his groan of pain when Ollie landed a kick square on his shin. "Fucker! God, you're lucky I'm tired or I'd kick your ass right now."

"Well, speaking of texting, I've got the phone ordered. Now, you should go sleep, boss. You worry me when you start talking about high school dances." Mike shook his head at the two of them like he didn't fuck around just as often, but the fake judgmental expression didn't bother Jake at all.

"Thanks, man, I was just about to discuss what colors we wanted to wear for homecoming." Grinning, Jake pushed up from the table, leaving most of his second sandwich untouched. "Don't eat my food, assholes. I'll crash for a bit and then come back for it, but come wake me up if anything happens."

"Sure thing, boss. I'll leave a note for Brendan too when I head upstairs," Mike said.

Ollie just flipped him off, which was his version of a good night. If they'd been in their house, he probably would have thrown the knife just to fuck with him, but since this was a rental Jake was grateful the idiot had some self-control.

Returning the middle finger, Jake headed toward the bedroom again, shutting the door behind him so he could strip down. As he set his gun and his phone on the bedside table, he had to admit that it made him feel a little better knowing Beth would have a way to call him soon enough.

But it was the low buzz of excitement in his veins at having an excuse to see her again that made him feel simultaneously good and horrible. Sure, it meant he'd be able to confirm she was safe again with his own eyes, and he'd have the chance to show her the video of Anthony's death... but he knew that wasn't the only reason he wanted to see her again.

He liked being around her. Hell, he liked *her*. The quiet strength that he'd only seen a glimpse of, the creative way she'd dealt with her lingering trauma, and the strange way she'd put her trust in him so quickly.

For someone who had been through so much shit to allow him to get that close to her, to bring him into her bedroom, her safe place — it was big.

Even if all she'd wanted was the information he'd offered, she'd still let him in. Listened to him, believed him, *trusted* him, and that came with the pressure to earn it.

And he would.

He'd do whatever it took to earn that trust because, as crazy as it sounded, he already felt responsible for her. He hadn't been there to stop Marcus from taking Thalia a second time, but he was here this time.

No one was going to get their hands on Beth again, and as soon as he knew which motherfucker had dared to try and come for her...

He'd kill them himself.

TEN

Beth

The black SUV across the street only moved once throughout the day. It wasn't gone long though, and two of the big guys stayed behind, sitting on the curb across from her house, watching.

It would have been unnerving if Jake hadn't explained it first, but knowing they were with him made their constant presence comforting. For the first time since she'd surfaced, she felt like she was… safe?

No, that wasn't the right word for it.

If anything, 'safe' should've been the furthest thing from her mind. She should have felt terrified someone was coming for her. Hell, a normal person would've had a meltdown and locked herself in her room with a knife — not started binge-watching Netflix with her parents in the living room like it was any other day.

But, while there was definitely fear over whoever was out there, along with the ever-present panic she always dealt with, she felt like there was finally some kind of hope inside all the darkness.

She'd tried not to think about the possibility of being taken again, but it wasn't like the idea had ever been far from her mind either. Marcus and Anthony had taught her a brutal lesson in just how easy it was to steal someone from their life, to pluck a human being out of a parking lot and make them disappear.

If it weren't for Thalia she would have stayed gone.

She would have died.

It was insane she'd survived at all, but even though Thalia had told everyone on the forum that both Marcus and Anthony were dead, she'd never quite been able to believe that Anthony was gone. Thalia had killed Marcus with her own hands, she'd watched him die, but all they'd seen of Anthony's death was a report from the prison and a few photos that could have been his body or a lookalike. He had the money to make something like that happen. He was evil enough to do it, to find a way out of prison and come after each of them again.

But when Jake said he was dead, that he'd seen it, that one of *his* men had done it... she'd finally believed it.

So, maybe it wasn't feeling safe, but a subtle relaxing of the constant tension she hadn't even realized she was carrying. A weight lifted. A sense of relief.

Relief that two of the monsters from her nightmares really were gone, even if another monster was apparently hunting her — but it wouldn't be easy now.

Last time she'd been alone, vulnerable, naïve. This time she had Jake and his team watching over her, she wasn't alone, and she definitely wasn't naïve anymore. Anthony had ripped that out of her long before the other monsters of the world ever got their hands on her, but she'd survived... and he hadn't.

"You seem good, honey," her mom said, breaking the internal spiral of dark thoughts and pulling Beth back to the softness of the couch and the glow of the television.

They'd spent most of the day like this. Beth curled up on the couch, her knees tucked to her chest, her mom lounging against the pillows on one side, and her dad in his recliner. It was nice to just sit with them, no expectations except choosing what to watch next. Beth closed her eyes when her mom reached over to fix a strand of hair and tuck it behind her ear.

"I've missed this."

"Me too," she whispered, smiling a little as her mom continued to run her fingers gently through her hair.

"Did that man bring good news about your friend?"

"Jake?" The question threw her off balance since her mom and dad had spent the entire day acting as if the early morning visit hadn't even happened. They'd asked if she was okay after he left, and then they'd dropped the topic altogether — which wasn't like them at all — but bringing it up during a binge-watch of 'Girl Boss' wasn't exactly a smooth transition.

"Yes, Jake," her mom clarified, but her voice was light, not strained or stressed as she repeated her question. "Did he have some good things to share about your friend? Thalia?"

Beth wet her lips, pressing them together as she shifted on the couch, pulling her knees a little tighter to her chest as she tried to figure out how to answer. Or, rather, how to *lie*. The disappointed look on her mom's face as she let her hand drop back to her lap made Beth's stomach twist, so she forced a small smile and guided her mom's hand back to her hair.

Just say what she wants to hear.

"Yeah, it was a good talk. He's really nice."

"That's wonderful, honey. It really seems to have helped." For once her mom's smile looked real, the tense lines on her forehead easing just a bit as she returned to playing with Beth's hair. "I'm glad he came by."

"Me too." Scooting a little closer, Beth laid her head on her mom's knee, closing her eyes again to soak in the soothing rhythm of her mom's delicate movements. Occasionally she'd pull one piece of hair from the rest, curling it around her finger a few times before letting it fall back. Then her short nails would brush over her scalp, gently seeking a tangle, or a strand out of place, before fixing it with the softest touch. Beth felt more of the tension ease, like her body was taking a breath after holding it for too long.

She almost felt... normal.

Her mom wasn't walking on eggshells around her or pressing her for answers she couldn't — or wouldn't — give. It reminded her of what life had been like before everything and tears stung her eyes. "You used to do this for me all the time when I was in high school."

"I remember," she replied softly, and there was more than a hint of sadness in the simple words.

I'm sorry I haven't sat with you on the couch like this since I came back.

I'm sorry I keep pushing you away.

I wish I was different.

I wish I was better.

There were too many things she wanted to say in that moment, but she didn't want to ruin it, and she couldn't get the words out anyway. Instead, she hugged her knees a little harder and went with something she wished she'd said more often before she was taken. "I love you, Mom, and… I'm really glad I have you."

"I love you too, Beth. So very much," she whispered back, pressing a long kiss to her hair. A short sniffle followed it, but Beth didn't lift her head. If her mom was crying, they were happy tears for once, and that was more than she would have dared to hope for when she woke up that morning. Her mom cleared her throat, toying with her hair again as she picked up the remote with her free hand. "One more episode?"

"Yeah," Beth replied, smiling a little even though only her dad could see it. "Another episode sounds great."

As she felt her mom gently rest her arm on her side, softly tracing endless circle patterns with her thumb on Beth's skin, she let out a slow breath. She didn't know what had caused the shift between them… but she was glad.

Even if it didn't last, a moment of normalcy was more than she could expect, and she wanted to take advantage of it.

"Wanna sit with us, Dad?" The offer brought back a tremor of tension, but the teary smile on his face as he got up from his chair was worth it.

"I'd love to," he answered, his face cracking a bit as he moved to sit beside her. He shifted on the couch a few times before finally leaning back, carefully leaving space between them, and she loved him for that. For his quiet caring, and how he never pushed her. Her dad clasped his hands in his lap, then pulled them apart, fidgeting for a moment. Almost reaching for her, before hesitating and moving back to his lap.

"It's okay." Beth laid her hand palm up on her leg, and she definitely heard him sniffle as he gently took it, not even squeezing. Her dad just wrapped his fingers to the back of her hand, but she knew this was something good. The rush of tension was easing off again, returning to a slightly more manageable hum in her veins, and if this wasn't progress… she didn't know what would be.

Maybe I can get better.

"I love you, sweetheart," he whispered, and she smiled a little as his Adam's apple bobbed.

"I love you, too, Dad." Keeping her eyes on the television, she could tell her parents were looking at each other over her head, but she did her best to ignore it. They were probably thinking exactly what she was — *this is good.*

It felt like a giant step forward even though it was pretty small in the scheme of things.

Other girls on the forum were dating, getting jobs, learning to really live… and Beth was celebrating sitting on the couch between her own parents.

Goddammit.

Swallowing down the self-criticism, she risked a glance up at her mom and caught her wiping a tear off her cheek. Her mom rallied quickly though, smiling again as she lifted the remote and adjusted the volume. "Would you want to watch Sherlock after this?"

"Yeah, Mom. That sounds good."

She'd soak in as much normalcy as she could handle before she had to go to bed and be reminded of just how fucked-up she still was with the click of a handcuff.

ELEVEN

Jake

Two Days Later

"How the fuck do we not have a single name?" Ollie snapped.

Brendan slammed his fist onto the table beside his laptop. "Fuck off, Ollie! You think this shit is easy? Come over here and do it yourself!"

"Maybe I should since you're not finding anything useful!" Ollie pushed himself out of his chair, but Mike caught his shoulder and shoved him back into it.

"None of this is helping," Mike growled. "Calm the fuck down."

"It just doesn't make sense." Rubbing a hand over his face, Jake paced along the wall near the front door, his cell phone still clutched tight in his fist. "I've reached out to everyone I can think of, and no one knows anything. How's that even possible?"

"There's a lot more freelance teams now," Brendan said, letting out a frustrated groan as he leaned back to stare at his laptop. Intertwining his fingers, he rested his hands on top of his head, brow furrowed in concentration. "A lot of this shady shit used to hit Infinity Consulting first, but they disappeared off the fucking map six months ago, and it's turned into a goddamn free for all."

"Has everyone got back to you, boss?" Mike asked, still lurking behind Ollie in case the asshole decided to go for Brendan again.

"No, but enough have reached back out with zero intel that it's pretty clear whoever took the fucking job is flying way under the radar." Shaking his head, Jake looked down at his phone again and felt the same itch he'd been fighting for two days. He wanted to be able to call Beth, to confirm she was okay voice-to-voice, but he kept putting off going to see her again.

"Listen, I'm digging through all the shit James and Thalia sent over from the Williams brothers' servers. The problem is that asshole didn't auction Beth off like the others." Brendan slammed his laptop shut; his face twisted with the simmering rage they were all dealing with. "I don't have a fucking clue where to start looking for who might be hunting her down."

"What about the brothel?" Mike pressed.

"I have the bullshit report from the Thai police that lists who *supposedly* ran that hellhole, but that motherfucker didn't have the resources to pull off something like this even when he was alive. Oh, and *yes*, that guy did die mysteriously shortly after her extraction."

"Just a fucking fall guy," Ollie grumbled.

"Yep." Brendan muttered under his breath for a minute, and Jake could tell he was fraying at the edges. Neither of them had slept since the afternoon before, but Brendan was carrying the weight of finding the info they needed, and it was wearing him down faster.

Ollie leaned forward suddenly, and Mike grabbed his shoulder, but Ollie shook him off and set the knife he'd been playing with down. Glancing back, Ollie waited until Mike stepped back before he spoke. "So *that* douchebag is dead, but what about potential partners? Investors? Property deeds?"

"No info on that. Hell, considering that part of the world and how corrupt some of the cops and politicians are, we're lucky we got one name," Brendan replied.

"One *dead* name."

"You're not helping," Jake said, giving Ollie a 'back-the-fuck-off' look as he approached the table again. "I know we're all frustrated, but Beth and her parents are still safe and at home."

"How long are we going to stay on the house though?" Mike grabbed the chair next to Ollie and yanked it away from the table so he could drop into it. "I mean, I'm not trying to be a dick here, but we've been on the place for three days and we haven't seen anyone suspicious rolling by. Hell, we don't even have confirmation that someone actually took the job, and you and Brendan have been turning over every rock you can find."

"You just want to leave her in the fucking wind?" Jake's question came out a lot sharper than he meant for it to, but the idea of leaving Beth vulnerable made his skin crawl. It didn't matter that it was a reasonable question... except it did.

"No, man— shit. That's not what I meant, I just—"

"It's fine." Waving a hand to cut off Mike's explanation, Jake forced a deep breath. "I know what you're saying, and I agree that we can't just live outside her house forever, but I'm also not comfortable pulling out yet. If someone took the job the day it posted, these assholes have had about four or five days to find out where she is and get a plan together."

"Which means they'd probably make a move soon," Ollie continued.

"But not necessarily today." Sighing, Jake looked around at each of the guys. "We all know how shit varies depending on what part of the world you're in and where you're trying to go, so we can't just bail out because nothing's happened *yet.*"

"But how long do you want to give it, boss?" Mike shifted in his seat, angling himself toward Jake instead of Ollie as he raised his hands up. "Look, I'm not pushing for us to back off now. I'm not even saying we need to decide on a timeline, but it's something to think about."

"I get what you're saying, and I'm sure you're not the only one thinking it." Jake looked down at his phone and knew that if his own men were getting antsy, Beth had to be climbing the walls, which meant the kindest thing to do would be to give her an update. And the phone.

And let her see with her own eyes that Anthony Williams was dead.

"Fuck it." Snapping his fingers, he pointed at Brendan. "Go get some sleep, Mike and Ollie can keep track of any updates that pop up on your screen."

"I'm fine," Brendan grumbled, but it was a lie and they both knew it.

"I wasn't asking, asshole. Rack out. I'm going to take the truck and give Beth an update on what's going on."

"You want to tell that girl we don't know shit?" Ollie raised an eyebrow at him, but as dickish as the comment was, Jake could see the man was serious. They all knew that would only make her panic more, but silence wasn't helping either.

"I'll phrase it differently, jackass," Jake growled. "We need to give her the phone anyway. Once we can contact her directly, without bothering her parents, all of this will be a little easier."

"What's your excuse gonna be this time?" Mike asked, and Jake rubbed at his eyes as the options spiraled through his head. Leaning forward, Mike braced his elbows on the edge of the table and shrugged a bit. "I don't think they're going to like the idea of a strange guy stopping by to give their daughter a cellphone."

"I'm not an idiot, I won't tell them about the phone."

"Then what are you going to tell them?" Mike's stare wasn't judgmental, but he hated just how much the guy was poking holes in his plans this morning.

"I'll figure it out." Clenching his jaw, he turned toward the bedroom to grab his stuff, calling back over his shoulder, "Go to bed, Brendan. I'm not fucking around."

"Fine," the other man called back, and the screech of a chair moving told Jake he was following orders.

As far as everything else the guys had brought up to him… he'd just have to deal with that shit later. There was still a chance one of their contacts would reach back out with information, and until then at least Beth would have a phone.

When he pulled up in the second SUV, the other guys were out and ready to move before he'd even shifted the vehicle into 'Park.'

"What's up?" Charlie called out, and Jake knew the man had his hand on a gun behind his back. Mike may have asked good questions, but even if the other guys were thinking the same things, it was clear that none of them were slacking. They were just as committed to keeping Beth safe as he was, and that knowledge lowered his blood pressure a little.

Grabbing the iPad and the stuff for the new phone, Jake climbed out of the car and walked over to them. "Everything's fine. I'm just bringing her the phone and giving her an update."

"*Is* there an update?" Benny asked.

"Not really, but I'm sure she's losing her shit with no updates," he said, lifting the iPad in his other hand. "And she wanted to see the Anthony video."

"That's good." Asaf nodded, relaxing a little as the other guys moved their hands away from hidden weapons. "She deserves to see the tape, and it'll be nice having a way to contact her. There is one thing before you go in, though."

"What is it?" Jake glanced at the front of the house, looking for anything out of place.

"We've been parked in front of the house for a few days now and people are starting to notice. Apparently, the Hernandez family lives in this one," Asaf tilted his head toward the house across from Beth's. "Luckily they've been out of town the last few days, but one of the neighbors walked over to ask us what was going on."

Fuck, fuck, fuck. "And what did you tell them?"

"I told the nosy bitch that we're private security and she didn't need to know why the fuck we're here," Charlie piped up.

Jake pinched the bridge of his nose. "Please tell me one of you assholes kept him from actually saying that."

"He managed to be less of an idiot in the moment," Benny clarified. "But it does mean people are paying attention, and I can't promise her parents haven't noticed us too."

"No one's called the police yet," Asaf added, but the shrug that came after told Jake that the man didn't think it was far behind.

"Okay, thanks for the update, guys. Just stay in the car. If the cops come, I'll make sure Beth knows we might send them her way."

"You going to give her parents a heads up?" Benny crossed his arms, leaning against the side of the SUV, and Jake wished that everyone would stop asking questions he didn't feel like dealing with on no sleep.

"Not yet." *That would just cause more issues.* "We'll deal with shit as it hits the fan, not before."

"You're the boss," Charlie said, giving a sarcastic salute before he turned back to hop in the driver's seat.

"Good luck," Asaf said quietly, squeezing Jake's shoulder before nudging him turned toward the house.

"Thanks." Heading up the walkway, he still had no fucking clue what he was going to say, or how he was going to explain bringing an iPad to her house this time, but he'd always been decent at thinking on his feet.

Jake checked his watch, glad to see it was after ten in the morning on a Tuesday so at least he wouldn't be waking them up with this visit. Rapping his knuckles on the door a few times, he stepped back and waited, but the door opened much quicker this time.

"You're back," Mrs. Doherty said, looking him over, and he turned on his most charming smile.

"Yes, ma'am. I'd told Beth I'd let her take a look at some stuff Thalia gave me before I left town." He lifted the iPad a little to try and bolster the bullshit explanation, silently praying the woman wouldn't ask any follow-up questions. "Does she have a few minutes?"

"Jake?" Beth's voice came from the stairs, and he leaned forward a little to be able to see her.

"Hey," he called into the house, offering a little wave as he watched her descend the steps. She was in a different shirt today, but the black yoga pants looked the same, and he was relieved to see a little color in her cheeks as she rounded the bottom of the stairs and joined her mom at the door. "Do you have a few minutes to talk?"

"Sure." Beth glanced at her mom, who opened the door a little wider, a small smile forming on the older woman's face.

"I'm glad you came back to talk again," Mrs. Doherty said, looking between him and her daughter. "I think Beth enjoyed having someone other than us to hang out with."

She enjoyed it?

"Th-that's good." Jake fumbled over the words, clearing his throat before he forced the smile back on his face to cover his surprise. "I'm happy to stop by anytime I'm in town."

"Great!" her mom replied, waving him inside so she could shut the door behind him. "You two can have the living room to yourselves, and I can make some coffee if you—"

"It's fine, Mom," Beth interrupted, shuffling backward on the tile of the entryway. "We'll talk in my room."

"Oh, okay, um… I can bring some coffee up?"

"I actually just finished a cup, and I promise I won't be in your hair long, Mrs. Doherty," Jake replied, feeling awkward as fuck standing by the front door making small talk with her mom like he was waiting to take Beth out on a date.

Why the hell are you even thinking about a date?

"Are you hungry?" her mom pressed, and Beth sighed loud enough for the older woman to notice. "Orrrr you can just tell me if you need something. I'll be in the laundry room, okay?"

"Thanks, Mom." Beth gave a tight smile and headed for the stairs, turning to look at him in a silent request to follow, which he did... even though it felt even stranger this time than it had the first day he'd visited.

No, it didn't just feel strange, it felt *wrong*.

The guys were right that he shouldn't be going to her room. He shouldn't be alone with her in her bedroom. It wasn't right. It wasn't appropriate.

He was there to protect her — end of story.

That's all.

Jake was so caught up in thinking about how he shouldn't have been there at all, that he didn't even realize he'd walked right into her bedroom until he heard her door click shut behind him.

Fuck.

He turned around to face her, and the way her brows pulled together — combined with how she'd crossed her arms and hunched her shoulders — told him all he needed to know about how anxious she was for news.

I should have done this yesterday.

"So?" Beth's voice was barely above a whisper, but it erased all the thoughts from his mind as if she'd shouted it.

"You, um, you moved the stuffed animals." He waved a hand at the empty surface of the chest tucked at the end of her bed, groaning inwardly at how impossibly stupid he sounded. *What the fuck, Jake?*

"Yeah, they're in the closet." She pointed toward it, and he actually turned to look like he gave a single fuck where she kept her old toys.

"Sorry, I just noticed it," he muttered, trying to explain away the weird comment, but it was probably too late for that. Digging in his back pocket, he tugged out the new cell and charging cord, holding them toward her. "Anyway, I brought you a phone. Last time I was here you said you didn't have one, and I just figured it would be easier if we could contact each other like this instead of me showing up here and making your parents nervous."

"You don't make them nervous." Beth moved a few steps forward and took the phone without touching his fingers, which he probably shouldn't have noticed at all, but he did.

Wait, what did she say?

"I don't?" he asked, a little stunned as she sat on the edge of the bed, a little closer to him.

"No." She swiped up to unlock the phone, immediately tapping on the 'contacts' icon. A second later she looked up at him. "You already put your number in here?"

"Yeah, I just figured it would be easier." Shoving a hand through his hair, he blew out a breath, but he couldn't shake the feeling that he was doing something wrong just by being near her. "I already put the number in mine too. That way if you have questions or need something you can just... call me. Or text, or not. I mean, *fuck*, you don't have to use it just to talk to me, you—"

"Thanks, Jake," she said, mercifully bringing his idiotic babble to an end. "I appreciate it."

"No problem."

"I've wanted a phone, but I never bothered mentioning it to my parents. I mean..." She huffed out a soft, bitter laugh. "Who would I call?"

"Whoever you wanted?" he suggested, and she shook her head.

"I don't have anyone else to call." Locking the phone again, she met his gaze, and he wanted to move closer to her. He wanted to have a *reason* to move closer to her, even though he absolutely shouldn't be in her fucking room at all, but the urge to wrap his arms around her and tell her everything was going to be okay was strong. Beth tilted her head a little, a few strands of hair falling into her face before she brushed them away. "Is this why you came by?"

"Partly." His voice came out stiff, and he cleared his throat, swallowing when he realized how dry his mouth suddenly felt. "I wanted to check in with you again and show you something."

"Show me what?"

"You were worried it was Anthony Williams coming after you when I was here last time, so..." Lifting the iPad, he unlocked it and navigated to the video file he'd saved, leaving it open on the screen before he held it out to her. "I thought you might want to see it for yourself."

"See it?" she repeated, reaching for the iPad, but her gaze stayed on his when he didn't let go of it.

"It's the footage from the prison. It's his death, and it's real, but it's your choice if you want to watch it." Jake's palm felt sweaty where he held onto the edge of the tablet, not willing to let it go yet. Not until she understood. "You don't have to watch it if you don't want to, Beth."

"I want to." She tugged it toward her, but he didn't let her take it, even when she looked up at him confused.

"It's just…" *Fuck.* "It's not something you can get out of your head once you see it, so I want you to be sure." Jake had never quite understood why Benny tried to shield the people they rescued from what his team did to the bastards responsible, but he was starting to get it. She'd already been through so much, seen so many terrible things… did she really need more horror inside her head?

"I want to watch the video, Jake." Her voice was velvet-coated iron. Soft, serious, absolutely confident. There was no doubt in her eyes, no waver in her tone, and he didn't have the right to question her anyway.

"Okay." Letting go of the tablet, he kept his distance as she set the phone down beside her and braced the iPad on her lap. Her hair hid her face, which he hated, but he saw the way her grip on the case tightened when she hit play.

He didn't need to see the screen to remember every second of the footage.

Two men, Ollie and a guard in disguise, walked into the prison showers where Anthony stood alone, and the bastard turned to face them. The attack was quick. Three swift jerks of an arm buried the shiv in the bastard's abdomen. Then, finally, he collapsed to the tile where his blood slowly spread, mixing with the lingering water on the floor as it slid toward the drain.

Jake stayed completely still as Beth watched, and then watched again, and again, and again. He lost track of how many times she played the short video, bent over the tablet, silent and unmoving except when her hand would move to tap the arrow and make it restart, but he didn't interrupt her. If this was what she needed, then he didn't care how long he had to stand there.

Although, her mom might get nervous and come check on them soon. Not that he would blame her for it. He'd shaved before he came over this time, but he was still a man in her daughter's room. A man she didn't know.

Shit, it wasn't like Beth knew him either.

And none of them knew who he really was, *what* he really was — although Beth was getting a taste of the truth right now.

He was a killer.

Sure, he'd killed for his country first, but then he'd killed for whoever paid the right amount of money, and that had lasted longer than he liked to admit. Even now, with his team focused on saving people, it wasn't that much different. His hands weren't any cleaner just because he thought the people he killed deserved it.

That was why he always pulled the trigger.

His team didn't need to carry any more bodies on their conscience than they already had, and he'd never regretted it — he still didn't regret it — but for a moment he wished he was a better man. A man worthy of standing in her room, of the trust she'd given him.

You should leave.

Looking her over one more time, Jake forced himself to turn away and move toward the door, but he'd only taken a few steps when her voice stopped him.

"You're leaving?"

"Yeah, I can swing by and get the iPad later." He cleared his throat. "You take your time."

He was just coming up with new excuses to put him back in her presence when he should have done the opposite. If all of Brendan's VPN shit wasn't on the tablet, he'd give her the code and let her keep the fucking thing, but that wouldn't be a good idea. There was too much on there. Things she didn't need to see.

"It's okay, you can take it."

He knew she was holding it out, and he knew if he took it, he had no reason to come back, which was all the more reason to grab it and go... but he didn't want to.

"Jake?"

Goddammit. His name in her voice was like a physical pull, and before he could even second-guess himself, he'd already turned around and taken the tablet back.

"I'll, um... I'll keep you updated," he mumbled, moving backward toward the door as he gestured at the phone beside her on the bed. "I mean I'll text you."

"Okay." She picked up the phone, cradling it in her delicate hands, and he had a brief flicker in his head where he wondered how small her hand would feel in his, but he pushed it away.

Grabbing for the doorknob, he was about to open it when he remembered what Asaf had told him, and he cursed under his breath. "Sorry, one more thing. Your neighbors have noticed the SUV across the street. No one's called the cops *yet*... but if they do, we might need to have you confirm we're here for your security."

"My parents—"

"I know, and I'm sorry." Clenching his jaw, he hated the sudden look of panic in her eyes, and he dropped his gaze back to the carpet like a fucking coward. "It'll be a last resort, and hopefully it won't come to that. But if it happens, just tell your parents I'm being an overprotective douchebag. You can blame me. You don't have to tell them what's going on."

"Have you found them? The person looking for me?"

You should have left when you had the chance, idiot.

"Not yet, but we will. I promise." The last word came out tight, like his throat knew he shouldn't say it, but it came out anyway, and when he looked up and caught her warm brown eyes again... he knew he meant it. Even if he had to let his guys take another job while he lived in a fucking car in front of her house, he wasn't going to let anyone get their hands on her.

"Okay. Thank you, Jake," she said, her soft voice wreaking havoc on his nerves as he tightened his grip on the doorknob. "For the phone, and for watching out for me, and for letting me see the video. All of it."

"No problem." Nodding, he yanked the door open a little too hard, forcing him to grab for it so it wouldn't bang into the wall. "Fuck, I'll, um, I'll keep you in the loop."

Beth stood up from the bed, but he backed into the hallway before she could move toward him. She didn't say anything, but he knew she'd followed him to the top of the stairs. He could *feel* her eyes on his back, and that urge to get away as fast as possible was warring with the need to stay beside her. To protect her. To stay between her and whatever monsters might be lurking — or not lurking.

Fuck, fuck, fuck.

He slipped out the front door without hesitating, not breathing until he'd shut it behind him again. The warm breeze and bright sunlight didn't feel right for how fucked-up his head was at the moment, but that was all on him.

Mike had been right to question shit. If someone was coming for her, they hadn't made a single ripple in the dark water his team, and others like them, spent their time in — and pulling that off wasn't easy.

They were either very good and very well-supplied… or they didn't exist.

It was possible whoever had posted the job had changed their mind or realized they didn't have the funds to make it happen. It was possible that Jake had just barged his way into this girl's life for no fucking reason at all. Scared her over nothing more than shadows from her past, which had probably made everything worse for her.

But her mom said she enjoyed it.

"Dammit," he growled under his breath, marching toward the SUV. The back door opened first, and Benny climbed out, concern etched into the deep crease in his forehead.

"Did something happen?" their medic asked, always concerned for the well-being of anyone he felt responsible for, and *shit*, maybe he should have been the one talking to her. Benny probably wouldn't have gone to her room or fucked up the process of explaining why they were there.

Hell, it really should have been Asaf. He always handled the families in situations like this, but instead he'd barged in like he had some kind of right to ruin her life personally.

"Jake?" Benny stepped closer.

"It's fine."

"You don't look fine," Benny retorted, and Asaf pushed his door open, narrowing his eyes in wordless agreement with their medic.

"I'm just tired," he snapped, hooking a thumb toward the SUV he'd arrived in. "One of you head back to the house and tell the guys I'm staying here. Keys are in the center console."

"Sitting out here isn't going to change anything, Jake." Asaf shaded his eyes as he looked past him toward the house. "We've got this. She's safe. You should go back and get some real sleep."

"I'm not leaving." It wasn't up for debate, and as he met each of his men's gazes, he could tell they realized he wasn't changing his mind. Benny was the first one to move, stepping aside and holding the door open for him.

"At least lie down in the back row," the man muttered as he climbed in, and he took the advice and slipped between the captain's chairs, dropping onto the back seat.

"Okay, so who's going back to the house?" Charlie asked, turning around from the driver's seat to look at him. "I vote me."

"Fine." Jake waved a hand at him.

"No way, Charlie." Benny leaned into the car with one hand braced on the frame. "I told you guys yesterday that I needed to make a supply run in case shit goes south. We were low on field supplies before we took the last job, and I'm not getting caught unprepared. I'll call the guys and pick shit up on my way to the house."

"You're a dick," Charlie grumbled, but Jake tuned them out. He didn't care who left, he just knew *he* wasn't going anywhere.

Twisting on the seat, he leaned against the window so he could still see the front door and stretched out his legs as much as he could. His gun dug into his back a little in this position, but he liked the reminder that it was there if he needed it. The guys talked back and forth for another minute, but eventually the door shut, and he saw Benny pull away.

"You can close your eyes, Jake. It's not like you won't wake up if we even crack a window." Asaf was trying to be helpful, and he knew he needed sleep. He'd lectured Brendan on the same issue earlier, but even though his eyes hurt, he was too tense to fall asleep.

"Maybe in a little while."

Asaf just nodded and faced forward in the front seat.

"I'll take a nap if he doesn't want to." Charlie laughed, angling the rearview mirror toward himself. "Can't look this pretty without some real beauty sleep."

"Fuck off, Charlie. No one thinks you're pretty," Jake grumbled, but the guy's laughter was always a little contagious and he found himself chuckling despite the shit mood all his overthinking had put him in.

And maybe that's all it was.

Maybe he was jumping at shadows, so intent on keeping the list of girls James and Thalia had provided safe that he'd overreacted.

Not that it made his actions any better. If anything, it made him charging into her life even worse, but if she was safe, and he was just being crazy... that would be fine with him.

No one had ever accused him of being introspective, but something about Beth sent him spiraling. Made him second-guess himself more than he ever had before, and that wasn't good. He needed to be on point if things 'went south' like Benny said, even if all their current evidence was saying everything would be fine.

But if everything really *was* fine, then they'd need to go back home to take another job.

He'd have no reason to see her again.

That's a good thing. That would be a good thing.

He repeated it over and over in his head, but there was a part of him that didn't agree, and it made him hate himself just a little more.

You're a bastard, Jake. An absolute bastard.

TWELVE

Beth

"Will you move the pork chops from the freezer to the fridge for tomorrow, sweetheart?" her dad called through the backdoor, but when her mom started to turn toward the refrigerator, Beth stopped her.

"Sure, Dad, I got it!" she called back, leaving her mom at the sink to finish rinsing off the plates from dinner while she dug out the package from the freezer. Setting it on a shelf in the fridge, she returned to the dishwasher and continued loading it for her mom.

"I could have done that, honey," her mom said quietly, and Beth tensed, holding tight to the pot she'd just taken from the sink.

"I can do things too, Mom," she replied just as softly, hands shaking from the possibility of confrontation, but for once her mom didn't push it. The sigh she earned in response was so much better than the fake cheerfulness she'd dealt with for over a year and a half. It was more real, more honest.

And they all needed more of that in this house.

Maybe Jake's presence had brought on the change. After all, he was the only visitor she'd had at the house since she'd come back — well, other than her sister, but Christina and her family didn't count. They weren't just there to see her; they were there for her parents too.

Jake had come only to speak with her, and he'd brought reality with him. Of course, it hadn't been good news, but at least he'd talked to her like a real person. He'd told her the truth. He'd let her see the video of Anthony's death.

And he'd trusted that she could handle it.

He'd believed she could handle it better than her parents.

God... It had been so long since she'd been treated like an adult instead of a breakable object. Everyone handled her like a porcelain doll, meant to be kept on a shelf away from anything that could damage it — as if she wasn't already damaged.

But Jake didn't seem to look at her like that. When he looked at her... it was like he really saw her. Like she wasn't a ghost.

Well, he *had* acted that way, until she'd zoned out on the murder video that morning like a complete psychopath, and he'd bolted. She'd probably freaked him out, but she hadn't been able to stop watching it. At first it was because she couldn't believe he was dead, that it was real — and then she'd kept replaying it because she knew it was.

The video was too grainy for the kind of detail she wanted, but it hadn't stopped her from studying every pixel. She'd wanted to see the pain on Anthony Williams' face when the knife went in, to see the emotionless robot feel a fraction of the hell he'd put her through. She'd leaned close to the screen, focusing on the blur of his face, and she'd imagined it. How he would have looked, how it would have sounded, how surprised the bastard probably was that someone had finally stood up to him. That moment of realization that he wasn't invincible, that he was going to die.

And then he did.

The pot slipped from her fingers into the dishwasher, making the plates on the bottom shelf rattle and her mom jumped. Flinching, Beth glanced over and mumbled a quick, "Sorry."

"Why don't you sit down, honey? I can finish cleaning up the kitchen."

No.

The damn word wouldn't make it past her lips, not with how her mom was looking at her. Like she was afraid the act of doing dishes was somehow too much for her to handle. Balling her hands into fists, Beth felt her nails dig into her palms as she tried to think of the right words that wouldn't hurt her mom's feelings but would still make her see her as something more like an adult.

"It's okay, I've got it," her mom continued, and Beth took a deep breath, remembering how Jake talked to her, how Jake trusted she could handle so much more than cleaning a fucking kitchen.

"I'm stronger than you think I am," she mumbled, but the rush of the water in the sink was too loud, and she knew her mom hadn't heard her when she looked over at her again, lips pursed with confusion.

"What, sweetheart?" Turning the water off, her mom waited, and even though her heart was racing Beth swallowed, preparing herself to say it again.

"I-I'm not weak, Mom." It was a little louder, but not as confident as she'd hoped. Licking her lips, she couldn't meet her mom's eyes, but she managed to stare at her chin as she repeated, "I'm stronger than you think."

"Oh, honey, I don't think you're—"

"You do," she interrupted, which only made the buzzing panic intensify, but all she had to do was think about the video and she felt strong enough to continue. "I can clean the kitchen. I can make my own food. I can *do things*."

"We know that." Her dad's voice came from the other side of the breakfast bar, and she turned to face him.

"We just don't want to push you," her mom added, and Beth made herself look back and forth between the two of them. She could feel how much they loved her, but along with it came the constant, crushing worry that had been present in every moment with them since she'd surfaced — and she couldn't handle it anymore.

"This doesn't help me." Shaking her head, Beth pressed her nails harder into her palms, feeling the reassuring bite of pain that reminded her she was alive, that she was really here. "Y-you have no idea what I can handle."

Her mom's gasp almost sounded like a hiccup, and she knew if she looked at her, she'd see tears threatening in her mom's eyes... so she didn't look. Instead, she stared down at the open dishwasher between them, skin tingling with nervous energy as she waited to see what they'd say now that she'd finally spoken up.

"I'm sorry." The words were hushed, muddled with the threat of tears, but Beth heard them easily in the uncomfortable silence of the kitchen. Her mom's breath shuddered slightly before she continued, "We're just trying to help, honey."

"What do you need, sweetheart? Just tell us." Her dad moved closer, standing on the other side of the bar where she and her sister had eaten breakfast on so many mornings years before. Before everything got so fucked up.

What do you need?

The question was too big. There were a hundred things that flooded her mind, drowning her in possible answers until she was tongue-tied and even more frustrated. It was this bullshit that made them think she couldn't handle something as simple as making her own coffee, or cleaning, or doing her laundry — but how could she make them see her differently when she couldn't even have a conversation about it?

Talking to them was so much harder than talking to Jake.

He'd trusted that she could handle what he needed to tell her without asking. He'd never doubted her, never judged her. Not even when she'd panicked over the loss of the zip-ties. Instead, he'd just accepted it, accepted all of her shit without question.

"I need you to trust me," she whispered, hating how stiff her throat was because it forced her to awkwardly clear her throat so that she wouldn't sound quite so hoarse. "I need you to believe I *can* handle things... otherwise how can you expect me to be normal again?"

She hadn't meant to say the last part, but it tumbled past her lips before she could stop it, and a louder sniffle from her mom confirmed she'd made her cry. *Dammit.*

"We do trust you." Her dad's voice was close, behind her, but he stepped into her peripheral vision, and she leaned back against the counter so she could see them both.

"That's right." Closing the dishwasher, her mom removed the barrier between them and held out her hand, offering it as she whispered, "And I've always believed in you, Beth. We both have."

Goddammit.

She wanted to take her mom's hand, she wanted to reassure her, but it was taking all her energy just to maintain this moment of bravery so she wouldn't back down and drop the conversation completely.

"Honey, I'm sorry I upset you. I never meant to hurt you like that, I just didn't want... I-I don't even know." Another sniffle as her mom's hand trembled in the space between them. "I just want to take care of you because I love you. I love you so much."

"I know," Beth mumbled, taking her mom's hand, and looking her in the eyes even though it hurt to see her crying knowing she'd caused it. "I love you too. I've never doubted that, but I..."

"You want to be treated like an adult," her dad finished for her, and she turned to face him. There was a small, sad smile on his face, and those brown eyes — the same eyes she'd inherited from him — were filled with understanding. He'd always understood what she wanted better than her mom, and she wanted to thank him for that, but her throat was too tight and all she could do was nod.

"We can do that," her mom said, squeezing her hand lightly.

"We absolutely can." There was a promise in those words that made the tension in Beth's chest ease off a little, and she took her dad's hand when he held it out. "We both love you very much, Beth. More than you could possibly understand."

She was trying to think of something to say when the doorbell rang, and before the chime had even finished someone was banging on the front door. Beth jerked, gripping both of her parents' hands tight as everything Jake had warned her about flashed through her mind.

"It's okay, sweetheart, it's just the door," her dad said, patting her hand as he tried to pull away, but she held on.

"No, wait—"

"Honey, it's fine, your dad will get it," her mom reassured her, but when her dad's hand slipped away, and he moved toward the front door she shook her head.

"Dad, just wait a second!" she called out, but it was muddled by another loud series of bangs, like someone was pounding their fist on the front door as hard as they could.

"What on earth is going on?" her mom asked, a mix of concern and irritation blending into her tone, but Beth yanked her hand free to rush after her dad because she had a pretty good idea what could be waiting.

She was barely out of the kitchen when she saw him opening the front door. A million terrible things went through her head, but when she stumbled to a stop a few feet behind him and saw Jake on the front porch, she was almost dizzy with relief... until she caught the intense look on his face.

"Jake? Is something wrong?" Her dad was still holding onto the door, keeping Jake outside, but he wasn't the only one there. Two other men stood with him, each of them looking just as serious.

"Mr. Doherty, I'm sorry, but we need to come inside." Jake stepped forward and her dad moved to allow him and the other men through the door. The second she met Jake's gaze Beth felt all the blood leave her face, a nauseating twist in her stomach threatening to return the dinner they'd just finished.

It was happening.

Someone was coming for her. Here.

"Can I speak with you and Mrs. Doherty?" one of the men asked. He was older and he had a slight accent, but the soothing tone of his voice did nothing to calm her or her parents down.

"Who are you?" her dad snapped at the guy, harsher than she'd ever heard him speak to anyone, and then he rounded on Jake just as angry. "Jake, you need to explain yourself right now."

"My name is Asaf, and I'm happy to explain everything while Jake talks to Beth. Is there somewhere we can sit down?" The man with the accent turned toward the living room. "How about in here?"

"No, you need to tell us what's going on right now," her mom demanded, moving close to Beth's side and wrapping a hand around her arm.

"Please, Mrs. Doherty," Asaf said, offering a restrained smile. "I understand you're concerned, but I promise I'll explain everything."

"Is this about Beth? Is something wrong?" her dad pressed, and she noticed how he moved in front of her, trying to protect her because he didn't understand that's exactly what Jake and the others were there to do.

"Dad, it's okay," she finally spoke up, wishing her voice had come out a little more confident. "You guys talk to him, and I'll talk to Jake."

"Talk about what!" Her mom's grip tightened on her arm, but Beth laid a hand over her mom's and squeezed until she faced her.

"This is one of those times I need you to trust me," she whispered, but it was clearly loud enough for her dad to hear because he turned around.

"But honey…"

"Fine," her dad cut off whatever argument her mom was about to start, but it was clear from the stiff way he moved that he wasn't happy about it. "We just told her we'd trust her, Tanya, so let's hear what they have to say."

Her mom stumbled over her words for a moment, but when her dad stepped forward and took her arm, she finally released Beth's.

"Thank you, let's sit down together." Asaf gestured toward the living room, leading the way, but her mom still hesitated, turning back to look at her.

"It'll be okay," Beth reassured her, but she was pretty sure that was a lie. It was just the good kind of lie that would let her mom handle the situation as well as she could.

For now, anyway.

"Charlie, stay on the door," Jake commanded, looking at the dark-haired guy who hadn't said a word. "If you see anything you alert us immediately."

"You got it, boss," Charlie answered, immediately opening the front door, and Beth was almost certain she caught sight of a gun as he reached for the back of his pants. The door closed again before she could confirm it though, and then it was just her and Jake.

"Are they here?" she asked quietly.

"Not yet, but..." He blew out a rough breath, looking over the inside of her house where the sheer normalcy of everything just seemed to mock the situation.

Fuck.

This is real. Someone is coming after me.

Swallowing, Beth tried to ignore the sharp, panicked sound of her mother's voice coming from the living room. "Do you want to talk upstairs?"

"I think that's best." Jake waved a hand toward the stairs, not that he needed her to lead the way since he'd been there twice before. Beth didn't say a word about it though, wordlessly moving up the stairs as her parents' worried voices followed her. The first of her mom's sobs broke just as she opened her bedroom door, and she flinched at the sound.

"How bad is it?" The question probably wasn't the right one for the situation, but Beth couldn't think of anything else to say as Jake marched into her room. He was clutching a cell phone hard in one hand, and for a second she wondered if he had a gun too.

Are they here right now? Outside?

"Jake?"

"I'm sorry, Beth." His voice was as intense as everything else about him. He was dressed nicely, but he looked like a coiled spring, too tense, unable to stay still, ready to go off any second. Pacing back and forth in front of her closet, he shook his head, mumbled something under his breath, and then looked up at her. "This is all my fucking fault."

"Your fault?" she repeated, confused, the panic rising inside as she moved back and bumped into her vanity table.

"I couldn't find them. I couldn't fucking find them, but we got word of a private plane landing today and a team gearing up locally." Jake slammed his fist into her closet door, and Beth flinched, grabbing onto the edge of the little table as he started pacing again. "Based on the chatter my tech guy has picked up, we think it's them, and if it is them…"

"Then they're coming for me," Beth finished, and he groaned, shoving his free hand into his hair.

"It's worse than that. We still don't know how many people are in the team, how well-armed they are… *fuck!*" Jake fisted his hair, clenching his jaw tight for a moment. "The truth is we don't know shit, Beth. Nothing except that they're going to know where you live, and they won't hesitate to go through your family to get to you."

The whole world seemed to tilt as Jake spoke, every word worse than the one before until she had to push herself toward the bed so she could sit down before her legs gave out. She was light-headed, unable to get a full breath as panic tightened her chest, squeezing her lungs until they burned.

How could I have been so stupid?

Of course, they wouldn't just come after her. She didn't leave the fucking house anymore, so they couldn't grab her in a parking lot like the brothers had. This time they wouldn't just hurt her, they'd hurt her parents. Probably kill them. Anyone willing to serve someone associated with a monster like Anthony wouldn't care about collateral damage.

"I am so fucking sorry, Beth." His voice was low, heavy with honest regret, but she didn't understand why he was apologizing. He was there, he was protecting her.

"So, you're telling my mom and dad what's going on?" It was strange how calm her voice sounded, because inside she was anything but calm. She was terrified, and the fear was hollowing her out with every horrible vision of her parents lying dead on the floor.

"Yeah, Asaf is explaining it. He's better at that shit than I am, all the hard conversations with parents, and…"

"And?" Beth looked up at him, instantly caught by the pained look in his eyes before he wiped it away, that serious expression from downstairs taking over again.

"This is definitely a hard conversation," he finished. "But I told him I'd explain everything to you, and then let you decide what you want to do next."

"Decide what?"

"If you want to stay here — and if you do, we'll do everything we can to protect you and your parents — or if you want to come with us." Jake swallowed, his voice calmer, more confident. In control. "If you come with us, we've got a place that will be a lot harder for them to find, and we can get your parents to go somewhere public. One of the big chain hotels with lots of cameras, so whoever is after you will know you're not with them. But it's up to you, Beth. No one's going to make you do anything you don't want to."

Up to me.

It was fucked up, but she felt a smile tugging at the edge of her mouth from the sheer insanity of it all. The monsters from her nightmares were back, coming for her, and Jake was leaving the decision in her hands… but the choice was clear.

She could tell by how upset he was that he'd told her the truth. He didn't know how many men were coming for her, what weapons they might have, and that meant he didn't know if his team *could* keep her and her parents safe.

Not here.

Not in this house where her parents had lived for over twenty years.

"Beth?" Jake took a few steps closer to her, but he stopped before he got to the end of her bed. Checking his phone, he let out a slow breath, and she mimicked it. Deep inhale, slow exhale. Calm and confident, just like Jake. "I hate to push you on this, but I really need you to decide."

"I'll go with you," she whispered, feeling her next inhale shudder as the reality of everything settled over her. It was really happening. The monsters were reaching out of the darkness, trying to drag her back, and she'd promised herself long ago that she'd never let that darkness touch her family. She'd never let it ruin them like it had ruined her.

"Are you sure?" He moved a little closer, the phone in his hand buzzing, but he ignored it. "We can figure out a defensive plan for your house if you want to stay. I can—"

When she looked up at him, Jake stopped talking, but his eyes kept searching her face, studying her like her therapists always did. He was obviously worried for her, brows pinched with concern, but his expression disappeared the moment she said, "I'm sure."

"Okay then. Do you have a suitcase? Duffle bag?" Jake immediately moved into action, taking control and tapping something out on his phone before opening her closet door. "Anything to pack stuff in?"

"Yeah, a little suitcase. It's blue," she answered, and a second later he tugged it out from the corner of her closet.

"NO!" her mom shouted downstairs, and Beth flinched. The other man must have told her parents what she'd decided, and it made her chest ache to think of how much she was hurting them.

It felt like all she did was hurt them.

First by being broken, then by not figuring out how to be normal, and now she'd brought the darkness from her past to their front door. Put them in danger. Put her sister and her nephews in jeopardy... all because she'd come back.

I never should have come home at all.

"Hey, don't think about them yet. Deal with one thing at a time," Jake commanded, and it was a lot like how he'd spoken to the one called Charlie, but... in a good way. The clarity of his voice cut through all the shit in her head, and she looked up to see him pulling clothes off hangers in her closet. "You need stuff to wear. Pack enough for a week, just to be safe. Where's your bathroom? I'll grab your shit from in there."

"At the end of the hall." Beth pointed, and Jake dumped the pile of clothes on the end of the bed before slipping out of her room. The suitcase was already open, waiting to be filled, and Beth moved, operating on automatic to do what he'd asked. Folding items and adding them, along with underwear, socks, a few pajamas, and then she grabbed the things that really mattered. The iPad that Thalia had given her, the phone Jake had given her that morning, and the chargers for both. The handcuffs were next, along with the tiny keys, and just placing them in the suitcase made her feel a little calmer.

Jake had given her those too, and they'd worked perfectly the last few nights. Leaving her parents was terrifying, but knowing that Jake would be there, that he knew Thalia and had already accepted her weirdness... it made it a little easier.

As long as she didn't think about it too much.

One thing at a time.

"You're going to have to go through this shit," Jake said from behind her as he nudged the door open, dropping an armful of stuff from her bathroom on the bed. "I just kind of grabbed everything I could find because I really have no idea what women need."

Beth tossed things into the suitcase as she came across stuff she knew she'd use, but she paused when she got to her toothbrush. "There's a toiletry bag under the sink. A pink one with a zipper. Can you get that, and..."

"And?" He paused at the door, looking at her, waiting.

"There's a box of band-aids. Can you get those too?"

"We've got band-aids, you don't need to bring any," he replied, and she bit her lip to stop herself from arguing.

"Okay." Turning back to the pile of stuff from her drawers and under the sink, she tried not to think about asking for a band-aid every day, or the fact that she'd have to explain it was for the goddamn tattoo and not a cut. Just thinking about the mark on the inside of her hip made her tense again, a cold sweat pricking to life between her shoulder blades.

"Beth." Jake's voice was firm, and she turned to look at him. "Do you need the band-aids?"

It took a second, but she eventually nodded, and he sighed.

"Next time just say so." The reply wasn't quite annoyed, but it definitely came across as chastising. That wasn't what surprised her though, it was that he hadn't asked *why*.

Focusing on the last items on the bed, Beth tried to make her cloudy brain think through what she might need. Not that she really *needed* any of it — except for the iPad. And the cuffs. And her meds. And the band-aids would make everything easier, but the other stuff didn't matter.

She didn't care what she wore, and she'd brush her teeth or her hair with whatever they had.

It was just the stuff that helped keep her sane that really mattered.

"Here you go," Jake said, tossing the last items onto the bed, and Beth made quick work of the rest of her toiletries. "Anything else you want to bring?"

"No, it's good." The suitcase wasn't full, but she thought it had enough until Jake grabbed more clothes from the closet along with a pair of sneakers. He set the shoes on the floor near her, and she pulled them on while he added the stuff he seemed to think she'd need. Except, he didn't even attempt to fold the clothes, he just shoved them in haphazardly before he closed the suitcase and zipped it shut.

"Okay." Lifting the luggage off the bed, Jake held it at his side and leaned down a little to catch her gaze as she finished tying her shoes. He waited until she was done and looking up at him before he spoke again. "We're going to go downstairs now. Your parents are upset, which is understandable, but Asaf has explained everything to them. They know you're leaving with us, and that we're going to keep you safe until we've eliminated the threat. All you need to do is tell them goodbye for now."

"For now," Beth repeated, a strange numbness spreading through her, as if she'd spent too long in cold water. She could almost feel it lapping at her ankles, the way it used to when she'd walk into the ocean after a volleyball game at the beach. Too late in the year and the Pacific could be freezing, but she used to walk in the water anyway, watching the surf until her toes were tingly and numb against the sand.

Except it wasn't just her toes now.

Everything was going numb. The ache in her chest, the whirling chaos in her head, the burn in her lungs — it was all fading into the background, but she tried not to slip under the water. She couldn't hide right now.

"Beth?" Jake was at her door again, waiting for her this time, and she was back on her feet before she even realized she'd told her body to stand. He nodded at her and then led the way to the stairs where her parents' voices drifted up, filled with tears and pain.

If she hadn't felt so numb, just the sound of it would have been enough to make her cry too, but she was doing the right thing. This was the only way to keep them safe, to keep the darkness from ruining their lives like it had already ruined hers.

Once the rest of the monsters were as dead as Anthony and his brother, then she could come back.

Maybe then she could figure out how to be normal, how to be their daughter again.

Maybe she'd even figure out how to live instead of just survive.

THIRTEEN

Jake

Beth was eerily quiet, and he was pretty sure she was in shock. Hell, he'd promised her just that morning that he'd find the bastards coming for her, and now he was back on the same damn day to rip her away from her parents. All because he couldn't keep the promise.

"Honey, please don't go, please," her mom begged, tear-streaked and barely able to stand. Her husband had his arm around her, helping to hold her upright as she pleaded with Beth. "I can't lose you again. I can't, baby. I love you so much, please stay."

Fuck. It was like a knife to the gut every time the woman sobbed. He'd been around plenty of sobbing mothers in his line of work, but he'd never been the reason they were crying before. For the first time he wasn't there to try and return a missing person — he was there to take one away.

"I'm sorry, Mom," Beth whispered, and Jake couldn't even remember how many times she'd said the phrase.

"Bill, you can't be okay with this! You can't let them take her!" Mrs. Doherty was swinging back to anger, turning to grab onto her husband's shirt as she shifted her focus onto him. "She's our baby! We already lost her once!"

"I know, Tanya, but this is what they do. They can protect—"

"No!" Beth's mom shouted, shoving her husband away as she turned back to her daughter. "Don't listen to them, sweetheart. You don't need to leave. We can keep you safe here! We'll call the police, and they'll—"

"Mrs. Doherty, I already explained that the police won't do anything," Asaf interrupted, and as usual Jake was impressed by how calm and collected the man could be while still sounding so empathetic. "There's no evidence, no threat to show them. If there was a way to guarantee all of your safety here, we would absolutely make that our first goal."

"You're not taking my daughter!" she screamed, but the anger faded back into sobs as her husband stepped forward and supported her once more, wrapping his wife in his arms as he whispered in her ear.

"I'm really sorry, Mom. I love you," Beth said, her voice still too soft, too calm. "I love both of you, and I'll be back as soon as I can."

"I can't let you go again. I can't let you leave." Mrs. Doherty slid to the floor and her husband followed her down, cradling her while she reached for Beth's legs, holding onto her yoga pants as she sobbed. "Please don't do this, baby girl. Don't leave. I would die before I'd let anything happen to you! I swear to you I won't let anyone get near you or hurt you. Not again. Not ever again."

"Mom, I know." Slipping to her knees, Beth ended up in a mirror image of her mother, their knees touching as she held onto her mom's hands. "I know you would try to protect me. I know you and Dad would both die to keep me safe — but *I* couldn't live with that. If anything happened to you guys, or to Christina, or her boys because of me... I wouldn't be able to live anymore. But Jake and his team helped Thalia when something like this happened, and they came here to help me too. They'll figure this out, but I have to go so we're all safe."

"I don't want you to go," Mrs. Doherty whispered through her tears.

"I'm so sorry, Mom." Beth's reply was just as soft, but when she reached her arms forward for a hug, Jake was surprised to see her parents hesitate for a moment before they embraced her.

Jake stayed quiet, looking at Asaf and then Charlie to make sure they gave the family space before he looked at the trio again. Mrs. Doherty was hugging her daughter tightly, pressing kisses to her cheek, while Mr. Doherty had his arms around both his daughter and his wife, his forehead braced against Beth's pale hair. Soft words buzzed between them until they faded into silence, broken only by the occasional sniffle.

He wasn't sure how long the embrace lasted, but eventually it was Beth's father who let go and helped the two women stand. Lightly touching his daughter's shoulders, he leaned down to look her in the eyes. "I love you, sweetheart. Please call us as much as you can."

"I love you too, Dad," she answered. "Take care of Mom for me, okay?"

Her father nodded, letting her mom step in for another hug, but it wasn't as tight as before. Jake could hear the woman telling Beth again and again how much she loved her, and the pain in her voice was like the slow twist of a knife between his ribs.

When he found the bastards who'd caused this pain, he'd make them suffer. He'd make them regret forcing him to tear this already wounded family apart again just to keep them whole. It was stupid to make another promise about Beth, even to himself, but he couldn't help it. No one deserved to hurt this much twice in one lifetime, and he would kill whoever was responsible.

Every single fucking one of them.

"I have to go," Beth said, pulling back from her mother who released her almost immediately. "I promise I'll call as often as I can."

"Okay, baby." Mrs. Doherty nodded a lot, leaning on her husband as he wrapped his arms around her again. "Okay. Just stay safe and come back to us soon."

"Jake," Mr. Doherty said his name and he stood up straighter, facing the man who was trusting him with his daughter. "Swear to me you'll keep her safe. I need to hear it from you."

"I promise I'll keep Beth safe." Jake said the words easily, because it wasn't anything he hadn't already said to her, or in his own head. "I swear it on my life, Mr. and Mrs. Doherty."

Shit.

He hadn't meant to say the last part, but it just... happened. Probably because he'd listened to Mrs. Doherty offer her own life for ten minutes while she'd begged, bargained, and pleaded with Beth to stay.

"I'll hold you to that," Mrs. Doherty said, and Jake had no doubt where Beth got that steel spine of hers. Her mother was just as strong, and he knew the woman meant what she said.

"Yes, ma'am." Jake picked up the suitcase again, signaling that it was truly time to leave now. Asaf moved toward the parents while Charlie went to the door.

"Remember what we discussed. Go for a large hotel, one with a lot of cameras, use your card and stay for a few days. Make sure the lobby cameras see you," Asaf reminded them, walking them through the plan once more.

It was the best way to keep them safe. If the other team was decent, they probably had someone that could track their credit cards and hack the camera feeds at the hotel, which was exactly what Jake wanted. He wanted the fuckers who were after Beth to know her parents weren't home, and that Beth wasn't with them.

He wanted them just as confused as his team had been. He wanted them desperate because that was when they'd make a mistake. Just one mistake and his team would find them.

Then they'd track them down, torture them for the info on who hired them, kill them, and then kill the motherfucker who thought he could come after a girl who had already survived too much. And the whole time

Beth would be safe, somewhere that no one was going to be able to find her.

At his team's compound.

Under his protection.

Beth had barely spoken beyond the occasional 'I'm fine' since they'd left her parents' house, and he and the other guys were giving her space, but her eerie calm didn't sit right with him. It wasn't that Jake expected her to break down — except, yeah, he did.

He didn't *want* her to be upset, and her stoic expression had made getting back on Luke's plane easier, but he was still waiting for something to make her snap like the zip-ties had. For her to start hyperventilating again. To panic. To freak out.

To realize she'd just willingly left her parents and flown across the state of California with a bunch of mercenaries without even fucking asking where they were taking her.

Goddammit.

The whole situation pissed him off in some ways and made him grateful in others. She'd trusted him enough to come with them, but she probably shouldn't have. What if the other team had tried to run a scam on her? What if they'd gotten to her first?

He couldn't waste time on what-ifs — and pointing out the danger she'd put herself in wouldn't make anything better. She needed to be with them anyway. It would be easier to keep her safe on their property, especially since no one would have a fucking clue where to look for her, but it still didn't mean she shouldn't ask questions. She should have at least asked where the hell they were taking her.

You're not her dad, Jake. That's the man you left crying on a porch in Carmel five hours ago.

Glancing over at her, he tried to ignore the way the headlights of a passing car highlighted her cheekbones and turned her hair to gold for a flash, but he noticed. He couldn't stop noticing her. Shit, he'd spent half the flight staring at her until Mike had jabbed him in the ribs with a pen and tossed a book at him, but even when he'd pretended to read, he'd continued sneaking glances. Checking on her, watching, and he couldn't lie to himself and say it was some version of fatherly concern.

Sure, he was concerned, but that wasn't the only reason he kept looking.

You're such a bastard.

Guilt dug at him for the hundredth time since he'd first seen the missed alert for her. He'd fucked up, and it felt like he hadn't stopped fucking up since. They still didn't have a real lead on who was after her, or who'd hired them, and he'd ended up yanking her out of her life even though he'd told himself he wouldn't.

"Fucking finally!" Charlie shouted from behind him as he slowed the car, stopping inside the short drive before the locked gate. "Home sweet home."

Charlie threw open his door, heading to open the gate while Beth leaned forward in the passenger seat, looking at the ancient sign that still curved over the entrance to their property. It read 'Wild Sierras Ranch,' or it was supposed to, but at some point the C had fallen off and now it was 'Wild Sierras Ran h.' He really should have fixed it already, but there was always something else that was more important.

"Hey Beth, look over there," Mike said, keeping his voice soft as he pointed into the endless dark outside the reach of the SUV's headlights. "The Sierra Nevada mountains are that way, and the views are pretty amazing in the daylight."

She looked where he was pointing, but Mike didn't get a response out of her, and Jake tightened his grip on the steering wheel to keep his mouth shut.

If she didn't want to talk, she didn't have to.

"Let's go!" Charlie called out, slapping the back of Jake's seat as he hopped into the truck and slammed the door.

Cracking his neck, Jake swallowed the threat he'd usually toss at Charlie for being a dick and moved the SUV up the long drive to their place. Benny was driving the other SUV and he knew they'd lock the gate up before they came to the house.

He parked and Mike and Charlie jumped out before he'd even shut off the engine, but Jake didn't move. Instead, he watched Beth. She was looking over the property, lit up only by the motion sensor lights his men were triggering and the oncoming headlights from the other car.

"You're safe here. I promise," he said, keeping his voice quiet, but she didn't turn back to look at him. Beth had her forehead leaned against the window, her muscles jumping when the guys opened the back of the SUV to unload. "There's no rush to go inside, okay?"

Still no answer. *Dammit.*

Jake climbed out, deciding that giving her space would be the best tactic, and at least inside the SUV the sounds of the boys talking shit to each other would be a little dulled. Grabbing the last bags out of the back, he slammed the hatch and kept his eyes on his men and not the girl in the passenger seat.

Coming home was always chaotic with his team, but it seemed like they all toned it down at least a bit as they unloaded their bags and filed into the house, calling out to each other as lights came on inside. The door was hanging wide open, a golden rectangle in the middle of nowhere, but Jake didn't move toward it. He stayed by the SUV with Beth, his duffle over his shoulder and her suitcase in his hand, waiting for her to be ready to move.

Eventually a shadow filled the doorframe, and Jake narrowed his eyes at it until he recognized the shape as Benny. *Of course* the medic would be the one to come out and check on her.

It was quiet out in the middle of nowhere, the silence broken only by the clicking of the engines cooling and the occasional buzz of an insect, which made the thuds on the wooden porch sound too loud.

Benny crossed the empty dirt quickly, but when he moved toward the SUV, Jake stepped to the side, making it clear he wouldn't let Benny get to her door.

"You can't leave her out here all night, Jake," he said, keeping his voice low.

"She's not ready."

"And you think a few more minutes in the car is going to make a difference? Her whole world fell apart today. She needs to lie down. Sleep," he insisted. "And so do you."

"She might want to eat something first," he muttered, not knowing if she'd had dinner before they got to her, but she'd barely touched the bag of trail mix they'd given her.

"You going to bring food out here to her?" Benny retorted, pushing his buttons, and Jake took the duffle off his shoulder and tossed it at Benny's chest, forcing the man to catch it.

"Go. I'll bring her in."

Their medic hesitated, gaze flicking between him and Beth, but eventually he shouldered the duffle and turned back toward the house.

Taking a deep breath, Jake approached her window, making sure she could see him before he lifted the door handle. He saw Beth jump at the *clunk* of the door opening, but he moved slowly. "Come on, time to eat and sleep."

Holding the door wide, he gave her as much room as he could, and after a moment she stepped down from the SUV, looking up at the big, two-story house that he and his men had made their own.

"After you." Waving a hand to the open door, he followed Beth, staying patient even though she walked incredibly slowly.

Maybe she doesn't actually trust us. Maybe she's regretting this.

Fuck, fuck, fuck.

When they finally made it through the door, several of the guys froze in place to look at her, but he could hear others making a racket in the kitchen. Jake closed the front door as quietly as he could, not sure how to break the awkward silence.

"I think we could all use a fucking drink," Charlie said, lifting a bottle of tequila in his hand. "How about it, Beth? Want a shot?"

"Are you fucking kidding me? She doesn't want—"

"Sure." The single word from Beth shut him up instantly, but he knew his mouth was hanging open as he looked at her.

You're not her dad.

You're not anything.

"Okay then." Jake walked past her and left her suitcase at the bottom of the stairs, more than a little annoyed that Charlie of all people got a response out of her. Not that it was a competition, except... dammit, it sure as hell felt like one.

"Come sit, I'll pour you a shot!" Charlie let out a whoop, raising the tequila in the air as he walked to their big ass dining table that dominated the area by the kitchen. It shouldn't have bothered him that Beth followed, but he swallowed it down and took his normal place at the end of the table, opposite Brendan's normal workspace.

Mike pulled out a chair in the middle of the table where Beth could watch the chaos in the kitchen, and she slipped into it silently.

"We should at least wait until she has something in her stomach," Benny said, but Charlie set a handful of shot glasses on the table and flipped him off.

"Blow me. She's had a shitty day. She can have some tequila if she wants it." Pouring liquor into the tiny glasses, Charlie called over his shoulder. "Who else wants a shot?"

A chorus of replies came from the team, but Jake kept his mouth shut. Benny was staring at him, jaw clenched tight, and he shook his head once to tell the man to stand down. Charlie was right. She'd had a terrible day, and if the girl wanted a drink, who were they to tell her she shouldn't?

"Hey Ollie, grab me some more shot glasses," Charlie shouted before pushing one of the full ones in front of Beth. "Here you go."

Her hands were so damn delicate, soft. Nothing like his, or any of the other guys, but when she turned the shot glass a few times and then tossed it back in one go, he wasn't the only one to go wide-eyed. Beth coughed, squeezing her eyes shut as she pressed the back of her hand to her lips, but then she pushed the shot glass forward again.

"Well damn," Ollie said through a laugh. "I think she'll fit in fine." Grabbing one of the filled shot glasses, Ollie tossed it back, and then Charlie handed out the others.

When Mike helped to slide one in front of Jake, he leaned over and whispered, "Take the shot, boss. You're going to freak her out if you keep staring like that."

Dammit.

Swallowing the tequila, Jake wished it was enough to ease the knot in his stomach, but it wasn't. He needed to act normal. She needed a dose of normalcy. Looking into the kitchen, Jake could see the guys were working on something to eat, and he called out, "What are you fucks making?"

"Lasagna, asshole!" Brendan called back.

"Asshole lasagna sounds terrible," Charlie shouted, and everyone laughed. There was even a small smile on Beth's face, and *that* told Jake all he needed to know.

She didn't want or need them to walk on eggshells around her, that was obviously what her parents had been doing since she got home. No, she needed to be treated like an adult. No purple room with stuffed animals and boy bands. She was twenty-eight, she'd survived hell, and if she wanted tequila and his team of asshole mercs cracking jokes… then that was easy.

"There's garlic bread in the freezer, I'll get it," he said, pushing his chair back to get up, but Asaf waved at him.

"Already got it, boss. Sit down and relax." Asaf lifted his tequila in a toast. "We're back home, we're all still breathing, and tomorrow is a new day."

"I'll cheers to that," Mike shouted, and more shots were swallowed. Charlie passed the bottle around the kitchen table, another bottle was opened in the kitchen, and Jake leaned back in his chair to look at all of them.

Asaf was right. His team was whole, Beth was safe, and that was better than a lot of their nights together. If he really wanted to help her, then he needed to focus on the mission, on finding the bastards behind it all.

Until then, they could at least give Beth a taste of life outside her parents' house.

Let her make her own choices.

Let her live like a real person.

An adult.

And I'll back off. I'll stop staring.

I promise.

FOURTEEN

Beth

Her head was pounding and the light pouring in the window wasn't helping. It was piercing through her eyelids, making the headache worse, but when she tried to turn over the clatter of the handcuff made her open them.

Then she jerked upright, panic making her heart race for a second until she remembered where she was.

Not at home.

She was with Jake and his team, in *their* house.

The night before came back in hazy flashes. She knew she'd stopped drinking after the fourth or fifth shot because her stomach had started churning, and she'd barely picked at the lasagna. Although she did eat the entire slice of garlic bread they'd put on her plate.

They'd arrived after midnight, but the guys had never eaten dinner, so they were starving. The meal had been really relaxed, and all the men on Jake's team had been so welcoming. No one stared at her or watched what they said around her. They'd even drunkenly moved beds around in the middle of the night because Jake told them to.

She traced her fingers over the chipped and scratched metal bars that made up the bed that used to be in one of the guy's rooms. Beth remembered him shouting at the other guys not to fuck up his stuff while they were moving it, and she'd listened from downstairs while they'd yelled at each other as they put the beds back together. No one had asked *why* Jake insisted on her having this specific bed… they'd just done it. Cursing and laughing and mocking each other the whole time.

They'd even made the bed for her, putting on sheets and bringing her a pillow and random, mismatched blankets from around the house. She was pretty sure she'd managed to say 'thank you' but she was so tired by the time they'd finished that all she could remember was digging out the handcuffs from her suitcase and climbing into bed in the same clothes she'd worn all day. Tipsy for the first time since before she'd been taken.

Scooping the key off the rickety bedside table, Beth unlocked the cuff and pulled out the drawer to tuck them away. The guys were already awake downstairs, she could hear the buzz of their voices and smell the coffee, but she hesitated on the edge of the bed as guilt tugged at her.

Her parents were probably sick with worry. Her mom probably hadn't slept at all, which meant her dad likely hadn't either. Thinking of them up all night in some hotel in town, crying and worrying about her, only made her feel worse. She'd drank tequila and slept, and she hadn't even called to tell them she was okay.

"You really are a terrible daughter," Beth muttered to herself, getting up to grab her shoes and tug them on. When she was tying the laces, she finally looked out the bright window and saw what Mike had tried to point out the night before.

Wow.

The mountains were breathtaking, impossibly beautiful in the distance, and the landscape stretched out far away from the house without another home in sight.

It had felt like they were in the middle of nowhere when they were driving, but it had been so dark she hadn't been able to tell for sure. Now, it was clear. This was nowhere near a big city. It was nowhere near *anything* as far as she could tell, which probably shouldn't have been comforting. After all, she was surrounded by open land, far away from help, and trapped in a house with seven armed men… but, as insane as it was, she felt safe.

Whoever was looking for her wouldn't find her here.

And she knew Jake and the others were committed to protecting her. Plus, they knew Thalia, they knew about the brothers, and while they'd given her space on the small plane they'd taken… once the guys were home they hadn't coddled her at all. They'd cracked jokes, insulted each other, cussed, drank, and basically acted like a bunch of brothers.

And Jake was their very attractive boss.

Stop thinking about him and go downstairs.

Then you need to call Mom and Dad.

Pushing herself off the floor, Beth moved to the door and listened for a minute. She couldn't make out what they were saying, but it wasn't like it mattered, they knew she was here. As quietly as possible, she eased the door open and headed for the stairs, but everyone fell quiet as she hit the bottom steps.

"Morning, you want some breakfast?" one of them asked, pointing into the kitchen, but she was too distracted to respond.

Had they all been so... *big* last night?

She'd been distracted, turning over the moment she'd had to say goodbye to her parents over and over, but in her mind the guys hadn't seemed so intimidating. Maybe it was the clothes. They'd worn button-down shirts instead of t-shirts, which probably hid how fit they were, how muscular.

Even the older guy with the accent — *Asa?* — had actual biceps.

"Or just coffee?" the guy behind the laptop offered, and she finally managed a nod.

"Come sit," another said, and she recognized the black guy that had pulled out the chair for her the night before. She just couldn't remember his name either, which was an awesome way to make a good impression.

"Um, thank you..." She sat down, tucking her hands between her thighs as she tried to keep the anxiety from creeping up while they all looked at her expectantly. "I'm really sorry, but I don't remember your names."

"Brendan," the guy that had been at the laptop said, setting a cup of coffee in front of her with a carton of cream next to it. "I gave you my bed."

"Thank you again for that," she mumbled.

"No worries." He flashed a smile and returned to his computer and the pile of papers at one end of the table. A moment later he smacked the guy beside him.

"Oh, shit, I'm Charlie. Easy to remember because I'm the good looking one," he added with a big grin, and she could remember how many jokes he'd cracked the night before.

"Don't be an asshole, it's too early," the black guy said from beside her. Then he lifted his coffee cup as he said, "I'm Mike."

"Benny." The man on her other side spoke up, rubbing at his light brown hair. "I'm the medic on the team."

"And he's a halfway decent shot," Jake added, and she smiled a bit as she turned to look at him sitting at the opposite end of the table from Brendan.

"I remember your name, Jake."

"That's good," he replied, grinning before he took a sip of his coffee. Looking up, he pointed at the older man with the accent who was still standing in the kitchen. "That's Asaf, and he's an *extremely* good shot."

"True," Asaf chuckled. "I hope you're feeling well this morning, Beth." The man inclined his head toward her, and she nodded.

"I'm fine." Looking around, she knew someone was missing, but she couldn't remember his name at all. "Wasn't there someone else? He was blond?"

"That's Ollie," Charlie said, rolling his eyes. "All you need to know about him is that he's batshit crazy, but we like him anyway."

"He's outside throwing knives," Mike added, and she looked over to see if he was joking, but after a few seconds she realized he wasn't.

"Really? Can I see?" she asked, and several of the guys glanced at each other.

"Sure," Jake answered, shoving his chair back. "Grab your coffee. Ollie loves showing off."

The act of adding cream to her own coffee without anyone trying to do it for her was such a small thing, but it really mattered. It almost made it a little easier to breathe, even though she was still surrounded by guys who she had no doubt were dangerous — but they were there to keep her safe. So, it was the *good* kind of dangerous.

"Sugar?" Mike offered, reaching across the table to slide a sugar container toward her that looked like they'd stolen it from a diner somewhere. *Maybe they had.*

Beth probably added too much sugar to her coffee, but she didn't care as she stirred it with the spoon Benny handed her.

"Thanks." She set the spoon back on the table since it seemed like none of the guys cared about using a plate or a napkin. Pushing her chair back, she stood up with her coffee, and it was almost impressive how loud it became as the guys got up too.

"Alright, let's go give Ollie an audience." Jake led the way outside, but she was escorted by the rest of them like some kind of celebrity surrounded by bodyguards. They never got too close though, and they weren't exactly crowding her, they were just walking near her, which was easier to handle.

When they came around the side of the house, Beth heard the *thunk* of something striking wood before she actually saw the blond guy. He was in a tight-fitting black shirt, black pants, and boots. All of that combined with the fact that he was covered in tattoos, and holding a knife, made him look like some dangerous biker, or a villain in a movie.

"What's up?" Ollie asked, flipping the knife and catching it without even looking at it.

"Beth wanted to see you playing with your little weapons," Charlie called out, and several of the guys chuckled, but when the knife landed between Charlie's legs a second later, making him jump, they really started laughing. "Fuck you, Ollie!"

"Not so little now, eh?" Ollie taunted, and Beth turned to watch as Charlie scooped the knife out of the dirt. Ollie spread his arms wide. "What? You wanna go for it?"

"I should kick your ass," Charlie growled, moving toward him, and she tensed when Ollie plucked another knife out of a thing wrapped around his thigh and beckoned Charlie forward.

Holy shit.

"Come on then!" Grinning like a madman, Ollie flipped the knife, catching it by the handle and angling it back along his arm as Charlie approached.

"Move." Charlie kicked dirt at Ollie, taking his spot in front of the target. There was a tattered outline of a person attached to a piece of wood on a post, and Charlie lined up with it. When he threw the knife, it looked good to Beth, but then it bounced off the target and everyone started laughing again, with Ollie laughing the loudest.

"Watch me, Beth," he said, winking at her before he turned to the target. His arm moved incredibly fast, and she heard the *thunk* of the knife embedding in the wood before she'd even seen it move.

Taking a few steps forward, she shaded her eyes against the sun and saw it was stuck in the target just a few inches from the other knife he'd thrown — while Charlie's was in the dirt.

"Such bullshit. A gun works better anyway," Charlie grumbled, flipping off Ollie as he stomped away from him.

"Guns work too, but knives never run out of ammo." Ollie tilted his head back a little, drawing another knife as he beckoned her forward. "Come on, you can get closer."

Her curiosity made moving forward easy, and she felt the other guys following her until she stopped a few feet behind him. Now that she was closer, she could see that the leather strap around Ollie's thigh had multiple slots for knives.

"Don't worry, I'm a lot better at this than fucknuts over there." Chuckling, Ollie turned back to the target and threw another knife. It landed square in the center of the body outline, and a second later another embedded itself in the wood amidst the others.

"Wow," she whispered.

Benny huffed beside her. "Don't compliment him, he's already way too cocky."

"Hey, don't tell her what to do, she can compliment me all she wants," Ollie said, marching toward the target to pluck his knives out, adding them back to his holster one by one. Grabbing the one Charlie had messed up from the dirt, he turned around and pointed it at her. "Your turn."

My turn?

Beth shook her head, backing up a step as she lifted her hands, but Ollie just closed the distance between them and grabbed her arm.

"Come on, it's not scary. I promise." His grip was light on her wrist, but Beth could tell that Jake's absolutely *wasn't* when he grabbed Ollie's arm.

"Let her go. Now." Jake's voice was a low growl, cold and dangerous, but Ollie didn't seem fazed at all as he looked down at Jake's fingers digging into his inked skin and then back to his face.

"Sure." He released her wrist, but didn't move, eyes still locked on Jake's as he spoke directly to her. "Beth, do you wanna try and throw a knife?"

"I—"

"Ollie, stop being a dick," Mike grumbled, his low voice just as serious as Jake's.

"Yeah." Her own voice surprised her, but the tension in the air wasn't helping her feel any better, and she only saw one way to defuse it. "I'll try it."

"See? Let the girl have some fun." Ollie tilted his head at the place where he'd been standing, yanking his arm out of Jake's grip as he led her to it. "You right-handed or left?"

"Right."

"Okay, put your right foot here, left foot back a little, and relax. Can't be too tense." He didn't touch her this time, he just showed her what the position looked like, and she mimicked him. "Fuck, wait, let's move you closer."

Ollie took a few big steps forward until she was only a couple of yards from the target, and then she got back into position.

"Now, you're going to hold the knife like this." Lifting it up, he held it by the blade, the handle aimed up, and then he gave it to her.

Her hands were shaky, and she kept worrying she was going to cut herself, but when he plucked another knife free and showed her the right way to hold it again, she did her best to put her thumb and fingers in the same position.

"You don't have to throw it hard, and you're just trying to get it to spin halfway so the point hits the board. A half turn. It's way more about your wrist than your arm, okay? Watch me." Ollie pulled his arm back just a little, and then... *flicked* the knife at the target. It stuck in, square on the bullseye, and she just shook her head.

"I can't do that."

"Just try it. When else in your life has anyone told you to throw a knife?" he asked, chuckling as he jerked his chin toward the target. "Go on. No one here gives a fuck if you land it or not. Charlie fucked it up and he's supposed to know how to handle weapons!"

Right.

"Fuck off, Ollie!" Charlie shouted.

"Love you, too," Ollie replied, grinning as he stepped up next to her and walked her through the steps again. "Ok, Beth, now just throw it. No one gives a fuck if you hit or not."

Taking a deep breath, she tried to do what he'd showed her, but when she threw the knife it just smacked into the target, sideways, and fell to the ground. "Shit."

"Here, try again." Ollie held out another knife.

"I bet you're better than Charlie," Mike called from behind her, earning a round of laughs and another 'fuck you' from the guy in question.

Ollie waggled the knife back and forth, tempting her with it, and she finally gave in and grabbed it. Taking the right pose again, she tried to picture what she wanted to happen. A half turn, the point of the blade sticking out of the person outline.

She threw, and it clattered against the target again, dropping lamely to the ground. Disappointment surged inside her and she felt a blush rolling up her neck. "I'm sorry I'm just not good at this."

"You've only tried twice," Jake said, and she turned to see him standing on her left. "Ollie, give me one."

Taking a knife, Jake held it closer to her, turning his hand so she could see all of his fingers.

"You don't want to hold it too tight because it'll tense up your arm, which will tweak the angle when you let it go." He mimed throwing the knife. "It's a smooth movement, and like Ollie said it's about tossing it with your wrist, not your whole arm. Also, I aim past the target. Think about hitting a space a few feet behind it."

"Show me?" she whispered and the grin he flashed was devilish. His usual intense, serious expression melted away into a playful, mischievous look that was... *really* hot. She was so distracted by his smile that she almost didn't pay attention to his hand as he turned back to the target, miming the movement a few times before he finally let go of the knife. It flew fast and stuck in the wood, a little outside the center, but it still would have hurt someone a lot.

"Try again," Jake said quietly, his voice carrying an edge that made her want to do it, want to try, but she couldn't think of anything to say back. So, she just nodded, taking the last knife from Ollie as she faced off with the target again.

Of course, she failed, but when she tried to walk away the guys kept telling her to try again, offering their own tips and suggestions.

Beth lost count of how many times she tossed the knives, no longer worried about cutting herself, but she'd yet to get a knife to stick no matter how many ways she adjusted her stance or her elbow or her fingers. Irritated with her utter failure, she accepted the next knife Ollie handed her and tossed it right away.

It was the roar of the guys cheering that made her actually look at the target, where her knife was sticking out of the wood. Angled, and definitely about to fall, but she still felt a rush of excitement, gasping as she covered her mouth and felt a real smile on her face. "Oh my God!"

"Fuck yes!"

"You did it!" Jake scooped her off the ground with a cheer, his hands around her waist as he lifted her effortlessly. She gasped in surprise, grabbing onto his arms to brace herself when he spun her in a circle. A laugh bubbled up past her lips, exploding in a burst of sound that was definitely the loudest she'd been since...

Just as the dark thoughts began to creep back in, Jake eased her down to the ground, but she was much closer to him now. So close that she could see the way his gaze drifted from her eyes to her mouth, and with his hands lingering on her waist she wondered if he was going to kiss her.

Did he want to kiss her?

Do I want him to kiss me?

The thought made her heart race and her chest tight, but she didn't want to run. She didn't even think she wanted to push his hands away.

"What did I tell you?!" Ollie shouted, and the moment was gone before she even had the chance to figure out if she'd imagined the whole thing. Jake stepped away from her quickly and the other guys moved in, giving her high-fives and compliments while teasing Charlie about her doing better than him.

It all seemed to happen in a daze though.

She managed to thank Ollie and the other guys, and she really was grateful when Ollie pressed the knife she'd thrown into her hand and told her to keep it, but the guys were more than a little overwhelming as they continued shouting and swapping insults while they herded everyone back inside for breakfast.

Between one breath and the next — or at least that's how it felt — Beth found herself back in her seat at the table, staring down at the knife in her lap, and wondering if she'd somehow dreamed the whirlwind of the morning.

"Beth?"

"Huh?" She looked up to see the medic guy, *Benny*, on the other side of the table, looking at her with a very furrowed brow.

"How do you want your eggs?" he asked, or more likely repeated because it was pretty obvious she'd missed it the first time he spoke to her.

"I'm not picky."

"Okay." Benny tilted his head to the side, but never took his eyes off her as he called over his shoulder, "She's good with scrambled."

"Got it!" Mike called back.

"What medications are you taking?" Benny asked.

Charlie stepped up next to him, set down a few glasses of water, and then punched him in the arm. "You're not her doctor, bro. Back off."

"Screw you, I'm the only fucking medic here!"

"And we're all so grateful when you're there to stitch us up, but she's not bleeding," Brendan said, gesturing at her from behind his laptop. "As you can see."

"Jesus Christ," Benny grumbled. "I just want to know if you have meds you need to take in the morning, Beth. We all slept in so it's getting late."

"Yeah, I do." She pushed her chair back, planning to go get them, but someone stopped her.

"I think breakfast is a higher priority." Asaf had both his hands on the back of her chair, carefully positioned so that even his knuckles weren't touching her back, but he wasn't letting her get up. "She didn't eat much last night."

"Another reason to be concerned," Benny argued.

"Hey!" Mike shouted from the kitchen. "Don't fucking talk about her like she isn't here. If she has meds she needs to take, she can handle that shit on her own."

She offered Mike a small smile, and he saluted her with his spatula before he turned back to the stove where he and Charlie were working on breakfast. It was sweet he'd stood up for her, but the truth was she *did* have meds she needed to take — but it was *also* true she needed something to eat. If she took her morning pills on an empty stomach they'd just come back up anyway, which would be a waste.

After that, breakfast rolled by without anyone pushing her to speak. The food was good, and the guys focused their attention on each other, discussing some fight that was going to be on TV later in the week. Although Benny did stare at her several times throughout the meal with that evaluating stare that doctors had whenever they had a problem in front of them they wanted to solve.

And she was the problem.

As usual.

In contrast, Jake was obviously avoiding eye contact with her — or maybe she was just being sensitive. He could just be distracted with trying to keep her alive, which made a lot more sense than some magical movie-like moment between them when he'd lifted her in the air.

Stupid, stupid, stupid.

Nudging her chair back, Beth stood and the guys' conversation stumbled to a halt, all eyes swiveling to her. "Uh, I'm just going upstairs to take my meds and call my parents. I forgot to do it when we got here last night."

"You shouldn't use your phone," Charlie said.

"It's not hers," Ollie replied. "Mike ordered it for her and it's not in her name."

"But her parents' phones are in their names." Brendan shoved his plate out of the way and opened his laptop. "It'll be best if you use my laptop to make any calls to them just in case their phones are being monitored. That way your position can't be tracked."

People can really do that?

"We can give you some privacy," Jake said, rising from his end of the table. "Come on, guys. Let's get the table cleaned up while she gets her meds."

"Thanks," she mumbled, unsure if anyone had even heard her over the sudden clatter of chairs and plates and silverware... but Jake did look at her. Unfortunately, his expression was unreadable. He had his 'business' mask back on his face, and she should be grateful for that. Jake and his team were keeping her safe, and just because he'd been nice to her didn't mean he thought of her as anything more than a victim that needed protecting.

That thought had a sour taste filling her mouth as she turned away from the table and headed for the stairs. Victim, survivor, whatever word people wanted to slap on it, it always came with the same baggage. Uncomfortable silences mixed with awkward glances and pitying expressions — and that was from the people who only had a rough idea of what happened to her.

Jake knew Thalia. Jake knew about the Williams brothers, which meant he had a pretty good idea what they'd done to her.

And why on earth would he want to kiss someone as fucked up as you?

Beth felt tears stinging her eyes, fueled by embarrassment and anger for being so damn stupid to be crying at all. She needed to get her shit together, call her parents, and be an adult. Shit, she'd been telling her parents how much she wanted them to treat her like an adult when Jake showed up and everything went to hell.

Time to walk the walk, Beth.

Sniffling, she stopped in the bathroom upstairs to rinse her face, but she cringed as soon as she turned on the light. The bathroom was disgusting, and she hesitated to even touch the knobs beside the faucet because everything seemed to be caked in a layer of grime and scattered leavings from them shaving. *Gross.* Grabbing a handful of toilet paper — which wasn't even on the roll — she shielded her hand and turned on the faucet. Splashing her face a few times, she avoided her reflection and eventually slapped off the light before she headed back to 'her' room.

She'd used the bathroom downstairs last night, and it was *much* cleaner, which meant she'd need to go down there to brush her teeth and stuff. Just seeing the one down the hall gave her a new appreciation for growing up with a sister instead of a brother.

Shit. Christina.

Had her parents said anything to her sister? She hoped they hadn't because there was no reason to worry her when she had her own family to look after.

And if Brendan was right about people being able to track or monitor calls to her parents, then telling Christina anything could put her in danger. That thought was more than enough to get Beth moving. She hadn't pulled anything out of her suitcase the night before except the handcuffs, so she had to dig for a minute to find where her pill bottles had ended up.

And you didn't bring anything to drink with you. Genius.

Groaning, Beth gathered the multicolored pills into her hand and rushed back downstairs to find the table already clean. Several of the guys were still cleaning in the kitchen, the three men taking up way too much room, but Brendan was smiling at her from behind his laptop.

"Hey, come sit here and I'll show you how it works," he said, beckoning her over with a tilt of his head.

Taking the chair he'd indicated, she noticed Jake was missing — but he wasn't the *only* one missing. Mike and Asaf weren't there either, and she needed to stop focusing on Jake anyway because he'd probably notice it.

"So, it's pretty simple. I've already got the software running, which will keep anyone from figuring out where you are if they're monitoring your parents' phones. All you need to do is put these on," he said, handing her a bulky pair of headphones with a microphone sticking out. "Then type their number in here, remember the plus one prefix for the US, and then hit dial and it'll work just like a normal call."

Beth had just set her small pile of pills on the table and was putting the headphones on when she froze. "Shit."

"What's wrong?"

"I don't know my parents' phone numbers," she groaned, dropping her face into her hands, and feeling like a complete fucking idiot.

"No worries, I've got them."

"You do?" She looked up at his screen as he switched into another window and a few seconds later she saw her dad's information appear. William Doherty, their address, and his phone number. "That's not exactly comforting."

"Privacy is mostly an illusion these days," Brendan said, shrugging a shoulder as he copied and pasted her dad's number into the other software. "There are a lot of services people can pay for that give them the ability to get basic info on just about anyone. A phone number or an address or car registration is basically public data now."

"Great," Beth mumbled.

He chuckled and gestured toward his laptop as he got up from the table. "That's why we're doing it this way. If anyone is looking, they'll get a shit ton of fake locations, but try not to worry about that stuff. That's our job."

"Okay," she replied, but she wasn't sure if any of what he'd said was really 'okay.'

"When you're done with the call, just click 'End' and give one of us a shout." He walked backward toward the stairs as he gave her a thumbs up. "Hope the call is good."

Beth nodded at him and switched to his chair in front of the laptop. Guilt gnawed at her as she moved the mouse over the 'Dial' button, because she knew she should have done this last night, but it had been really late. Still, delaying now wasn't making it any better so she clicked and closed her eyes.

The phone only rang a few times before her dad's voice came over the line with a tense, "Hello? This is Bill Doherty."

"Hey, Dad," she said, cringing when she heard his explosive exhale, as if he'd been holding his breath since the moment she'd left the house.

"Oh my God, Beth, we've been so worried."

"Are you okay, honey?" her mom shouted.

"Hold on, let me get this— uh, I think that's it. I think it's on speakerphone now," her dad muttered. "Can you hear us, pumpkin?"

"Yeah, I can hear you guys, and I'm so sorry I didn't call last night. I'm fine."

"Thank God," her mom said, blatant relief in her voice. "Have they found these people yet? When are you coming home?"

"It hasn't even been a day," her dad answered for her. "I'm sure they're doing everything they can."

"I just hate this so much…" Her mom's voice cracked, and Beth winced. She'd probably made her mom cry at least once a day since she'd been released from the hospital. To be fair, she'd probably been crying while Beth was in the hospital too, but at least Beth hadn't seen the pain she was causing back then.

"How are you doing, pumpkin?"

"I'm fine, Dad." She shrugged a shoulder like they could see her. "How are you guys? Did you find a hotel?"

"I'm not worried about us!" her mom said, raising her voice. "I don't like being away from you like this. I feel so... s-so damn helpless!"

Did she just cuss?

Her mom never cussed, and both her parents had always lectured her and Christina about it, so hearing even a tame word like 'damn' out of her mother's mouth was beyond weird.

Fuck. Christina.

"I'm really sorry, Mom," she mumbled. Clearing her throat, Beth sat up straighter and tried to sound more composed, more like an *adult*. "I know this is really hard, and I know you're not happy, but Jake and his team are working on everything. I did learn something this morning though, so I wanted to—"

"Did they find them?" her mom interrupted, and Beth heard her dad mumble something to her.

"Sorry, pumpkin, what were you saying?"

"I'm calling you on one of the guy's laptops using this special software they have because there's a *chance* these people could be monitoring your phones. So, even if they are, they won't be able to track this call back to where I am, but they might be able to track other ones, so if Christina calls..." Her mouth went dry as she thought of her older sister in the hands of someone like Anthony Williams. Would they hurt her sons to get to her? Her husband?

Beth's stomach roiled, threatening to return everything she'd had for breakfast. She clenched her jaw tight, pinching her thigh through her yoga pants, and the blip of pain helped to push back the rising panic.

"We shouldn't say anything that could put her in danger." Her dad was so much more observant than she gave him credit for, and she couldn't help but be impressed at how calm he sounded as he acknowledged the horrible situation she'd put her entire family in.

And he was holding her mom together too. She could hear how upset her mom was, but Beth couldn't make out what she was saying over the speakerphone. It was obvious she was crying though, and Beth caught Christina's name in the mix, and then Cole and Parker — Christina's boys.

Her dad had grasped the danger quickly, and he'd managed to stay calm, but her mom wasn't handling their new reality well. Not that Beth blamed her. No, she only blamed herself.

All of this was her fault.

"I'm really sorry," she muttered, unable to keep the croak out of her own voice. "I'll call you guys again tomorrow."

"Beth?" Her dad was back at the phone.

"I'm still here."

"Okay, pumpkin. Thank you for calling us and giving us this warning. We're at the Hilton downtown, and I promise we'll be safe."

"Thanks, Dad. I love you both so much." She had to swallow past the lump in her throat to manage more words. "And please take care of Mom."

"Always. I've got your mom, you take care of yourself, okay?"

"I will." She nodded even though he couldn't see her, and then forced out a stiff, "Bye," before she ended the call.

Prying the headphones off her head allowed the clatter of the kitchen to return, but she knew they'd heard her call even though Ollie, Charlie, and Benny were doing their very best *not* to look at her.

She appreciated the effort, though. It gave her a moment to compose herself, swiping at the tears lingering in her eyes. She'd managed to keep herself from crying, but she didn't know why she was trying so hard. Losing it in this situation would be a normal response.

But she wasn't normal.

And she was so fucking tired of crying.

FIFTEEN

Jake

"If there's no footage at all then it has to be the guys we're looking for," Jake said, leaning back in his desk chair. "What were you able to get out of the staff?"

"Not much."

Jake groaned. "Just tell me."

"You're not gonna like it. It's generic as fuck," Brian said. "Three men, all physically fit. The guy they spoke to was American but—"

"Wait, there were only three of them?"

"Yeah."

"Fuck," he muttered. His first instinct was that the team didn't seem big enough, but then he remembered why they'd shown up in California in the first place. *Beth*. A tiny, traumatized girl that couldn't have fought back. Hell, Marcus Williams had abducted women by himself without getting caught so bringing three trained mercs for one woman was more than enough.

"Were you expecting more?" Brian asked.

"No, never mind. Keep going."

"I'm telling you, Jake, this shit isn't going to help you. It was three guys, physically fit like I said before. Only one of the guys spoke to anyone and he was definitely American, but they said he could have had a slight Hispanic accent."

"What did they look like?"

Brian sighed heavily. "All three had dark hair. One was a white guy, the guy who talked to them was tan enough to potentially be Hispanic, and the other guy looked more Middle Eastern."

"Fucking useless," Jake grumbled.

"I told you we didn't get much."

"How hard did you try?" Jake pressed, but he felt a smile tugging at his mouth when he heard Brian's dark chuckle roll over the line.

"Come on, man, you know I put in some elbow grease to try and help you out." With Brian in the mix that could mean a lot of different things. On the lighter end, someone might be missing a few teeth, or they could be looking at reconstructive surgery and rehab. He wouldn't have killed a witness over this shit, but Jake knew the man would have made sure the witness had nothing else to share before he gave up.

"I appreciate the help. My guys and I owe you one, okay?"

"Not sure I earned a favor on this one, man. These guys you're looking for know what they're doing, which means you're not up against the usual sick fucks you hunt down. You're up against some assholes with actual training."

"We knew that going in," Jake admitted, but hearing Brian say it brought the reality back to the forefront of his mind.

"Just watch your six, okay?"

"Always do," he replied. "Thanks for trying, I'll hit you up after this job is done."

"Sounds good." Brian ended the call and Jake rested the phone on his chest so he could rub his dry eyes.

Another dead-end.

These bastards were ghosts, and Jake didn't want to think too much about what that could mean, but Brian had recognized it as well. Whoever wanted Beth hadn't sent out some goons from organized crime or some wannabe. No, they'd clearly offered some real money, which had attracted a real team of mercenaries.

Soldiers of Fortune willing to do anything as long as someone paid them for it.

In this case, if the witness was right about the accent, then the mercs could be American ex-military — men he might have served beside — and that made him sick to his stomach. Pulling a trigger for money was something he could understand because he'd done it… but *this*? Taking a woman from her fucking family and delivering her to some monster, knowing what they'd do to her?

No fucking way.

There was a line and those bastards had crossed it.

Jake shoved himself out of his chair so hard that it rolled back and almost fell over from the force. It hadn't helped him, though. He wanted the bastards in front of him so he could take out his frustration on the ones who actually deserved it.

"Motherfuckers!" he shouted, kicking his desk before he grabbed his notepad and threw it across the room. He wanted to scream, or get in a fight, or break shit. He needed to do *something* because sitting around on his ass was going to drive him crazy.

Or is the girl the one driving you crazy?

Fuck.

Someone knocked on his door and he growled under his breath before snapping out a harsh, "What!"

The door opened so smoothly that Jake knew who it was before he even turned around. Asaf stood in the doorway, the tips of his fingers lingering on the door as he lifted one eyebrow.

"Don't start with me," Jake muttered, waving a hand at the man who he earnestly respected, but he really didn't want someone trying to calm him down right now.

"I'm not starting anything," Asaf replied, crossing his arms as he leaned against the doorframe, obviously getting comfortable.

"I mean it, Asaf," he grumbled, trying to burn off the furious energy by pacing in the limited floorspace of his room. His fists were clenched so tight that he could feel the skin stretched taut over his scabbed knuckles, but he pushed back the urge to put a hole in the wall. It wouldn't make him feel any better and he'd just have to repair it at some point.

"I know you're not interested in my opinion right now, but I do think you'd benefit from leaving your bedroom at some point today."

"You're right," Jake growled. "I'm not interested in your opinion right now."

"Did you get bad news?" Asaf asked, as if Jake hadn't made it abundantly clear he didn't want to talk about shit right now. "I'm going to take that as a yes."

"Just get out."

The older man didn't move an inch. In fact, he looked completely unbothered, dressed in a button-down and crisp jeans — which was about as 'casual' as Asaf got when he wasn't in tactical gear.

"What the fuck do you want, Asaf?" Jake snapped.

"For you to be honest with me, but since you're obviously not in a *sharing mood*, then I'll settle for you getting out of this goddamn room and updating the team."

"There are no updates."

"Then tell them that."

"They already know," he argued, but Asaf just lifted his eyebrow again. "You're really fucking annoying, you know that?"

"Me?" Asaf asked, laughing a little as he pointed at his chest. "I'm fucking charming, Jake. That's why you have me handle the families and organize shit."

Rolling his eyes, Jake scooped his notepad off the floor and noticed he'd dropped his phone during his tantrum too. He stomped over to his desk and picked it up, tapping the screen to ensure it was still alive. Luckily, it wasn't broken.

That's the last thing I need to deal with right now.

"We're up against another merc team," he said, staring down at the notepad as he put it back on his desk. "It's not one hundred percent but based on the cleanup for their arrival in Carmel, I don't see many other possibilities. A witness from the landing field said the one who spoke sounded American."

"Makes sense."

Jake turned to look at him. "That doesn't piss you off?"

"Every job we take makes me angry, Jake, but I know anger isn't going to get shit done. We look for information and when one source doesn't pan out, we *keep looking*. Patience and persistence will—"

"Don't feed me your sniper shit right now." Shaking his head at Asaf, Jake grabbed his desk chair and dragged it back in place so he could drop into it.

"You know it's true," Asaf pressed. "And you also know a good general does everything they ask of those they command."

"And *you* know I've never been a general."

"That wasn't the point, asshole," Asaf said, rubbing his temple where his dark hair was beginning to turn silver. "It's a quote from General Patton, and I thought you could use the reminder."

Ouch.

"Tell me how you really feel," he grumbled, wondering for the hundredth time why he'd put together a group of guys that treated the team's chain of command like a fucking suggestion.

Not like he could pretend he was being a good leader right now.

He'd always had a temper, but usually he was able to channel that anger into something productive. It made him work harder, made him more driven, and cleared his mind to find a path to the solution — but his mind was anything but clear on this job.

It wasn't just the anger though. It was her.

Beth.

Groaning under his breath, Jake leaned forward, planting his elbows on his thighs so he could cover his face with his hands as he muttered, "I'm sorry."

"You realize it's incredibly tempting to ask you to repeat that, right?"

"Bastard," Jake mumbled.

Asaf's chuckle confirmed that he wasn't really pissed at him, but Asaf wouldn't have brought the issue to his attention if his absence hadn't been noticed and commented on by the guys. Unfortunately, he couldn't tell any of them that the reason he'd spent most of yesterday and today in his room was because he couldn't stop thinking about how Beth's bottom lip was so fucking plump and biteable that he'd almost kissed her after she'd finally nailed her knife throw.

A swell of shame immediately overshadowed the trickle of arousal that thinking of her mouth caused, and he was glad he already had his head in his hands because he couldn't look anyone in the face with those thoughts active behind his eyes.

Still, he knew he needed to go back to the living room. He never worked in his bedroom when they were in the thick of researching a job, so hiding in here was probably making the guys more suspicious than if they caught him staring at her.

Or you could just be a decent man and not leer at the girl.

"Why don't you take a break from all this and come with me to pick up the ammo from Burt's?" Asaf offered.

"You're not sick of my shit?" he asked, finally sitting back up to look at him.

"I can just turn up the radio if you start whining again." Asaf moved away from the doorframe and tilted his head down the hall. "Come on, boss."

"Deal."

Jake hopped up, tucking his phone into his pocket and his gun into the back of his jeans as he followed Asaf toward the front door. A few of the guys acknowledged them passing through, but everyone in the living room was busy looking through something Brendan had sent them.

If he was a better leader, he'd sit his ass down on the couch and join them right now, but he was taking the coward's way out instead... just because it would give him another couple of hours away from Beth.

He hadn't seen her in the living room, but it wasn't like any part of the property was off-limits. She deserved to enjoy herself, and the other guys were doing good with her. Maybe one of them was showing her around, which didn't bother him at all.

His skin definitely wasn't crawling at the thought of one of them alone with her.

Climbing into the SUV, Jake was pretty sure he could hear his teeth creaking from how hard he was clenching his jaw. He didn't even glance at Asaf when the other man started the truck and headed for the gate.

Jake did have the decency to hop out and handle the gate, though. He just didn't want to talk, which Asaf honored for a little while. The road noise filled their silence, helped by the quiet country music on the radio — not that he was listening to it.

He was thinking about Beth again.

Not about her situation, or the men hunting her, or the fact that her own mother had hesitated to touch her so he never should have laid his hands on her. No, he was thinking about how she'd laughed when he picked her up the day before like an absolute idiot. For one tiny moment he'd seen the happy girl from the old photo in her file because her grin lit up her face like a supernova.

Then he'd realized what he'd done, and he'd tried to fix it by putting her back on the ground, but she'd just looked up at him with those big, brown eyes and her perfect mouth parted and waiting for him and—

"Wanna hit the range while we're at Burt's?" Asaf asked quietly, keeping his eyes straight ahead.

"Hell yes," he said, tempted to thank Asaf for asking the question because it had mercifully ended Jake's spiraling thoughts, but that would bring up the wrong kind of questions. Taking a deep breath, Jake felt himself relax a fraction. "Shooting some shit sounds like exactly what I need."

"I figured." Asaf glanced over at him, a smile spreading over his face. "Wanna make it interesting?"

"You think I'm as dumb as Charlie?" Jake laughed. "Like hell I'd bet you a fucking dollar at the range. What was your record again?"

"Fourteen-hundred meters," he replied casually, as if nailing a shot at that distance was normal.

"Christ, man."

"The world record is over twenty-eight-hundred," Asaf said, shrugging his shoulder. "My record isn't that impressive."

"Fuck off," he said, laughing again. "You know, you really shouldn't give Charlie hope that he can beat you."

Asaf chuckled. "But it's so fun to listen to the kid talk trash when I lay a few shots on the outside, because it makes it so much better when he loses his shit after I wreck his best."

"You're diabolical," Jake replied, feeling his chest relax as they joked, and the road rolled by beneath them. "How much does he owe you now?"

"About four grand."

Jake almost choked as he tried to gasp and laugh at the same time. "Are you fucking kidding me?!"

"Nope," Asaf said, tilting his head with an even bigger smile. "He keeps training and challenging me with double or nothing. It's not my fault. 'Pride goeth before the fall' and all that."

"Shit, Asaf. You're always so professional around the clients that sometimes I forget just how fucking merciless you can be." Reaching across the console, Jake smacked Asaf in the arm and held on for a second. "Thanks for getting me out of the house, man. I needed some fresh air."

"Anytime, boss."

SIXTEEN

Beth

_____

Two Days Later

"Fuck you, Ollie!" Mike said, tossing a napkin at him. "Swanson is going to wipe the floor with Lobov."

"You didn't even see the match I'm talking about!" Ollie shouted back.

"Shut up!" Brendan groaned, shoving Ollie. "This guy is supposed to be awesome. He'll be on the main card in a year or two."

"Is he in the featherweight?"

"Bantamweight."

What the fuck? They may as well have been speaking another language.

All the guys had been yelling similar things for over an hour while different fights happened on the screen, but Beth still had no idea what any of it meant. For the last few days, whenever the guys had mentioned 'fight night,'

Beth had assumed it was like any other sport where two people or groups would compete and then a winner was declared.

But this was an all-night thing with over a dozen fights, different competitors, and before the fights there was commentary and predictions — and she had completely given up on trying to figure it out.

The guys were happy, though. They had pizza, beer, liquor, and men beating the shit out of each other on the TV, and it was like all the anger and frustration of the past few days had never happened.

If only it was that easy for me.

"Get the fuck up! Get up!" Charlie shouted, jumping to his feet. "Move, motherfucker!"

"He's in an armbar," Jake said, pointing at the screen, and she looked to see one of the men holding the other's arm straight.

"I could get out of that shit." Charlie dropped back onto the couch as the guys busted out in laughter. "I could!"

"Yeah, right," Brendan said, and Charlie kicked him in the shin.

Watching them from her spot on the floor made her smile a little. They hadn't liked her sitting on the floor at first, but after she'd accepted a pillow to sit on, and another to shove behind her back, the guys gave in. It was probably weird, but she honestly liked the little place where two of the couches met and she was surrounded by the guys' legs. It felt safe.

Plus, the big, mismatched couches around the coffee table barely fit the seven of them, but that didn't seem to bother the guys. They really were like brothers. More of a family than a team.

Family.

Just when she thought she'd managed to distract herself from everything, that one word made her remember how much her mom had cried on the phone that afternoon. Even her dad was starting to sound less and less confident in his assurances that they were fine.

She knew they weren't fine. They were miserable.

And the calls were getting more and more painful, but it was all her fault.

Beth tilted the bottle of rum up again, swallowing another mouthful to try and kill the memory of her mom's broken sobs. She'd started the night with tequila, but the rum was much better. It didn't burn her chest or make her want to cough. No, the rum was smoother, and she liked the warm blankness it gave her.

Holding the rum in her lap, she tried to zone out, to let her mind go quiet, but every few minutes she'd remember something. The guys arguing the day before, Brendan's exhaustion, or the angry call she'd heard Charlie making last night.

All of it was about her.

They were all stressed and frustrated because there weren't any answers. No clues. No updates. There had probably never been a threat at all, and now she wasn't just hurting her parents by staying here; she was wasting the guys' time. Time they could be spending saving someone else. Someone trapped in a new hell, suffering… hoping and praying someone will come.

She'd been that girl in Anthony's fucked-up rooms.

She remembered waiting for someone to save her.

And she remembered feeling the hope drown in her chest.

I can't keep doing this.

Beth tried to chase the dark thoughts with more rum, but even as the warmth spread, there was no escaping the truth — she was the problem. She'd been the problem at home, and she was the problem here, only now she was stopping Jake and his team from saving lives.

Looking over at him took effort. He'd been so kind to her at her parents' house, but since she'd come to their compound they'd barely spoken. It wasn't like they were friends, but somehow it still felt like rejection. Especially because every time she looked at him, she remembered the way he lifted her into the air. And his smile. And the way he talked her through a panic attack ten minutes after meeting her for the first time.

Shit.

Tears burned her eyes, and she ducked her head to wipe them away with her shirt, grateful the room was relatively dark except for the huge TV. Beth took a deep breath and tipped the rum back again, building up her courage to do the right thing.

He's probably just trying to figure out how to tell you they can't do anything.

You'll feel better if you just get it over with.

Rip it off like a band-aid.

Turning to look at him again, she willed her body to move, but she was frozen in place, watching the light from the TV play across his features as he laughed at something someone said.

He hasn't looked this happy in days.

It was his smile that finally gave her the courage to get up, but she lost it as soon as everyone looked at her. *Dammit.* Slipping past the guys, she headed for the downstairs bathroom and used it, taking her time as she turned over the words she could say. She'd left the bottle of rum on the floor and she regretted it, because she could feel her anxiety building like ants marching through her veins.

Do it. Go. Now.

Beth had to practically throw herself out of the bathroom to make her legs move, but the darkness helped her keep moving until she was standing behind the couch Jake was on. He glanced back at her, concern flickering over his features for a second.

"You okay?"

She hesitated. Her tongue suddenly felt too big for her mouth, but she managed to lean down and whisper, "C-can I ask you something?"

"Sure." Jake nodded and climbed over the back of the couch instead of around, joining her in the dim space by the kitchen table. "What's up?"

"Um..." Beth had no idea why she'd thought they could sit at the table. It was right beside the living room, and it was way too loud. Plus, the guys would probably try to argue with her if they heard her say any of it. Jake would understand, though. "Upstairs?"

"Is everything okay?" he asked, but she didn't answer him. Instead, she went straight for the stairs.

Her heart was beating so loud in her ears that she wasn't even sure he was following her until she got to the top and saw him climbing after her. She felt like her whole body was buzzing as she finally made it into her room, leaving the door open for him while she sought the edge of the bed.

Maybe if she sat down her pulse would chill out.

"Beth?" Jake hesitated in her doorway, his arms stiff as he awkwardly shoved his hands in his pockets. "What's going on? What do you want to ask me?"

Rip off the band-aid, Beth. Just fucking do it.

Talk!

"I, uh, I know I'm causing a lot of issues, and I really appreciate you wanting to help me, but…" Her voice wasn't anywhere near as confident as she wanted it to be, but she closed her eyes and spat out the rest. "I know you were trying to help, but I'm just taking up your time and my parents are really stressed without me anyway, so I should go back home. Then you and your team can get back to saving people."

"But you can't go home yet, it's not safe."

"I heard Charlie say you guys haven't found any new information," she mumbled, pinching the side of her thigh until the sting registered and gave her something else to focus on. "But I don't blame any of you. I know how hard you all have been trying, and I can see how stressed everyone is. Maybe it was a mistake, or an error, or... something. I don't know, but I can't stay here forever."

The floor creaked as Jake moved, then she heard the door close, and Beth opened her eyes expecting him to be gone... but he wasn't. He was closer, and he was looking at her just like he had the first time he'd shown up at her house. Intense. Focused.

"We're going to figure out who is coming after you, and once the threat is eliminated, I promise you'll be back to your life." He took another step toward her. "Back home, with your parents, safe and sound."

She thought that was what she wanted until she heard him say it out loud.

Back home, with your parents, safe and sound.

A better daughter would be comforted by those words, but she wasn't. All she could think about was how much more alive she'd felt in their compound. No one had babied her, or tried to make her coffee for her, or told her she couldn't walk outside. She'd liked living with the team. Hell, she apparently wanted to stay even though it was tearing her parents apart and keeping the guys from saving someone else's life.

Christ, you're selfish.

Pinching her thigh again, Beth closed her eyes tight to try and block out the thoughts that wouldn't go away. It didn't matter if *she* liked it here, she was a problem. She was in the way, and she was hurting her parents by staying here, which made the solution clear.

"Hey, don't do that," Jake said, gently moving her hand away from her thigh before he let go and took a seat at the very edge of the bed, as far as he could get from her. He sighed heavily, rubbing the back of his neck before he looked at her again. "You're not causing issues for us, Beth. This is what we do, and I don't want you hurting yourself, got it?"

He was waiting for her to respond, but she couldn't think of anything to say. She knew he was lying, that he was just trying to be nice, but she'd already brought her issues home to her parents... Jake and the other guys didn't deserve to be weighed down by her darkness, too.

"Do you believe me?" he asked, prompting her again, but the silence stretched between them. "Beth... will you at least look at me?"

Staring at the floor, she *wanted* to look at him, she just couldn't make herself do it. Even if he wouldn't admit it out loud, Jake had to recognize the problems she'd brought to his doorstep.

His team had been spinning their wheels for days, and they hadn't found a single bit of evidence on who could be coming for her. Brendan wasn't sleeping, the guys were stressed, *everyone* was on edge... and it could all be for nothing.

If all of this was just a mistake, then she'd never been in any danger at all, and every minute she spent in their home was another minute ticking away for someone they could be saving. Another minute her mom was crying in a hotel room, another minute her dad was suffering alongside her.

And if someone really was coming after her?

As fucked up as it was, she wasn't sure if that possibility changed her mind. She didn't want to go home because she was nothing more than a ghost there. Not a real, living person, just a memory haunting and tormenting her parents. It wasn't the first time she'd thought how much better off her parents would be if she'd never come home at all.

"Beth." Jake touched her chin, turning her face toward him, and she felt her entire body tense up. His forehead creased a little more as he trapped her chin between his thumb and forefinger. "Say it."

"Say what?" she whispered.

"Say that you know you're not causing issues for us." The pressure on her chin increased as he shifted closer, his intense gaze flicking between her eyes. "Why do you think you're causing us problems?"

"B-because I am." It was easier to answer him like this, with his touch anchoring her to him, keeping her from sinking into her thoughts. No one ever touched her because she'd always flinched, but *this* was helping.

"But you're not," he insisted, and she noticed his gaze had dropped to her mouth, but he quickly corrected himself, pinning her with his stare. "I want to hear you say it."

"I can't." Clenching her eyes shut, she shook her head a little in his grip, and she was disappointed when he let go. It felt like a punishment. "I'm sorry…"

Jake sighed again, muttering a curse before he said, "You don't have anything to be sorry for, Beth."

"But I do. All I do is cause problems," she insisted, sniffling. "For you guys, for my parents, for… everyone."

He grabbed her hand and squeezed hard, not letting go even though the sudden touch made her jump. "That's not true."

God. Why was he making this so hard? She was just trying to do the right thing.

"You need to listen to me, Beth, because I don't bullshit, and I don't lie. You're not a problem and you're not causing any issues. My men and I choose to do this, we *want* you here, we *want* to keep you safe, and I want…" Jake muttered a curse as he released her hand, and a second later he grabbed her face in his hands turned her toward him until she had no choice but to meet his gaze again. "There is no way in hell I would have fucked with your life if we weren't sure you were in danger. This isn't a game, and I don't play around with this shit. I may not know who they are yet, but I'm going to find the bastards coming after you and make them regret ever learning your name."

Okay, so the threat is real.

She knew that should make her scared, she knew she should be feeling panic and anxiety… but all she felt was relief. How could the idea of going home upset her, but the thought of monsters hunting her down simply made her feel better? It was insane. *She* was insane. But as she looked into Jake's eyes, she felt the whirlwind of thoughts inside her slow.

"Do you believe me?" he asked, voice so intense it captivated her. His hazel eyes were laser-focused on her, tracing her face, studying her, and all she could do under his scrutiny was nod.

Somewhere in the back of her mind she knew it was naïve to blindly believe Jake would find the ones looking for her... but if anyone could do it, it was him. And then he'd make them pay, just like he made Anthony pay.

When her lips parted on a shaky inhale, his gaze zeroed in on the subtle movement, and the whole world seemed to hold its breath.

Beth could feel the goosebumps rising on her skin as Jake's warm palms cupped her face, his fingers teasing her scalp while one of his thumbs brushed her cheekbone where she knew a blush was surfacing. Everything tingled, buzzing in expectation as her gaze dropped to his mouth just in time to see Jake's tongue trace his bottom lip in slow motion, leaving a slight shine behind that caught the light from her bedside lamp.

It seemed to take forever, but it probably only took a few seconds for him to tilt his head to the side, close the narrow gap between them, and press his lips to hers.

A kiss.

He's kissing me.

The flutter of panic in her stomach was irrational. She wasn't afraid of Jake, and she didn't think he'd hurt her, but her body locked up anyway. She wanted to respond, to kiss him back, to do *something* because this was what she'd imagined when he'd had his hands on her waist.

She'd thought about this, she wanted it… but her damn body wouldn't move.

She really was broken.

Any second now he'd realize something was wrong with her and she wouldn't even be able to argue it. She'd never be normal. Not like the other girls on the forum. They were moving in with guys, and she couldn't even kiss someone without adrenaline rushing through her veins and panic crawling up her spine to lock her ribs in a vise.

Beth couldn't make a sound, she couldn't even breathe, but there was no mistaking the soft, satisfied sigh that escaped him just before he pulled back. His next exhale brushed over her lips, drawing her attention to the way they hummed, echoing the sensation of his tender kiss again and again.

She tried to memorize it, to etch it into her memory forever because as soon as he realized she was broken, he'd know it was a mistake and then it would never happen again.

SEVENTEEN

Jake

Fuck, fuck, fuck.

He needed to let go of her. Right now.

Dropping his hands from her face, he fought the urge to launch himself backward, to apologize, because those were all things he _should_ do… but he didn't want to. He'd been fantasizing about kissing her for days, and the reality was even better. Her lips were so fucking soft, so perfect, but he couldn't tell if she'd kissed him back.

Had he just forced himself on her? _Shit._

She was looking down again, her endless gaze focused on something far beyond her lap or the blankets, and there wasn't even a hint of what she was thinking in her expression.

"Please look at me," he whispered, afraid he might see something damning in her gaze.

She didn't even twitch. It was like she hadn't heard him at all.

"Beth, look at me." It wasn't until he put a hard edge in his tone, the kind he used on the guys when they weren't listening, that her eyes finally snapped to his.

Empty.

Her gaze was empty, like she'd stepped out of her body and left it with him, and his stomach turned as he studied her warm brown depths. That was all he could see for a long minute, until something else flickered in her eyes.

She wasn't gone yet.

Half of him wanted to ask if he'd pushed her, if he'd crossed the line like one of the fucking animals that had touched her before, but the larger part of his brain — or at least the loudest part — knew if he asked... it would be over, and he'd probably never get another chance.

Reaching for her hand again, he caught it and wove their fingers together. Tight. A little harder than anyone would call *romantic*, but her shoulders relaxed the slightest amount as he applied the pressure.

Shit.

Fucking shit.

"Don't run, Beth. Stay with me," he said softly, but despite the gentle tone he saw some of the tension return. "I'm not going to do anything you don't want me to, hear me?"

Her eyes stayed wide, slightly unfocused, and he gripped her hand tighter until she seemed to come back a bit from wherever she was drifting. *Catatonic.* He remembered that word from her file, and right now she almost had the same faraway look from the photos they'd taken after she was recovered. The look that had haunted him and brought him to her door unbidden, unwanted, and unwelcome.

Don't run, Beth. Stay with me.

"Did you like it when I kissed you?" he asked, barely a whisper, but it was like he'd shouted. She flinched, tugging a bit at his grip on her hand, but he refused to let go. "Beth. Look at me."

The hard tone brought her gaze back to his again. Pained and haunted as she let him hold her hand even though her posture told him something terrifying was going on behind her eyes. There was a solid chance she wasn't even seeing him right now, but he wasn't going to give up. He'd never forgive himself if he set her progress back over a kiss. She'd gone through too much to get here.

She was a survivor. *Fuck, she'd survived more than most.*

He couldn't help remembering Thalia in that freezing warehouse, covered in blood, beat to hell, and so fucking terrified — but she'd given him the same damn look. Scared, traumatized, and still willing to fight. Women were stronger than men, *himself included*, ever gave them credit for... which was why he went with his instinct instead of what every logical thought in his head was screaming.

"Answer me." Rough tone again, and she almost leaned closer. *Fuck.* He hated himself for it even though being harsh seemed to soothe her more than any kindness. Her lips even parted like she was trying to obey, tongue tracing dry lips, but no words left them. "Your choice,

Beth. All of this is your choice. Answer me now, right now, or I'm getting up and you can go to sleep."

His cock twitched against his thigh, and he almost twisted to crush his own balls in his jeans just to keep the fucking thing in check. When she didn't speak, he knew he had to stand up or he was going to ruin everything. The last thing she needed to see was him with a hard-on, backing her into a corner with harsh words, but just as he sighed and stood up — he felt another tug on his hand.

"Yes." It was almost inaudible. Had he taken a step the shift of his weight on the floorboards could have smothered it... but he'd heard it, and only God fucking knew the strength of will it had taken her to say it from wherever her mind was drifting.

In for a penny, Jake.

Taking a steadying breath, he forced himself to turn and look at her. The rings under her eyes looked a little darker than they had at her house, but when her gaze lifted, it was like a cheap shot in a fist fight. The blatant need sent his head reeling, made his feet unsteady, and his dick went fully erect behind his zipper.

Careful, asshole.

"You liked that?" he asked, squeezing her hand tight again as he held the eye contact like the damn lifeline it was, because as long as he had her on the line, he could pull her back up from wherever his first clumsy kiss had sent her. Leaning closer, he watched as her head tilted back, her neck craning until the long slope of her throat was exposed to the light — and then she nodded. Just once, but it was all he needed to move his other hand to the side of her head, winding his fingers in her hair to hold her still.

Hold on, Beth. Don't run.

"I liked it, too."

She barely blinked, breaths coming in short little pants as he felt her fingers tighten painfully on his hand, but she wasn't pulling away again. Wasn't shutting down, turning off, disappearing. She was there behind those haunted eyes, trusting him not to hurt her.

Ignoring the way his stomach tightened and his cock twitched, he closed the gap and kissed her again. He poured everything into it, because he'd lost the eye contact, but he wasn't going to let her slip away this time. It wasn't just a kiss; it was a full-on offensive maneuver. Teasing his way past her lips with a flick of his tongue until she opened and he could claim her mouth.

New territory, *his* territory, and when she let out the softest little moan, he tightened his fist in her hair. With any other woman he'd been with, the sudden grip on her hair would have earned a yelp at best, a slap at worst, but Beth didn't even make a sound. Instead, her body bowed toward him, and it was an offering he couldn't even pretend he didn't want to accept.

Leaning her backwards, he used his hold on her hair to make it as gradual as possible, to give her every opportunity to jerk away, to stop him, but she laid back on the bed without a pause in the kiss. He had to brace his knee on the bed beside her thigh to continue it, but he kept every muscle in his body taut — and away from her. This was already way farther past the line than he'd ever thought to go, but Beth leaned into the kiss. Her tongue was tentative at first, teasing his, until he nipped her lip and she sighed against his mouth and sought him out.

Her free hand caught in his shirt, twisting in the fabric to pull him closer, and he pressed their entwined fingers into the bed, letting her feel his weight there and nowhere else. There was no way in hell he was touching her clothes, or really climbing on top of her, or between her thighs, no matter what the soft sounds coming from her throat might hint at.

She tasted sweet, like the rum she'd swallowed with such abandon downstairs. Like heaven, wrapped in a shell that had been through hell. In a body that didn't deserve to be in pain no matter how much her body arched when he craned her head back farther just to hear another soft sound from her lips.

They should have taken the damn bottle from her. They shouldn't have let her drink so much as thin as she was. She was probably tipsy, if not bordering on drunk by now as the liquor he could still taste on her tongue processed. Every one of the guys had watched her like overprotective big brothers as she sat on the floor, knees tucked to her chest, staring through the TV as she drank — every fucking one of them had watched her with concern... except him.

He'd been imagining *this*.

If one of the guys came upstairs to find him right now, he'd deserve every punch, every hit, every cursed shout as they dragged his ass outside and reminded him of what they all stood for.

Easing back, he didn't break the kiss immediately. Instead, he shifted it down a gear, and then another as he teased her lips with a lick, another kiss, and then a nip. When he finally relaxed his hold on her hair and looked down, he saw cheeks flushed pink, swollen lips, and vibrant, warm brown eyes. Just as her brows pulled together, he felt her knees close around his thigh.

When the fuck did my leg move between hers?

Get up. Right fucking now.

Swallowing, he slid his hand from her hair and stroked the back of his fingers over her cheek. But just as he leaned up, she followed and kissed him again, and he both loved and hated the way she clung to him. Fist twisted in his shirt, legs tight around his thigh, and her nails driving into the back of his hand with little spikes of pain that so clearly begged him to stay.

Helpless to deny her, he kissed her back, tilting his hips away so she wouldn't brush his erection with her thigh as he took control of the kiss.

And he was a total bastard for it.

Climbing farther onto the bed, he felt her shift backward, the kiss breaking and reforming again and again as she spread her legs, but he ignored the offer and slipped to her side. Still fully dressed, he nudged her until she lay on the bed properly.

It was a special kind of torture when he broke the kiss again and she stared up at him from her back. Offering him everything with a single look that didn't require words — but that look made his decision for him. "Turn over."

There was a flicker of something in her expression he couldn't identify, and then Beth slowly rolled all the way to her stomach. Her knees pulled under her as she started to lift her ass from the bed, and he had to clench his jaw at the sight. The delicate curve of her back, the round of her ass in the yoga pants, barely a tug away from being bared to him.

"No. Come here, Beth," he demanded, planting one hand on her hip to pull her back to the bed, on her *side* like he'd wanted in the first place. And then, because he was already manhandling her like a bastard, he wrapped his arm over her waist and tugged her against his chest. She was stiff, tense, and he cursed his hard-on because he knew she could feel it. "It's time to sleep."

When she shifted her ass, rubbing against his erection, he adjusted until he could get a handhold in her hair, and then yanked. Hard. She barely gasped, more reflex than real reaction, but she stilled and he let the horror reel of every fucked up thing he'd ever seen play in his head until the damn thing died in his pants. Going cold, he trailed his fingers over her scalp where he knew he'd hurt her, and then tucked his arm under his head.

"Go to sleep." It was an order, said in the same tone that had first pulled her back from wherever the first kiss had sent her, but now he wanted her to sleep. *Needed* her to sleep before he did something unforgivable. Settling into the bed, he made his own body relax, aiming for a combat nap, but she was still moving.

Legs sliding on the sheets, breathing still far too rapid to be anywhere near sleep, Beth wouldn't stop moving even as the minutes ticked by, and Jake's noble plan was fraying at the edges.

"Be still and sleep. It's obvious you haven't been, and you'll feel better with a solid night's sleep, I promise." *Promises, promises, why the fuck do you keep making promises to this girl?*

Another full body twitch, a wiggle, a shift of her head that almost popped him in the nose and left him with a face full of hair. Lifting his head, he sighed and resettled, tugging the pillow down for them. A hard squeeze at her waist made her go still even as it brought all of those soft curves tight to his front. Her breath caught, and for a second he thought he'd finally done it. Crossed the wrong line and ruined everything, but then she whispered, "I can't sleep. I…"

Guilt was a gut punch he hadn't been expecting, but he should have known better. He'd been the one to give her what she needed after all. "Where are they?"

"The drawer."

He placed a kiss to the back of her head before he could stop himself, and he wanted to kick his own ass as he rolled backward to tug the flimsy drawer out of the bedside table. There was nothing inside it but dust and a pair of shiny handcuffs. Beth tensed as the metal jingled and scraped across the wood, and he felt a fresh wash of rage toward every bastard that had ever touched her. Still, he forced his voice to be as gentle as possible as he asked, "Do you want the light?"

"Will you stay?" she asked, so damn quiet he couldn't deny her even though he'd had plans to get out of her bed like a decent man.

"Yeah."

"Then no light." She was still curled on her side where he'd put her, the rise and fall of her curves a terrible temptation he knew he could have with a touch, a word — and it would be so wrong. Worse than the kiss, worse than holding her against him in bed. It would be a betrayal.

It would make you even more of a bastard.

"Okay." The word came out tight, strained, but he flicked the light off then reached down to the end of the bed to pull a blanket over them. A second later he felt her stretch, her body shifting as she reached for the metal headboard, but he stopped her. "Wait, let's try this."

Pulling her close again, more gently this time, he slid his hand up her arm until he found her wrist and eased it back down. With a flick, he swung the cuff open, keeping two fingers inside the metal as he tightened it so that it wouldn't cut into her.

It turned his stomach the way she relaxed, sinking into the bed, into *him*. A red haze of violence filled his head as he stared down at the dim outline of her on the bed, and before he could change his mind, he latched the other cuff around his own wrist.

Beth tensed again for a second, and then her breath shuddered as she melted against his front. "Thank you," she whispered.

"I'm right here, Beth. I'm not going anywhere." *Even though I should.* A good man wouldn't be enjoying her body against his, wouldn't have ended up in her bed in the first place. A good man would have told her she was being ridiculous trying to go back home, put the tipsy, traumatized girl to bed, and gone back downstairs to finish the fights.

Instead, he was handcuffed to her, his arm draped over her ribs, and because God was a cruel bastard, he'd probably wake her up with morning wood like a real monster. That thought almost had him turning to his back, but then Beth wound her fingers into his, gripping tight as their cuffs clattered together in the dark. With a sigh, she pulled his arm tighter around her, planting their bound wrists against her chest like she was hugging him to her.

The softness of her breasts and the delicate scent of her hair were all he could think about as he got comfortable behind her. Both of them lying on the same pillow, right wrists in handcuffs, still fully dressed. Nothing about this was normal, or good, or healthy.

But it felt so fucking *right* that he bit his tongue and closed his eyes.

EIGHTEEN

Beth

Someone was shouting in the house, maybe more than one person, but Beth tried to block the guys out because she was warm and comfortable and all she wanted was to drift back into empty sleep.

Then someone opened her door.

"What the *fuck*!" a man shouted, and by the time Beth opened her eyes Mike was already halfway around the end of her bed. "You fucking bastard!"

"Whoa, whoa, Mike! Wait!" Jake said, trying to raise his hand, but they were still cuffed together and her arm stopped his — which left him completely defenseless when Mike hit him, a brutal punch that snapped Jake's head to the side.

Panic rushed through her chest, choking off the shout in her throat, but then she saw Mike rearing back for another one, and she threw herself across Jake to shield him.

"Fuuuuuuck," Jake groaned.

"Get the fuck out of her bed!" Mike wasn't even looking at her, he was looking right through her, and he was furious.

Speak, dammit. Say something!

"Holy shit, what the hell is going on?" Charlie asked from the doorway, blocking it as more of the guys showed up.

"Nothing!" she yelled, or at least she *tried* to yell, but the word came out thin and tight and no one was listening to her anyway.

By the time Charlie joined Mike beside her bed, there wasn't a hint of humor left in his face. "Move, Beth."

She shook her head hard, but Jake nudged her, mumbling, "It's okay."

"Take the fucking handcuff off and get out of her bed." Mike was fuming, but it seemed like he didn't plan on hitting Jake again. At least not yet.

"I need the key," Jake said, talking through a bloody mouth as he shifted and sat up. Pointing his left hand at the bedside table since their right hands were still linked, he added, "Please?"

"I can't believe this shit," Charlie grumbled, stepping past Mike to yank the drawer open. He handed Jake the keys a second later, and then Jake met her eyes.

"Everything is going to be fine," he said, talking softly as he unlocked the cuff. "Just stay in here for a bit, okay?"

"Don't fucking talk to her," Mike growled, yanking Jake off the bed by his arm as soon as the cuff was loose. "Downstairs. Go."

"Go!" someone shouted in the hall, and she could see the guys heading for the stairs.

Say something.

Speak up.

She opened her mouth to try and explain, but Mike and Jake were already at the door, and Charlie was following after them, although he was at least looking at her. There was a dark shadow over his face as he scanned her, and she knew why. She knew what he was looking for, she knew what they all thought, and she had to make them understand... but all she managed to do was shake her head.

He didn't do anything.

That's what she wanted to say, but nothing came out, and Charlie turned away.

For a minute, Beth couldn't move. She imagined jumping out of bed and chasing after the guys, shouting at them, but her body was locked up, panic choking her just as effectively as a hand around her throat.

It was just like the night before.

When Jake kissed her.

But he didn't give up on you.

Closing her eyes tight, she focused on her breathing, remembering how he'd crouched in front of her bed the first day they'd met and talked her through the panic.

This wasn't exactly the same. The panic attacks came when her mind chose to fight a situation, but sometimes her mind went for flight instead of fight.

That's how Ailsa described it anyway. Fight or flight. Panic or escape.

Both were equally out of her control, but she couldn't just wait for her mind to surface this time. She didn't have time to sink under the water and hide. She needed to move. *Now.*

Get up. Get the fuck up.

Her hand twitched and she felt the cuffs shift. A shaky inhale and then she managed to grab the keys, remembering how Jake had chosen his wrist instead of the bed... and she'd never slept so well.

I didn't have any nightmares.

That realization helped her move, her mind reaching for her body, surfacing faster than ever before because for once she *wanted* her body back. As broken and damaged and fucked-up as it was, she needed to get downstairs. For Jake.

The cuffs dropped away, and she climbed off the bed, still moving stiffly, but she could hear them shouting downstairs. They were just trying to protect her, but they didn't understand.

No one ever understood... except Jake.

He'd seen her, even when her mind slipped under the surface, even when the darkness tried to drag her away.

'Don't run, Beth. Stay with me.'

Those words, his voice, his touch — all of it had held her up, lifted her, kept her close enough to the surface to feel his kiss, to kiss him back. And for a few minutes she'd felt real.

She wasn't a ghost with Jake.

He hadn't hesitated to reach into the dark for her, and if he was willing to do it for her, the least she could do was return the favor.

Beth was shaky as she moved down the stairs, holding onto the railing while the shouts echoed up.

"There's no fucking excuse!"

"What the hell were you thinking?"

"I was just trying to help her," Jake said, much calmer than the others.

"No, you were just trying to help yourself *to* her." That was Mike's voice, still furious, and she hesitated near the bottom step as she listened to them moving around. Heavy, male footsteps switching between the tile where the big table was and the carpet of the living area.

"We should drag your ass outside for touching her," Charlie said, talking over the others' grumblings. "You know that, right?"

"I get it," Jake replied, his voice still calm, flat, and she moved forward, building up her courage to confront the guys.

"You obviously don't get it," Benny shouted. "Did you forget everything she's been through? Maybe you need to look at her details again. Pull it up, Brendan. Make him fucking look at it."

The words registered just as she made it to the big doorway, and she saw Benny standing next to the table as Brendan turned back to his laptop.

"I didn't..." Jake trailed off, and although she couldn't see him, she could hear the guilt in his voice.

"Didn't what?" someone snapped.

"You know you crossed the fucking line," another guy said, and she was pretty sure it was Ollie as he raised his voice. "You'd castrate any one of us if we touched a girl on a job!"

"Bring him over here, Mike," Benny said, pointing at the laptop. "He needs to fucking read her file again, then he can try and look us in the eye and say he didn't do anything wrong!"

My file?

"What does it say?" she asked, taking the last few steps past the doorway, and this time they heard her.

An awkward silence descended as she looked at them. Mike had one hand on the back of Jake's neck, the other on his arm, halfway between the couches and the table. The other guys were scattered around, their faces a mix of anger and shame and sadness.

Looking back at the laptop, she moved closer and asked, "Is that my file?"

"You really shouldn't... I mean, you don't want to look at this," Brendan said, clearly uncomfortable as she closed the gap between them. He reached for the laptop screen like he was going to close it, but he froze when she touched his shoulder.

"Please."

Muttering a curse, Brendan let go of the laptop and dropped his head. He hesitated, clearly torn, and then he turned and got up from the chair… and she sat down.

Missing Person. Elizabeth Amelia Doherty.

Her parents had filed the report three days after she was taken, but she'd already known that. They'd apologized to her so many times in the early months for not responding faster, for not getting the police involved sooner — but she knew it wouldn't have mattered. The police had never found anything. Still, her heart pounded in her ears as she read through the clinical description of herself. Hair color, eye color, height, weight, last known location. It was all so official, so detached, but it brought back the memories of that day. The setting sun, the warm air on the walk to the public parking lot after work, and then… *poof.* Nothing until she woke up tied to Anthony's bed.

She scrolled down farther, reading the updates in the police department's files.

They'd never found her car, and there was no footage of her arriving at her apartment building. No activity on credit cards, or bank account, or phone.

In her peripheral vision, she saw Mike leading Jake back toward the couch, making him sit against the back while the other guys found places to perch. Brendan was leaning against the wall by the kitchen and Asaf was hovering near the opposite end of the kitchen table. The others were probably nearby, too, but she couldn't look away from the screen as her life unrolled with the scrollbar.

They didn't have any information on who had raided the brothel in Thailand, but there were photos of it, and it was surprising how innocent it looked. From the outside it looked like a hotel, but not a rundown, dirty one. It was the kind of hotel tourists would go to... and maybe they had.

Her stomach clenched, bile rising up her throat as flashes from her nightmares replayed behind her eyes. She could feel the rope on her wrist, the sting of a lash on her back, the weight of someone on top of her, inside her, crushing her.

Stop it, stop it, stop it.

Shaking her head, she felt the allure of the dark depths in her mind, but she forced herself to refocus on the screen in front of her. She'd wanted answers, wanted this information for so long, and she didn't want to run from it.

That plain looking, five-story building had been home to so much suffering, not just hers, and she hoped when they'd taken her out of it, some of the others trapped there had escaped too.

With that thought, she scrolled down... but the next page was worse. Photos of her at Ramstein Air Base, even thinner than she was now. Just bones and bruises and scars. She skimmed the notes on every injury, the notations of the scars, the tattoo, and descriptions of her mental state.

Next were the records from Greenwood Psychiatric in California, but she was surprised to see an additional document after her intake paperwork that showed billing information for 'James Hawkins.'

Thalia's husband paid for it?

She'd never even thought about the cost of her months at Greenwood because her parents had never discussed bills or anything — but it was naïve to think it would have been free. Universal healthcare wasn't a thing in the US, and her dad made too much for the hospital to just write it off... but why hadn't Thalia ever mentioned it? Did she even know?

That question disappeared when she scrolled to the next page and saw her doctors' notes. They were blunt, brutal, cruel. The harsh truth behind whatever false comfort the doctors had fed her parents.

Severe post-traumatic stress disorder. Consistent catatonic state.

Unresponsive to medication.

Unlikely to recover.

The notes seemed to completely write her off, giving up on her almost immediately after she'd arrived. They mixed in their diagnosis with casual references to her 'repeat sexual and physical assault' and 'sex trafficking' as if that made it okay for her to stay catatonic.

The more she read, the angrier she got, tears blurring her vision that she had to swipe away so she could see the same shit from a different doctor. One after another they reviewed her case, evaluated her, and came to the same conclusion. 'Unlikely to recover.'

Broken. Damaged. Ruined.

Even after the iPad showed up and Thalia's words brought her back to the surface, even after she'd proven them wrong, the tone of their notes didn't change.

They'd seen the truth from the very beginning. They'd known she'd never be normal again, even if she woke up, even if she could talk and walk and move. The doctors knew she couldn't be fixed.

Which was exactly why she shut down when Jake kissed her.

It was why she couldn't function day-to-day.

The same reason all the other girls on the forum were making real progress, improving, *healing*, and she hadn't. She was just conscious. Not catatonic, but not better. Still 'unlikely to recover' no matter how hard she tried.

A sob choked her as she stared at those words, and raw anger rushed upward on the heels of it, turning the sob into a scream of rage as she picked up the laptop and threw it, knocking the chair to the ground in the process. The laptop crashed onto the kitchen floor, and it was Brendan's shout of, "Oh shit!" that made her realize what she'd done.

"I-I'm sorry," she murmured, voice breaking as she stumbled backward, and then bolted for the stairs.

NINETEEN

Jake

Beth ran and he moved to follow her, but Mike yanked him back against the couch. He wanted to shove him off, to tell them all to go to hell, but he understood why they were pissed.

Watching her cry as she looked at her file had been fucking torture for him — for all of them — but he didn't want her to be alone. Not after what she'd just read, because he still remembered every bit of it.

"Fuck…" Benny sighed, rubbing his neck as he followed after her, and Brendan was right on his heels.

Charlie side-eyed him hard as he headed for the hall, and he both hated and understood the way his men were looking at him. It wasn't right, and he wasn't trying to pretend it was, but he still didn't regret it.

And he was pretty sure Beth didn't either.

Why else would she have blocked Mike?

Asaf didn't look at him at all as he moved toward the stairs, and Jake tried to follow again, but Mike dug his fingers into his shoulder, muttering, "Don't."

"Dammit, Mike," Jake growled, looking up at the man who he knew was his friend, his brother, no matter how much he'd fucked up. "I just want to hear what she says. I won't even go in the room, but I need to know if she's okay. Don't you?"

"Motherfucker…" Mike grumbled, shoving him forward without taking his hand off Jake's shoulder. "Fine, but you're not going near her. I'll make sure of that."

"Fine," Jake agreed, shaking off his grip as he got to the steps. He couldn't hear anything at all until he got to the second floor, but even then, the voices were too low to make out until he stopped next to Asaf who was blocking her doorway.

There was raw disappointment in Asaf's gaze, but Jake didn't have the energy to deal with it. He just leaned against the wall and closed his eyes to listen to Brendan.

"Seriously, it's a virtual machine, like a copy. You didn't ruin anything, I promise."

"It's true," Benny confirmed, but there was no response from Beth.

"Honestly, you helped me out," Brendan added, chuckling. "I've been wanting a new laptop anyway and now no one can bitch at me for getting one."

His chuckle died slowly, making the silence that followed even more awkward — and then Benny cut through the bullshit.

"Beth, we need to know if Jake did anything... *wrong* with you."

He was pretty sure his heart stopped, and his lungs seized as he waited for her response, ears straining, and as the seconds ticked by, he wondered if he *had* crossed a line. No matter what she said, or how she'd reacted, the answer could still be 'yes.' With all the hell she'd experienced, maybe she couldn't consent to a kiss because she'd forgotten she could turn someone down. Maybe he'd—

"Are you sure?" Benny asked, and since Mike hadn't tossed him over the railing, Jake was pretty sure that meant she'd said he *hadn't* hurt her.

"He helped me sleep." Beth's voice was so fucking soft, but no one was making a sound as she spoke, and he finally took another breath when she added, "And stay asleep. He kept the nightmares away."

I did?

His heart rejoined the party, pounding against the inside of his ribs as he fought the urge to look in her room just so he could see her face and confirm what he'd heard. He wanted to see her expression, to know if he'd actually helped her, but he knew the guys wouldn't let him.

"But are you okay?" Benny pressed. "Mike said you were handcuffed together and—"

"I need the cuffs," she answered, cutting him off, and Jake bit the inside of his cheek to keep from smiling. That was her iron core showing through again. "I can't sleep without something on my wrist, anchoring me, it's just… it's just how I am. I need it, and he gave me those so I didn't have to keep using the zip-ties."

"And Jake?" he prompted.

"He helped me. I asked him to stay," she said, a long pause following before she said, "Last night was the first time I haven't had any nightmares since before… before everything."

It's true.

Jake opened his eyes, glancing at the doorway as warmth spread through his chest, but he felt the guys looking at him and he met their gazes. There was doubt warring with cautious acceptance in each of them, some leaning more one way than the other. Ollie still looked like he wanted to hit him, but Mike was where his gaze eventually stopped.

"That's what she pulled you away for last night?" Mike asked, his arms still crossed, but there was less anger in him now.

"She wanted to talk." *Not a lie.* "Everything else just… happened."

Leaving out the kiss — *kisses* — felt wrong, but he didn't want to try and explain it. Hell, he didn't even have a good explanation. He'd just followed his instincts, and he was relieved to hear they'd been right, but the entire situation could have just as easily gone the other way.

And if she'd said he crossed a line, if she'd said he hurt her, he would have walked himself outside for the guys to beat the shit out of him.

"She's asking for you," Asaf said, and Jake whipped his head around in disbelief.

"What?"

Stepping back from her doorway, Asaf jerked his chin toward it. "She wants to talk to you."

"Jake?" Benny called, and a second later the man appeared. There was still anger in his gaze, but it was obvious he'd begrudgingly accepted Beth's answers. "Go on."

He swallowed hard, nodding at their medic as he and Brendan stepped out of the room, making room for him. Beth was on her feet when he stepped inside, and they both froze for a second, but she recovered first.

Jake moved out of her way, stepping farther into the room, and he was surprised when she grabbed the door and looked around at the team before she shut it in their faces.

Shit.

With the guys outside, eavesdropping, he wasn't sure what to say or not say. There were all the things he *should* say, and then there were a whole lot of things he *wanted* to say, but probably shouldn't.

Definitely shouldn't.

Beth climbed onto her bed, crossing her legs, and it was obvious she wanted him to sit with her, but he hesitated. Getting back on her bed was asking for trouble, and even though the morning had been a fucking mess so far... he couldn't deny how much he wanted to hold her again. Kiss her again.

Dammit.

"I…" Looking over the door, he clenched his jaw, remembering the guys standing just outside, listening. The things he needed to say, they didn't need to hear, so he joined her, but made sure to keep some space between them on the bed.

"Your mouth is bleeding."

He wiped at the corner of his mouth and his hand came away with some dried blood, but he shrugged it off. "It's okay," he said, keeping his voice low. "I would have done the same thing."

"I'm sorry I didn't explain everything earlier, I just… couldn't."

"You have nothing to apologize for, Beth. I'm the one who should apologize," he whispered, dropping his gaze to the blanket. "I shouldn't have taken advantage of you."

Silence stretched between them, and he eventually gave in to the temptation to look at her. She looked hurt and confused, her brown eyes dewy from tears as they met his. "Why would you say that?"

"I'm supposed to be keeping you safe," he explained, keeping his voice as low as possible while a fresh wave of guilt crashed through him. "I'm not supposed to be leering at you, and I'm definitely not supposed to be kissing you."

"Why not?" That hint of iron was back in her tone as her brow furrowed, little wrinkles appearing in her forehead. "I'm so tired of everyone treating me like I'm fragile. I know I'm fucked up. I know I'm a mess, but I'm just… I'm so fucking sick of being reminded about it all the time."

"I get it," he said, remembering how she'd reacted the night before when he'd felt her receding inside herself. It hadn't been sweet words or gentle touches that had brought her back to him.

"Do you regret kissing me?"

He almost laughed at her whispered question, shaking his head. "Me? Not at all."

The corner of her mouth twitched with the slightest hint of a smile before she asked, "What about sleeping in here?"

"Why do you ask?"

Beth just pointed at his face.

"Mike always pulls his punches. I'm fine," he lied. Mike had absolutely landed his punch, and there were more than a few teeth that felt loose. Jake honestly felt lucky he'd been in the process of sitting up, because if Mike had nailed a better angle, he probably would have fractured his cheekbone.

"Well…" She hesitated, picking at the blanket between them as she took a slow breath in and out. "Would you be willing to stay again? In here?"

What?

The question took him by surprise, and he bounced between too many thoughts. He obviously wanted to say yes, but the guys might try and kill him, and no matter what she'd said… it was still really fucked up that he was moving in on her in the middle of this shit.

"It's just I slept better with you here, and I know everyone is mad about it, but I didn't have any nightmares, and I *always* have nightmares," she babbled, talking fast, a hint of panic in her tone as her breathing picked up, but he felt like a fucking predator taking advantage of her blatant anxiety. She wanted him in her bed to keep the demons at bay, but he couldn't even pretend that's why he wanted to say yes.

"I don't know if I—"

"Please," she begged, and every bit of his will power buckled.

"Okay." The word was barely out of his mouth when she launched herself at him, clinging to him like he was a life raft, and even though he knew he shouldn't... he wrapped his arms around her back and pulled her closer.

"Thank you," she whispered against his neck, squeezing him tight.

He couldn't form any words. The scent of her hair coated his next breath and his brain just turned off. She felt so perfect against him, so *right* even though everything about this was wrong — but he didn't have a single urge to be noble.

A better man wouldn't accept this offer.

A good man wouldn't be thinking of how incredible she'd felt pressed against him in the night.

If he had any decency at all, he'd keep his hands — and his lips — to himself, but he knew if she even hinted at another kiss, he'd give in.

She's worth the damnation.

Jake's eyes were crossing as he scrolled through another website Brendan had sent over. It was another nightmare hole on the dark web, but after hours of scrolling through the same shit, even the worst side of humanity could become monotonous.

Leaning forward, he grabbed his coffee from the table and took a swig.

The whole team was scattered around the kitchen table and the couches, everyone working, and it was a relief that they'd found some level of normalcy after their morning. Of course, he wasn't in the clear. Every time he tried to sit next to her, or even get near her, one of the guys would *somehow* get in his way.

It was obvious they were still pissed and trying to keep him separated from her, but he didn't blame them. He'd crossed a line, and if the roles had been reversed with anyone else on his team, he wouldn't have let them get away with it — no matter what the girl said.

He was only getting away with it because he was the boss. Their leader.

And you're setting such a great fucking example.

There was another trickle of guilt inside him, but it wasn't anywhere near enough to deter him. He couldn't even lie to himself and claim this was him trying to comfort her. No, he liked her. He was attracted to her, and he was pretty confident she wasn't looking at him like a big brother. She'd reciprocated, she'd asked for him, and she wanted him back in her bed tonight.

To keep the nightmares away.

Right. That was all she'd said upstairs. Nothing about another kiss.

Nothing about wanting him.

Taking another drink of coffee, he angled his head back on the couch and used the movement as an excuse to glance over at her. She was sitting next to Asaf at the kitchen table, scrolling through her iPad, and he wondered if she was on the forum.

Is she telling Thalia about me? About the kiss?

What would Thalia think about it?

For some reason that made him feel worse than everything his team had shouted at him that morning. He respected the Badass too much, and it would gut him if this changed the way she thought about him.

But Beth kissed you back.

He sighed, hating the way his mind kept him running in circles every time he tried to process what the fuck was happening between them. Turning back to his laptop and all the terrible shit waiting for him, he got back to work.

The hours dragged by, as if time itself was trying to keep him out of her bed, but eventually it was dinner time, and he jumped at the chance to ditch his laptop and cook.

Jake had just slid a tray of taco shells in the oven to crisp up when Asaf returned and headed straight for Ollie. The resounding *smack* as he whacked the back of his head, and Ollie's shout, grabbed everyone's attention.

"What the fuck was that for?" Ollie snapped.

"You left the seat up in the bathroom, dipshit," Asaf replied, jerking his thumb toward the hallway. "There's a girl in the house now."

"Fuck you! I did not!"

"You were the last one in there, Ollie. I passed you in the fucking hallway." Another *smack* to the back of Ollie's head. "Don't be such a pig."

Ollie shoved his chair back, facing off with Asaf. "Hit me again and I'll bludgeon you with the goddamn toilet seat."

"No thanks, I'm not sure I've had enough shots for that," Asaf retorted.

"You're a dick," Ollie snapped, flipping Asaf off as he grabbed for his chair and dropped back into it.

"No, I was just raised by a mother who taught me basic manners." Asaf rolled his eyes, heading for his seat at the table. "Speaking of which, all you mongrels upstairs should take a look at that bathroom and remember you're sharing it with Beth now."

"It's not that bad, right?" Charlie asked, looking over at her, and Jake could tell by the way Charlie's expression changed that Beth agreed with Asaf. "Damn... sounds like we've got chores after dinner."

"Sorry, Beth," Ollie mumbled.

"Yeah, we didn't think about it," Brendan said. "We're sorry."

"We'll get it cleaned up," Mike added, and Jake turned back to the stove to hide the smile creeping over his face.

Asaf had always been a neat freak about the bathroom, so Jake and Benny had just kept up with it in the downstairs bathroom, but he could remember the last time he'd stepped in the upstairs one and even he'd been surprised by how trashed it was.

Watching the guys react to her discomfort reminded him of how protective they'd been since she arrived. They gave a shit about her happiness... and her safety. Which was why he'd earned more than the punch Mike had delivered that morning. The guys were just being good men, taking her on like a little sister and making her feel included in their messy version of a family.

He was the anomaly.

The odd one out.

The bastard who absolutely didn't think of her like a little sister.

But he could still protect her in his own way. He could keep the nightmares at bay, help erase those dark circles under her eyes with a few good nights of sleep, and he'd take the blue balls as punishment for wanting anything more.

Getting to have her in his arms was more than he deserved anyway.

TWENTY

Beth

_____

Three Days Later

Tapping on another forum post, Beth skimmed through the pictures of JL0312's dog. It was ridiculously fluffy, and apparently only nine months old. Between the photos the other girl talked about finding some pillows from her couch shredded on her birthday — but the dog was definitely cute enough to get away with it. Smiling to herself, Beth typed out a quick comment before switching back to the main list.

Unfortunately, the last two posts she hadn't caught up on were *both* about relationships.

Don't read them.

You know it'll just piss you off.

Of course, they probably wouldn't bother her if she could just get up the nerve to kiss Jake again, but she kept fucking that up. She'd come up with so many things she could say, so many plans for what to do, and then it would be time to get in bed and… she'd freeze.

She was so frustrated with herself that when she'd woken up before him yesterday, she'd actually contemplated kissing him in his sleep just to get over her nerves — which was extremely creepy.

And pathetic.

Groaning to herself, Beth slumped lower on the couch, sulking. Obsessing over this really wasn't helping, but her brain wouldn't drop it. Jake hadn't even tried to kiss her since the guys freaked out on him, which she kind of understood, but he'd told her he didn't regret it.

He could have lied, though.

Or maybe he hadn't regretted it then, but he did after?

Stop it.

Rubbing the heels of her hands against her eyes, Beth took a deep breath and let it out slowly. She needed to stop focusing on this. No matter what was happening between them, she was sleeping through the night now, which was a huge improvement. Having a few days without nightmares was like a vacation from her normal life and she needed to just suck it up and be grateful.

Beth stared at the forum for a minute, debating if she should read the new posts or not, but she just didn't have the energy to read about people falling in love. Instead, she scrolled back to the last post from Thalia. It was short, just a quick one about her yoga studio, but Beth liked her posts.

Everyone did.

Thalia was basically the patron saint to every woman who'd survived the Williams brothers. Hell, she'd killed Marcus with her own hands, and then her husband had hired Jake's team to kill Anthony.

Taking out the brothers would have been enough of a miracle to canonize her, but that didn't even begin to cover everything. Thalia had created the forum with James' support and sent out the iPads to each of them — but none of them would even be on the forum if James hadn't used his resources to tear down the brothers' operation in the first place. That single act led to all of them being rescued, and it wouldn't have ever happened without Thalia.

But that wasn't why Beth looked up to her so much.

Thalia proved that no matter what horrors they'd been through... they could still become someone *real*. Someone whole enough to fall in love, someone strong enough to work through the trauma, someone normal enough to have a job, a life, a future.

She was hope.

A bright light in the dark that kept Beth afloat on her worst days.

When she was in Greenwood Psychiatric, still catatonic, drowning in her own mind, and written off by her doctors, it was the arrival of the package from Thalia and James that first pulled her out of the darkness.

Actually, it wasn't even the whole package, it was the letter Thalia sent with it, read aloud by an uncomfortable orderly who'd stumbled over the references to Marcus' death and Anthony's imprisonment. Those words had pierced the depths she was lost in, reached down deep and yanked Beth to the surface, slamming body and mind back together for the first time since Anthony Williams had drowned her on a table.

She'd never told Thalia how the letter had affected her, but it wasn't exactly a pretty story.

Beth barely remembered those first days when all she could do was scream and sob until her throat was too raw to continue. She held onto the letter through all of it, though. Clutched it to her chest like a life raft until being on the surface didn't hurt so much.

Then she'd followed the directions and logged into the forum. *BD0211. Beth Doherty, February 2011.* Her name and when they'd taken her. She'd reached out into the abyss with her first post, sharing her name and searching for anyone who might understand — and Thalia had reached back.

Always kind, always understanding. Thalia had showed her she wasn't alone.

Her forum brought all the survivors together, and she'd filled in the gaps about the brothers and everything that led to their rescues. Then she'd shared her story to prove they could, too. Not just the brave moments, but the terrible ones. The moments of weakness, the shame of finding pleasure in the horror, and the hate she still carried for herself as a consequence of all of it.

That was how the forum started.

As a private place just for them where they could say the things they never wanted to tell their families or their doctors or their therapists.

But that was almost two years ago, and over time the forum had become more about successes and life updates than the dark shit they all felt or remembered and...

Oh.

Self-awareness hit her like a blow to the chest, and things clicked into place she hadn't even realized were connected. Back when the posts began to change, she'd started posting less and less. It hadn't been a conscious decision, she just hadn't wanted to bring the other girls down with *another* post about bad nightmares, or panic attacks, or how fucking useless she felt.

Even when they tagged her or asked for updates, she just lied and said she was fine.

But she wasn't fine.

The whole point of the fucking forum was to have a place to vent all the bad shit no one else understood, and for some reason she'd just... stopped. Even though having the validation she wasn't alone, that she wasn't the only one who felt crazy or broken, had been so damn helpful in those first months.

And it hadn't just been Thalia responding to her back then. All the girls had.

Beth was the one who stopped reaching out, stopped sharing, and that one stupid decision had changed everything. The forum went from a place where she felt connected, to a place she only logged in to see how different she was.

She'd isolated herself.

You fucking idiot.

Groaning under her breath, she thought back to different posts that had upset her or sent her spiraling, and she no longer had to wonder why her mom hated the forum so much. It wasn't about Ailsa — it was about *her*.

She'd done exactly what Ailsa and so many other therapists had said not to do... she'd compared herself to the other girls. Every success someone else posted instantly became a failure for her. Another reason she'd never be okay, never improve, never be a real person.

But she didn't have to let her mind keep lying to her.

And if she really wanted to figure out what the hell to do about Jake, there were a bunch of other traumatized and fucked-up women literally at her fingertips.

Swiping back to the top of the screen, Beth opened a new post and took a steadying breath. The blank box was waiting, but she started and stopped and erased multiple times before she figured out how to approach the questions that mattered.

She didn't want to freak everyone out with the potential danger she was in, and since Thalia knew Jake, she didn't really want to name him either — so she kept the post simple. An apology for not posting in a long time, with a shorter version of her realization about why she'd stopped, and then she went right for the issue. She'd met a guy, he knew some of her history, and he was being really nice, but they'd kissed once, and she'd sort of... locked up. They'd worked through that, though, or at least she *thought* they had, and they'd sort of made out, but he hadn't kissed her since and she had no idea how to work past the anxiety and panic and her fucked-up brain to try and move forward.

Of course, kissing was the earliest stage of her problem, but she wasn't sure if she wanted to unload everything in one post. Some of the other girls had retained their sex drive through everything, and she knew that came with its own guilt... but there were others like her that hadn't, and they might have answers or suggestions.

They could make you feel less alone, at least.

She debated it for a few minutes, re-reading her post a few times as she wrote and re-wrote a few more sentences about feeling broken *physically*. Her cheeks were on fire as she attempted to explain how she'd tried to touch herself a few times since she got out of the hospital and her body hadn't responded... but she *had* responded to kissing him. It'd been the first time she'd felt any kind of arousal since she'd been rescued, but she wasn't sure if that would make her body work or not.

Hell, she wasn't even sure if she'd ever get to kiss Jake again, but every idea she'd come up with had failed miserably, so what did she have to lose? It wasn't like she had a reputation to protect.

Beth hovered her thumb over the post button, heart pounding as she re-read it one last time to make sure she'd at least made sense.

"Is that really how you feel?"

She jumped, twisting around on the couch to find Jake lurking behind her.

Oh God, he was reading over my shoulder.

Nausea and panic warred as she looked down at the screen in her lap and realized she'd posted the damn thing on accident.

"Beth, I—"

No, no, no.

She launched herself off the couch, so desperate to get away from the situation that she practically ran into the hall and up the stairs. Her face was on fire, and it wasn't until she shut the door to her room that she realized she was deep in a panic attack. Lungs burning, she dropped her iPad on the floor and folded her arms over her head, pacing the room as she gasped for air, trying to figure out how the hell that had happened. The wheezing whistle of her throat closing told her she was fighting a losing battle as the panic only got worse. But she'd thought she was alone in the house. A bunch of the guys had gone to the grocery store, and the rest were working on some project outside in their workshop.

The house had been completely silent, so why the fuck hadn't she heard him come inside?

This can't be happening.

The panic had its claws in deep, the vise-like grip tightening around her lungs, and no matter how many times she told her body to breathe slow, she kept gasping while her throat clamped shut around the rush of air.

Fuzzy darkness was eating away at the edge of her vision, hiccupping gasps echoing in her ears, and then there was a hand on the back of her neck and another on her arm. The strong grip turned her around, moving her back to the bed, and a moment later she was sitting on the edge and Jake forced her head between her knees.

"Breathe slower, Beth. Listen to me!"

She recognized his boots, although they were dirtier than the last time she saw them, and that seemed like such a strange detail for her to notice right now.

"Beth!" he snapped, and his fingers dug in at the back of her neck, a faint pinch amidst the chemical chaos occurring in her veins, but it helped. "Stop gasping and breathe slowly."

She listened to him inhale and did her best to mimic it, but her lungs stopped short, head spinning with her desperate need for oxygen.

"Again," he commanded. "Slower."

Jake made it sound so easy. He breathed in slow and deep, and then let it out just as slow. Then he did it again, and again, even though she was taking two or three breaths for every one he showed her.

"Better," he lied, and she rolled her eyes where he couldn't see it.

"I. Don't. Need. Your. Pity," she said between panicked gasps.

"What?" Jake sounded sincerely confused at first, but there was irritation mixed in when he elaborated. "What the fuck are you talking about?"

"Stop it," she grumbled, shoving his hand away from her neck so she could sit up and drag in a few more desperate breaths.

"Stop what? Helping you breathe?" he asked, sarcasm tainting his tone, which only made her angrier.

"No." She shook her head, looking up at the ceiling to stretch out her neck in a desperate attempt to convince her body to let more air into her lungs.

"Stop what then?" he snapped, raising his voice before he corrected it. "Goddammit. You need to breathe slower, Beth."

"I'm. Fine."

"Oh, really?" Jake huffed. "Yeah, you sound fine. That wheeze in your lungs is completely fine."

Asshole.

She tried to slow her breathing, but the panic and the adrenaline in her veins had control, and the black was creeping in again. *Fuck.* Buckling forward, Beth put her head back between her knees, and she probably would have slipped right off the bed if Jake hadn't caught her shoulder.

"Christ, Beth!" he shouted, crouching in front of her with one hand on her shoulder and the other hovering near her leg. "You ready to listen to me, yet?"

No.

It was childish, and she knew it, but she shook her head. All she wanted was to be alone so she could finish her panic attack and then melt into the floorboards or teleport or something equally improbable that would allow her to escape whatever conversation was lurking on the other side of her ability to breathe normally.

"I swear, Beth... don't push me right now."

She lifted one hand and raised her middle finger, and he had a fistful of her hair a second later. With a quick jerk, he bent her head back and she was practically nose-to-nose with him.

"Is this what you want?"

"No." The word came out on a pant, and she had a front row seat to the way Jake's intense hazel eyes widened, the green flaring around his dilating pupil, leaving barely a hint of the brown visible.

"You—" He let go of her and pushed himself off the floor, his boots thumping over the wood as he paced away and back and away again. "I wasn't trying to read what you were writing. I was just coming inside to check on you, and then I saw your screen, and—"

"Stop."

"We need to talk about this!" he argued, moving closer, but she shook her head back and forth, doing her best to breathe evenly.

"No... Go back... Outside." *Slow and even. Breathe slow. Picture a balloon filling up in your chest.*

"Where the fuck did this attitude come from, Beth?" he snapped. "I know I shouldn't have looked over your shoulder downstairs, but it's not my fucking fault I saw it."

Shut up, shut up, shut up.

"Goddammit!" Jake shouted, pacing away from her again, and she heard his groan that encapsulated exactly how she felt. This was the fucking worst. "You want me to talk about the kiss? Fine. I'll talk about the kiss."

"No… Just go… Go away." She looked up at him, but felt her head spin from the quick movement, and as soon as she wobbled, he was there.

"Put your head between your fucking knees," he growled, making her obey with a fist in her hair.

Fuck. It was definitely more evidence of just how twisted everything was that the sting of her scalp and the commanding edge of his voice made her entire body tingle. Like his rough touch was a live wire hovering over her skin.

"I'm going to assume you're listening, because I really don't have the patience right now for another one of your shitty responses." Jake shifted his hand in her hair, winding it just a little tighter without allowing her to sit up at all. "You want to know why I haven't kissed you again, right?"

She tried to shake her head, embarrassment setting fire to her face, her neck, her chest. All she wanted was to spontaneously combust so that she didn't have to listen to him try and let her down nicely.

This has to be a nightmare.

"I'm supposed to be helping you, Beth. Keeping you safe and— You know what? I've been so worried about crossing a line with you, but I've already crossed that line."

She managed a breath, and then another, enough to say, "And you regret it… I get it."

Jake snapped her head back, forcing her to meet his gaze again, and she couldn't ignore the fierce heat behind his eyes. "Don't put words in my mouth. I *never* said I regretted kissing you."

"Then why... haven't you... kissed me... again?" The need to gasp every couple of words wasn't helping her make a convincing argument, but this wasn't how she'd planned this afternoon to go at all.

"Because I—" Jake tensed, his jaw twitching as he clenched his teeth around whatever he almost said. He searched her eyes for a moment, looking back and forth before he exhaled roughly. "I don't want to take advantage of you."

Anger spiked in her chest, expanding her lungs as she narrowed her eyes. "Fuck you."

He jerked back like she'd slapped him, but he recovered fast. "I'm trying to do my job."

"Fuck you!" she shouted, shoving him back, and he let go of her hair to catch himself with a hand while she sat up straight. "If I'm just a job"—she dragged in another breath—"then get out."

"Beth..."

"Stop it," she snapped, finally getting control over her breathing. *Slow in, slow out. Repeat.* "I'm a person. Not a victim. I choose who I want." *Slower breath.* "I thought you saw me for me... I guess I was wrong."

TWENTY-ONE

Jake

Beth was still struggling to breathe evenly, but he felt like she'd just turned off his life support with a handful of words.

I guess I was wrong.

He wanted to argue, to tell her that he did see her, but he couldn't make his tongue move. On his ass on the floor in front of her, he saw everything he'd felt instinctively. She was so fucking strong, her brown eyes blazing, fingers gripping the edge of the mattress as her hair formed a messy halo while she glared down at him.

"I do," he mumbled, raising his voice as he repeated himself, "I do see you."

"But you don't want me?" she asked, and he was relieved to hear her breathing better, but the words were like a knife between the ribs.

"That's not it."

"Then what!" she snapped, pain lacing her tone, and he hated himself for hurting her.

"I don't *deserve* you." The truth sucked to say out loud, but he couldn't deny it as he shifted to his knees in front of her. "You deserve someone else. Someone good. Someone who will—"

"What? Someone who will *what?*" Beth grabbed his shirt, clinging to it, pulling until he looked up at her again, or at least in her direction, and she let out a half-hearted laugh when he didn't answer. "Who do you think I deserve, Jake? Someone who might see me as something other than a victim? Someone who might like me anyway, despite knowing every fucked-up thing that's happened to me?"

"Beth…"

"Or, wait, maybe I'm supposed to wait for someone perfect. Someone who doesn't judge me for being crazy. Someone who doesn't think I'm ruined and isn't afraid to touch me," she continued, tugging at his shirt like she wanted him closer, but he couldn't make himself move. "What about someone who sees a broken zip-tie on the ground and knows exactly what the fuck I've been doing? Someone who cares enough to give me a pair of handcuffs so I don't have to hide a hundred broken zip-ties."

The tears were brimming over her beautiful eyes, marking shining tracks on her cheeks before she managed to swipe them away, but each one was like acid on his skin.

She shoved him back again, her voice cracking as she pushed her tangled hair out of her face. "But maybe that asshole doesn't want me after all, maybe he realized I wasn't worth the bullshit involved in—"

Jake had no idea what he was doing as he covered her mouth, but as he stood up and wound his other hand in the hair at the back of her head, he just knew he didn't want her to finish. "Stop. Don't you dare say that."

Beth mumbled against his palm, and he stared down at her, instinct warring with logic, but then she huffed and rolled her eyes, and he gave in.

Lifting his hand just enough to allow her to speak, he cautioned her with a simple, "Be nice."

"If you don't want me like that, just say it," she whispered, and he knew she was referring to the post she'd written for Thalia's forum. Just the idea Badass might be reading what Beth had written about him made him feel… confused. Some mix of pride and shame that didn't balance each other out. "Please just tell me," Beth continued. "I can't handle not knowing. I can't do *this*. Take me home, or take me to someone else who can protect me, but—"

"You really think I don't want you?" He covered her mouth again, grabbing the lower half of her face, and she looked up at him with that tear-filled, accusatory look. "Trust me, Beth. I want you. I *have* wanted you, and I'm sure I'm going to hell for it, because every time I'm near you… all I want to do is kiss you. I want to touch you. I want to fall asleep with you in my arms so I know you're safe because anything that comes for you will have to go through me."

Another muffled response against his palm, and he let her go, prepared to get shut down. Instead, she whispered, "Then kiss me."

Fuck.

How was he supposed to resist that?

Catching her by the waist, he tossed her onto the bed, instantly covering her as he shifted a knee between hers and planted his arm beside her shoulder so he could cradle the back of her head. A fistful of hair had her lips parting, and he wanted to taste her again... but he hesitated, struggling to think with his brain instead of his dick.

"Jake?" she whispered, and hearing his name in her voice was a special kind of hell. "I want you... I want this."

"Goddammit." He closed his eyes, trying to forget the way she looked underneath him. "I'm not a good man, Beth."

"What? Yes, you are," she argued.

Jake shook his head, but he didn't move, which helped to prove his point. "No, I'm not. A good man wouldn't be in this bed right now, and you... you deserve a good man."

"Who?"

"Fuck, I don't know," he grumbled, dropping his head against his arm as he forced a breath that he hoped would kill the growing erection behind his zipper. "Someone good, someone who knows how to be respectful and gentle. Like Benny, or Mike. Hell, Asaf would—"

"I never said I wanted you to be gentle," she whispered, and he would have sworn his heart actually stopped. "And they didn't kiss me, Jake."

"I know," he croaked, his body too tense.

"And they aren't in this bed."

He almost laughed. "That's because they're better than me."

"No," she said, and he felt her hand on his cheek, gliding toward the back of his neck to pull him down. "They aren't here because I don't want *them*."

Fuck. Jake swallowed, eyes drifting open on a sinful sight. "Part of me wishes I was better than this, but it's getting pretty fucking hard to listen to that part of my head right now."

"Why's that?" The question itself was a tease, every syllable wrapping around her tongue in the most delectable way possible, but it was the way she shifted on the bed underneath him that finally broke him.

"Because a good man wouldn't do this," he answered and kissed her. She arched into him, but he just pressed her back to the bed, giving in to every urge he'd had that first night as he tasted and nipped and teased, claiming her mouth again and again.

Every tiny sound she made was perfection, and the pricking of her nails on the back of his neck was all the encouragement he needed to continue. Tightening his fist in her hair, he expected a whine, but her hips rolled upward instead, and he dropped down so his thigh rested between her legs.

"You okay?" he asked, craning her head back so he could lick and nip down the column of her throat. She moved her head against his grip on her hair, but he wasn't sure if it was a nod or not until he felt her shift against his thigh, subtly grinding. "Feel good?"

"Mmhmm," she murmured, her breathing picking up again, but it definitely wasn't panic this time — it was arousal, and he couldn't deny the bolt of pride he felt after what she'd written downstairs.

"Good girl," he praised, capturing her mouth again, just in time to feel the buzz of her quiet moan as he rocked his thigh between her legs. Jake couldn't remember the last time he'd made out with someone like this. Probably not since high school, which was stupid because feeling Beth writhing under him was incredibly fucking hot. Moving a hand to her waist, he felt as nervous as a teenager, constantly questioning himself, waiting for her to panic, but she didn't.

Instead, she ran her hand up his side, nudging his shirt higher, and the feeling of her fingers brushing his skin was electric. His pulse raced as she nipped his bottom lip, mimicking him as she kissed him back, urging him on.

He was trying to be careful, but she'd reached out to the forum about this. She wanted him, she'd written it in her own words, and he'd almost fucked everything up by holding back.

Steeling himself, he shifted to her side, and her little whine of complaint as he took his thigh away gave him enough confidence to slide his hand from her waist to her hip and then between her legs. He moved slow, tracing the seam of her yoga pants, gradually applying a little more pressure until she gasped against his mouth.

"I really don't want to fuck this up," he whispered, and she opened her eyes, so much fucking vulnerability in her gaze, and she was trusting him with it.

"You won't." Her voice was soft, breathy, as the flush in her cheeks darkened. "It might not work, though."

"Does this feel good?" he asked, rubbing in firm circles as he sought her clit through the layers of fabric, but he knew he'd found it when her hips twitched, and her brow furrowed.

"Yeah…" Beth didn't sound confident, but she didn't trust her own body… which made sense. After everything she'd been through, he wasn't surprised she struggled with anything sexual. Shit, that was why he'd tried to be a good guy, and why he was second-guessing every move he made.

"If it feels good, nothing else matters, okay?" He leaned down to taste her skin, tracing his lips up her throat as he alternated between licks and kisses and playful bites, all the while listening to every hushed sound she made. Every muscle twitch, every noise, every breath — he was studying all of it, making sure she was okay.

He glanced over at the door, grateful he'd thought to close it when he followed her upstairs, but he wished the thing had a lock on it. If the guys came back in the house, they might look for them, and that would be bad… but stopping would be worse. She was kissing him back, lifting into his touch. She was present and participating, and he couldn't risk losing that.

Eventually they found a rhythm, her hips moving in time with his fingers as their lips crashed together again, but he knew it wasn't enough for her. If he wanted to prove to her that she wasn't broken, he needed her to come.

"You can tell me to stop, Beth," he whispered, moving his hand to the waist of her yoga pants, and then he felt her push one side off her hip as she met his gaze and nodded. It was consent, but he still moved slow, working her pants down one bit at a time.

"I want this." Three words, almost too quiet, but he really needed to hear them.

"Thank God," he groaned, sitting up enough to shove her pants out of the way, and when he brought his hand between her legs again, he muttered a curse. She was wet enough that he could feel it through her underwear, and he wasted no time seeking out her clit again.

"Jake," she whined, letting out a needy little gasp that had his cock twitching as she arched.

"That's it. It feels good, doesn't it?"

She nodded, lips parted as she panted and sighed, torturing him with every arch, every roll of her hips, every desperate noise, but this was the kind of torture he'd sign up for any day.

Beth was gorgeous stretched out beside him, one of her knees bent as she opened herself for him, her legs bare because she'd worked her yoga pants off with all her writhing, but he'd never wanted the ability to read minds more than he did right now. He could tell she was close, but just when her breathing would pick up, her brows pinching together as she hovered on the edge of an orgasm — she'd suddenly pull back.

The hesitation was like tripping a breaker, and it meant she had to start all over, building back to the precipice… which he didn't mind. Listening to her pleasure and watching her was a gift, despite the ache in his balls, but he could tell she was getting frustrated.

If he said anything about it, he knew she'd shut down. It would confirm every fear she had about herself, but she was wrong. She'd soaked her underwear, and her body knew exactly what to do — every flick of her hips proved that.

No, this was all her mind getting in the way.

You know what she responds to.

Shifting, Jake slipped his other hand under her head and back into her hair, grabbing a fistful just as she got close again. The sharp tug forced her to look at the headboard, earning him a blissful sigh instead of a cry. Lowering his voice, he intensified the circles over her clit and spoke right against her ear, "That's it. Just like that. Ride my fingers like a good girl."

Her whines got louder as she clutched at the sheet, her other hand finding his t-shirt again, pulling at it as that wrinkle appeared between her eyes again.

Stop holding back.

"You're so fucking wet, baby," he groaned, nipping her ear, and she moaned quietly. "I'm going to taste you in a minute. Hear me? I'm gonna lick and suck and taste you until you flood my tongue because you make the most perfect fucking sounds when I touch you, and after this

I'm not going to be able to keep my hands to myself when you grind your sweet ass against me in your sleep. I want you to—"

Her back arched, body tensing as the sweetest little gasp escaped her lips, and she twisted against his hold on her hair as she finally came, but he didn't let go. Even as her thighs clamped together over his hand, he kept circling, her underwear turning slippery as the orgasm rolled through her. Waves of shuddering tension followed, and her quiet mewls had him leaking precum, but he had no plans to even touch his pants.

It was tempting to push her into another orgasm, though, but instead he slowed down, gentling his fingers, letting her enjoy it as he relaxed his hold on her hair.

Trailing kisses up her neck, he took his time getting to her ear. Jake stroked his fingers over the soaked fabric between her legs, cupping her as he whispered, "I don't think you're broken, baby."

TWENTY-TWO

Beth

———

Holy shit.

She couldn't think straight yet, but she heard what he said, and she was having trouble arguing it. There was a point when she'd almost told him to stop and give up, but she was so fucking glad she'd kept her mouth shut because she was pretty sure she'd never come that hard in her life.

You've waited long enough.

The thought made her laugh, but only a little bit actually made it out.

"What's funny?" he asked, and Beth looked up at him. He had that same mischievous grin on his face she remembered from when she'd asked him to throw the knife. A mix of pride and playfulness that melted her all over again. "Still not talking?"

She wasn't sure she could.

Her brain seemed to be rebooting.

"Hmm…" he mused, pulling his hand from between her legs. His gaze shifted to his fingers just before he put them in his mouth, the sexiest groan rumbling in his chest as he closed his eyes and tasted her. "Fuck, you taste so good."

He'd said he was going to taste her. It was one of the devious things he'd whispered just before she came — and he'd said *so many* incredible things. All those whispers had pushed her over the edge, and now his eyes were back on hers, burning, intense, and hungry.

"You want to stop?"

No. Please no. She shook her head, and he chuckled.

"You're going to have to speak if you want me to do anything else." It sounded like a tease, especially with that devilish grin lingering on his face, but she could tell he meant it, which just proved she was right about him being a good man.

Wetting her lips, she took a breath and managed to say, "I want you."

"Want me to what?" he pressed, propping his head up on his hand as he looked down at her, his other hand skating across her stomach, over her shirt and then under it.

"Anything," she whispered. *As long as it's you.*

"Tsk, tsk." Jake shook his head, playfully chastising her as he traced patterns on the skin over her ribs. "That's not an answer I'm going to accept."

"Why?"

"Because *anything* isn't an answer." His hand inched higher until his thumb brushed the underside of her breast. "Want to try again?"

"Jake…" She arched, reaching for his hand when it started to drift away from her chest, but she hesitated.

"Go on. Show me where you want me to touch you," he commanded, and she obeyed.

With his hand under her shirt and her hand over it, she guided him back to her breast, sighing when his warm, calloused palm covered it. Then she squeezed his hand, and he squeezed her breast — not that there was much to grab — but he didn't seem to mind.

"What next?"

Anything. That's what she wanted to say, because all she wanted was for him to touch her, to keep touching her, and she didn't care how.

"This?" he asked, brushing his thumb over her nipple. They were already sensitive, hardening into little nubs when he'd had his hand between her thighs, but then he pinched it lightly and she arched into his touch. "Speak or I stop, Beth."

"Harder," she whispered. Jake hesitated, but it was only for a second, and then a zing of pain rang out from her breast, rushing through her veins like a shot of something decadent and dangerous.

"What next?" he repeated, quickly pinching her other nipple on the heels of the question, which made it impossible to think. "Tell me what you want. Now."

"You."

"I'm right here."

She whined, frustrated because he knew exactly what she meant. "No, I want _you_."

"Not an option." This time there wasn't any humor in his tone, and he took his hand from under her shirt like he was punishing her for asking again.

She'd always been stubborn, though, so she had to push. "Why not?"

"It just isn't," Jake said, sitting up with a frustrated sigh. "Pick something else, or we can go back downstairs."

"That's not fair. I want you, and you said I'm not broken, but I just want to know for sure."

"I think I've already proved your body works perfectly fine," he growled, leaning over her again. "Do you need another example?"

"I'm saying yes, Jake. I want you and—"

"And _I_ am saying no," he interrupted, a sharp edge to his voice. "I'm not going to risk fucking everything up by rushing this with you, okay? So, since you're being stubborn, I'll give you options. We can stop now, or—"

"I don't like that option."

"Okay…" A low chuckle softened the seriousness of his face, and she watched him try, and fail, to hide his smile. "Well, I really want to see you come again, but it's your choice. My hand or my mouth?"

The words made her blush, but she went for it anyway. "You said you wanted to taste me, right?"

"I absolutely fucking did." Jake grinned, moving quickly to hook his fingers into her underwear and yank them down as he shifted down the bed. "Just try and be quiet for me, okay?"

Her stomach dropped, remembering the guys might come inside, but when she looked down at him, she saw the band-aid covering the fucking tattoo that would probably remind him of why he hadn't wanted to touch her in the first place. She tried to cover it with her hand, but realized that was awkward, although Jake didn't seem to notice at all as he tossed her underwear to the side and rested his hands on her knees, waiting until she slowly spread them.

"Hell yes," he whispered, sliding his hands up her thighs as he settled himself between her legs. His shoulders were big, forcing her legs even farther apart, as he peppered her inner thighs with kisses. "We can stop anytime you want to…"

"I don't want you to stop," she whispered.

A low groan was his only response before he dove between her thighs. There were no more gentle kisses, no teasing licks, he just hungrily dragged his tongue through her wetness before latching onto her clit.

"Oh fuck, fuck, fuck," she babbled, fisting the sheets on either side of her as he flicked his tongue over that crippling bundle of nerves. Pleasure bowed her spine, ripping a desperate whimper past her lips. It was too intense. She was still too sensitive from the first orgasm and instinct had her twisting away.

She'd expected Jake to let her go, but he just grabbed her hips and pinned her back to the bed, holding her exactly where he wanted her so he could continue. A satisfied groan buzzed against her as he focused mercilessly on her clit, winding her up faster than she thought possible.

"Please, please," she whined, not even sure what she was saying it for, but then he stopped, and she instantly regretted it.

"You taste so fucking good..." Looking up at her from between her thighs, Jake ran his tongue over his bottom lip before flashing that wicked grin she was definitely falling for.

You're in so much trouble, Beth.

Moving his hand, Jake found her clit with his thumb and pressed, creating slow, tiny circles that were absolute torture. "Are you okay if I use my fingers *here*?" He dipped his head down and dragged his tongue over her entrance, making eye contact when he repeated it, taking his time before that grin took over his lips again. "Answer me, baby."

"Yeah, it's okay," she whispered.

"Say please again."

Oh fuck. Yeah. So much trouble.

Her mouth felt so dry, her pulse was racing, but she couldn't do anything except look into his eyes and obey. "Please."

"Mmm, such a good girl. Bite the pillow if you need to make noise." Groaning, Jake descended on her clit again and she bit back a cry, scrambling for the pillow to muffle herself as he eased one finger inside her. He moved so slow, which was an insane contrast to the way his tongue was attacking her clit, but that just made everything more overwhelming.

When he worked a second finger in, immediately curving them to match the magic he was working with his mouth, she arched off the bed, moaning into the pillow to stay quiet.

It was like he knew her body better than she did.

Screw that, he *definitely* knew her body better. There wasn't even a competition. Every twitch, every sigh, every moan was because of him, and she felt the wave rising inside her, swelling, threatening to crest — but she was stuck again. Pinioned between want and oblivion.

"Please, please, please," she begged into the pillowcase, unsure if he could even hear her as she fisted the other side of the pillow, reaching for the orgasm, desperate to fall.

Then she felt his hand on her breast and with one pinch of her nipple, he freed her.

That sharp zing shot through her, stealing her breath away with a flash of pleasure and pain as it pushed the wave over. It didn't push her down though, it carried her, lifted her up, spinning her head around as light exploded inside her veins, lighting up every nerve with glittering ecstasy. An impossible, breathless rush of bliss that was even better than before.

Shivering, she couldn't hold still as Jake licked and sucked, lingering even though she was sensitive and every flick of his tongue sent another ripple through her body. Eventually he stopped, kissing her thigh, her hip, moving up her stomach before he left her shirt in place and moved the pillow away from her face.

"Convinced?" he asked, pure pride on his face as she panted, but he didn't wait for her to answer before he kissed her again. She tasted herself on his lips, his tongue, and knew what she wanted now.

Reaching between them, she found the button of his pants and managed to pop it open just before he caught her hand and jerked back. "No."

"But it's my turn to taste you."

"There's no *quid pro quo* on this, Beth. This was about you, not me."

Propping herself up on her elbow, she pointed at his pants. "I can see you have a hard-on, Jake."

"Yeah, obviously."

"So, I want to return the favor!" she argued, sitting up on the bed to face off with him.

"It's not happening."

"What if I just use my hand?" she offered.

"Nope."

"That's ridiculous!" she growled, trying to stay quiet. "It's not fair that you made me come, but you won't let me do the same for you." She didn't know why it was making her so mad, but she felt the heat rushing to her face, stupid tears brimming up as she realized the most likely reason. "Do you really think I'm so fragile that I can't even touch a dick? I was with men before he—before everything happened. I was twenty-two, Jake, I wasn't some naïve virgin, and I'm definitely not one now."

He leaned forward and captured her face in his hands, pulling her closer until she had no choice but to look him in the eye. "The absolute *last* fucking thing I'd call you is fragile. I know you're strong, Beth, and my dick is hard because I want you, but if you want this to continue, then we're doing it on my terms."

"What terms?" she whispered, trying her best to keep the tears at bay.

"We both have to be ready before we do something, and you may feel ready to cross another line today, but I'm not. Got it?"

"Okay." She swallowed, feeling like shit that she'd been such a bitch when he was just trying to help her. He'd *already* helped her, and kissed her, and helped her come, and she was pushing for more anyway. "I'm sorry, I just feel guilty."

Jake kissed her, softly, gently, and then she felt his sigh against her lips. "You want me to come?"

"Yes…" Her response was cautious, wary, because he'd just made his stance painfully clear.

"Move back against the headboard." Jake released her, and as she shuffled backward, he moved closer to the end of the bed. "If you want me to come, then you're just going to watch… and give me a little motivation."

"Watch?" *Motivation?*

"Yep." Working at his pants, Jake shifted, and then he had his dick in his hand... and Beth was staring. She was staring a lot as he slowly stroked the hard shaft, up and down, before running his thumb over the head, spreading the shiny pre-cum. "Here's the deal, Beth. Are you listening?"

She nodded, forcing herself to look at his face instead of his lap.

"It's simple. You touch yourself, I touch myself. You stop, I stop."

"But I can't." She shook her head, pressing her thighs together. "I've tried... it doesn't work."

"You can do it, Beth," he answered, grinning. "You just did. Twice."

"Because it was *you*."

"Then pretend it's me." He tilted his chin toward her. "Go on. Spread your legs for me."

Leaning back against the headboard, she obeyed, slowly spreading her legs, and his low groan made her feel a little better. The hunger in his expression wasn't faked, and neither was his grip on his shaft, and as soon as she moved her hand between her thighs, he moved his — up and down.

"You're still so wet, baby," he purred, stroking himself at a steady pace. "Rub your clit for me. Come on, I really don't want to stop yet."

Don't stop.

Her movements were tentative, unsure, but he was right... she was wet. It made it easier for her fingers to move over her clit, and she tried to do it like he had. Although, she wasn't exactly focused on her own pleasure. Jake was way too distracting. One hand braced behind him; he wasn't tentative at all. Every pump of his hand had purpose, and she imagined what he felt like. Softness over steel, hot and hard.

"Good girl," he purred, and she realized she was so caught up in Jake's hands that she'd let her fingers continue the repetitive little circles over her clit without thinking about it. He sucked his bottom lip between his teeth, his eyes focused between her thighs, and she knew he was still tasting her on his mouth. "Tell me what you're thinking about."

"You," she whispered.

"Say it out loud. What am I doing?"

"Say it?" The heat in her cheeks became an inferno as he nodded and grinned at her, trailing his gaze from her face to between her thighs, down to his shaft, and then back. "Um, I'm thinking about when you were licking me," she mumbled, feeling her core clench at the memory. "With your fingers inside me."

"What next?" *Of course he asks that fucking question.*

But this time, the answer was her decision because it was her fantasy, and as she closed her eyes, she had no trouble imagining what she wanted. "You're on top of me. Kissing me," she said, panting, feeling a pulse come to life between her thighs. "Then you're inside me, moving."

"Fuck…" He groaned, and she opened her eyes to see his hand moving faster. "Tell me more. What am I doing?"

"You… um…" *God, I can't say this.*

"I can see how wet you are, Beth, and I want to know what has you so turned on. Tell me. Now." That commanding edge in his voice was bliss, pushing away the trickling anxiety.

"You're kissing me, and you sound just like that," she mumbled, that pulse getting stronger in her clit. Needier. "And you've got your hand in my hair, pulling it, and…"

"Don't leave me hanging," he pleaded, his need building with her own.

Some brief flash of bravery made her meet his gaze as she said, "And you're not treating me like I'm breakable. You're thrusting inside me, and you're not holding back, and… and I want it."

"Christ, *yesss*…" Jake moaned low, the muscles in his arm contracting again and again as he jacked-off, and she imagined him thrusting inside her at that pace. Filling her, brushing all those same places he had with his fingers, but it would be so much better with him.

"Your turn," she said, riding her momentary bravery. "What are you thinking about?"

He clenched his jaw, growling low before he finally said, "You."

"Yeah?" Somehow, in front of Jake, with him staring at her like a starving wolf, she actually felt beautiful. Desirable. Taking a shuddering breath, she slid two fingers inside, completely intoxicated by the almost pained look on his face as he watched her move them in and out. "Tell me what you're thinking. Please."

Tracing his lower lip with his tongue, he shook his head a little. "Keep doing that and you're going to kill me, baby…"

"I'll do whatever you want me to if you'll just tell me what you're imagining."

"I keep thinking what it would be like if this were your hand," he said, groaning low. "And what your tongue would feel like… your mouth…"

"Keep going," she encouraged, sliding her fingers back to her clit, the heat slowly building as her hips twitched, seeking more.

"Fuck… I'm imagining just how incredible it would be to kiss you when I slide inside you for the first time and feel your body squeeze my cock." He squeezed his shaft, just like he described, and then his hand was moving faster. "Tight and hot and soaking wet."

All she could do for a moment was nod, her body reacting to him even though it was her fingers on her clit making her whimper. "I-I want that."

"Picture it for me," he urged, his pace picking up, his breaths turning rough, as he continued. "Imagine how good it'll feel when I'm inside you."

Yes, please.

Leaning forward on the bed, she'd barely moved when Jake's hand froze at the base of his cock.

"Put your hand between your legs, Beth. Now." The command was like a shiver rushing through her body, and she obeyed. Back against the headboard, fingers on her clit, but she was chewing on her lip, waiting, because he wasn't moving his hand at all. "Look at me."

She met his gaze, knowing she'd broken the rules, but she didn't even feel bad as she slid her fingers deep again, wordlessly pleading with him to continue.

"Imagine this with me, okay? Because this is exactly how it will be." Jake moved his hand again. "Eventually, when we're *both* ready, I'm going to eat your perfect pussy until you come for me, until you soak the damn bed, and then I'm going to look into your eyes, so I know the only person you're thinking about is me. *Then* I'll fuck you, and I promise I won't treat you like you're fragile. I'll make damn sure you come for me, because I want to feel you squeeze my cock as you fall apart underneath me."

Oh my God. She couldn't look away from his hand, moving up and down, and he was imagining her. He wanted her, to be inside her, just as much as she wanted him.

"Go on. Come for me, Beth. I want to watch you come."

The wave was there, warm and building, but it was wobbly. Nowhere near what it was like when he touched her, and no matter how much she rubbed the little bundle of nerves... she wasn't getting any closer. "I can't," she whined.

"You can. That's my hand, not yours. Imagine I've got your hair in my fist, bending your head back so I can taste your skin, so I can hear every sweet sound I pull out of you every time I thrust deep inside you." He groaned, his body tensing, and she knew he was close, which meant she was holding him back.

It's not you. It's Jake.

Pressing herself against the railing of the headboard, she let the metal dig into her back, imagining it was Jake pinning her there, thrusting inside her. Every whirl over her clit merged in her mind with his thrusts, her body rocking in time with the strokes of his hand she could hear.

"Fuck, Beth… all I can think about right now is just how amazing you're going to feel when you come on my cock. Picture it, me buried deep, pressing you into the bed and—"

"Jake!" she gasped, stunned when her body jolted, the orgasm surprising her as pleasure locked her muscles, forcing her to fold forward, curling around the fluttering waves of bliss pulsing outward from her clit as she made her eyes stay open so she could watch.

"God, yes." Jake stroked faster and faster, clenching his jaw tight, and then he jerked as he came, a muffled shout swallowed in his chest as the first shot hit the blanket, and then another as his hand slowed. The last few pulses rolled down his shaft, over his fingers, and she crawled forward, breathless. "What are you doing, Beth?"

"Can I…" She moved a little closer, using his words to make it easier. "Can I please taste you?"

"Just a taste?" he offered, and she nodded, stopping in front of him on the bed as he looked at the mess he'd made on his fingers. "Here."

"Thank you," she whispered, opening her mouth, and the second he slid two of his fingers over her tongue, she sealed her lips to his skin, letting her tongue tease him, just to make it clear what she *could* have done.

And he clearly understood.

Jake's lips were parted, his intense gaze focused on her mouth as he growled under his breath. "You really are going to kill me, Beth. *Fuck.*"

He took his hand away a second later, and she tilted her head, about to ask why, but he silenced her with a kiss. It was brief, but it felt like a promise that there would be more chances. More opportunities to explore and prove she wasn't as broken as she thought she was.

"You know, if you somehow manage not to kill me..." he said, laughing low. "My team is probably going to finish the job."

"But I didn't tell them anything."

"The kiss was one thing... this is way different." Grabbing the blanket, he wiped himself off, glancing between the door and his hands. There was a new tension in his shoulders, and she could tell he was deep in thought as he climbed off the bed and wadded the blanket up before putting his pants back together.

"You still want me, though, right?"

He chuckled. "Beth... you have no fucking idea how much I want you, but I want you enough to not fuck this up any more than I already have, okay?"

"Okay," she nodded, feeling better that his thoughts weren't wandering in the direction of avoiding her again, but it still didn't explain the heaviness that had settled over them. "Are you upset?"

"No, but I want you to stay in here for a bit. We were pretty quiet, but there's a chance one of the guys heard us, and—"

"You *were* exaggerating about them killing you, right?"

"Hopefully," he said, but the laugh that followed wasn't comforting. "Either way, I'm gonna have to tell them, because there's not enough room in this place for secrets."

Shit.

"Are you telling them now?"

"If Mike and Asaf are back from the store… yeah." He nodded, picking up the blanket, but his face didn't look as confident. "Just stay in here."

"Okay." For once, she really didn't want to argue, but she also didn't want to leave him alone, or watch him get hit again. "Maybe I should—"

"It'll be okay," he assured her. Taking a few steps toward the door, he leaned down and picked up her iPad, bringing it back to the bed with him. "I promise."

"If I hear violence, I'm coming downstairs, because I don't want them to think that—"

"Deal." Jake wrapped his hand around the back of her neck, pulling her into another kiss. As he leaned back, he pointed at the iPad and said, "You should probably share your new situation with the forum while I'm handling the guys."

"New situation?" she asked, watching him gather up the blanket and walk backward toward the door.

"Well, I don't think you have to worry about me kissing you," he said, grinning as he reached for the doorknob. "And you're *definitely* not broken."

TWENTY-THREE

Jake

"You hiding from us or from Beth?"

Jake leaned forward, peeking around the edge of the workshop to find Charlie standing there like he'd been waiting for Jake to notice him. Sighing, he sagged back onto the old bench. "You training to be a stalker? I didn't even hear you walk up."

"That's because you need hearing aids," Charlie said, moving into his peripheral vision before adding, "And you didn't answer my question."

"I'm not hiding, jackass. I just came out here to think."

"You're sitting behind the workshop, on that rusted piece of shit, in a nest of weeds. That's hiding," Charlie retorted, tucking his thumbs into his pockets, and Jake looked over at him because it was clear the man wanted his attention before he'd get to the fucking point.

"Well?"

"Still waiting on an answer, boss. You out here because of us, or because of her?"

Neither. Both.

"Please just fuck off," Jake grumbled.

"Okay, since you want to be a little bitch about this, I'll lay it out," Charlie began, striding over to plant himself right in front of him. "Is the team pissed at you? Yeah. Mike and Benny are a lot more likely to throw you a blanket party than the rest of us, but I don't think anyone is particularly happy."

"Wow. Thanks. You can go back inside now."

"I'm not done. No matter how any of us feel about it, it's pretty goddamn clear that she's got it bad for you, so…" Charlie spread his arms.

"So?" Jake prompted.

"Honestly, I don't have a fucking clue what to say about that. You're the dumbass that saw the line and decided to pole vault over it, and now you've landed in a goddamn minefield." Charlie shrugged, sounding as disgusted with Jake as most of the guys had. "Just know that if you fuck up with her, there's going to be fallout. So… try not to fuck it up, I guess."

Godfuckingdammit.

The entire reason he'd come out here was to think through all this shit, but whatever sixth sense Charlie had for annoying people must have activated, because it hadn't taken long for the man to find him. Taking a deep breath, Jake resisted the urge to pick a fist fight, and simply asked, "Anything else?"

"We're all up shit creek in a sinking canoe when it comes to the actual fucking job."

"That's not new," Jake muttered, leaning back against the workshop.

"Well, I figured since you're out here with your thinking cap that you might spare a few minutes coming up with ideas for how we can keep your new fuckbuddy safe."

Clenching his jaw, Jake counted backward from ten, cracking each of his knuckles on the way down, but when he got to one he still wanted to knock Charlie's teeth out. "Go inside. Now."

"Yes, sir," Charlie shouted, snapping to attention and saluting him just to be a dick. As the man walked away, he heard him mutter something about lunch and Jake checked the time on his phone.

10:46.

He knew he should just suck it up and make the phone call, but he'd hoped sitting outside and looking at the mountains would bring him some clarity. Then Charlie had fucked up his head even worse than it already was.

Jake didn't regret telling the team the day before, though. It was the right thing to do, and shit would be ten times worse if they'd found out some other way.

And Beth doesn't deserve to be your dirty little secret.

Not that he'd ever seen that as an option.

When they'd just kissed, and he'd promised himself it would never happen again... it was just simpler to keep it quiet. But even that was stupid because he'd never stopped fantasizing about her. He was still fantasizing about her while trapped between his dick and the last scraps of sanity in his head.

Just call him.

"Fuck me," he muttered as he hit dial and pressed the phone to his ear, listening to the ringing while he stared out at the Sierra Nevadas.

"Jake?" Dr. Hawkins answered. "Is everything okay?"

"Hey James." Blowing out a breath, he realized he wasn't sure how the hell to start this conversation, so he delayed. "Everything's FUBAR, but nothing to do with Thalia. How is she?"

"She's doing well." That aristocratic English accent didn't do much to hide the suspicion in the man's voice, but it must have been the manners that had him wait an awkward minute before finally asking, "What exactly are you calling about, Jake?"

"Well, you know how you gave me and my team all the info on the girls the Williams brothers took?"

"Yes…"

Jake cleared his throat, already knowing this conversation was going to be just as bad if not worse than the one he'd had with the guys. "We got an alert that someone was looking for one of the girls, Beth Doherty, and we—"

"Beth Doherty?" James repeated, his tone intensifying. "What happened?"

"We went and got her because we haven't been able to identify who put out the job or who took it."

"So, she's safe?"

"Yeah," Jake answered. "We're at my team's compound, and we've been hitting dead-ends everywhere, but that's not why—"

"I've got contacts who can help out. Just have your technology lead contact me and I'll get it organized," James interrupted, and Jake clenched his teeth. He usually didn't have a problem with James Hawkins, but the man had a terrible fucking habit of interrupting the moment he had something to add to a conversation.

"Sure, thanks," he muttered, but quickly corrected himself. "Sorry, I really am grateful for the help because we've been banging our heads against the wall on this one, and I'm honestly running out of trees to shake. That's just not exactly what I was calling you about."

"Well, whatever you need to handle the situation, just bill me for it. All I ask is that you don't mention any of this to Thalia," James said. "Now, what were you calling for?"

Dammit.

"I appreciate the offer to take on the expenses but—"

"I'm assuming Thalia will *eventually* learn about whatever is going on, and then she'll learn that I was aware, which she won't be happy about," James explained. "So, for my sake, let me handle the expenses so I have something in my pocket to convince my beautiful wife that I did all we could to help."

He's a fucking billionaire, just take it.

"Okay, James. I get it, and I appreciate it. I'll have Brendan reach out to you today, and I'll make sure to send you a bill after this shit is handled." Jake sighed, hating that this was sounding more like a business meeting than what he actually needed. "I have to be honest, though. I won't tell Thalia anything, and I'll make sure my guys don't… but I'm not going to tell Beth what she can or can't post on that forum."

"I can accept that," he replied, apparently shrugging off the potential issue. "So, what else were you calling about?"

"Um… it's more of a personal thing." The silence was uncomfortable, and at one point Jake actually checked the phone to see if the call was still on. "James?"

"I'm here, and I have to admit I'm interested," he said. "What personal things do you want to talk to me about?"

Just spit it out.

"So, Beth is here with us, like I said, and I've been spending time with her," he babbled, knowing he sounded like an idiot. *I blame Charlie.* "I mean, we've had the opportunity to spend time together, and— Shit. Okay, I'm just trying to say that we've gotten close, so I wanted to give you a call and see what advice you might have for me."

"My advice is simple, Jake. Keep your bloody hands to yourself and do your job. Kill whoever comes after her and then return Beth to her family."

You've got to be fucking kidding me.

"Keep my hands to myself?" he repeated, not even bothering to hide the anger in his voice. "You mean like you did with Thalia?"

"I made mistakes, and it almost cost us everything we have now," James replied, doing a decent job of obscuring how pissed he was behind his fancy accent. "However, Beth is more damaged than Thalia was, and I still didn't handle things well. Do you really think you're—"

"I think that at a minimum, I never helped fund the motherfuckers that did this to either of them."

James' next words were ice cold. "You called me asking for advice, Jake, and I've given it."

"So, that's it?" he snapped. "I'm just supposed to treat her like everyone else has? Like she's too fucking damaged to ever have anything normal? To ever have anyone interested in her?"

"You've already touched her, haven't you." It wasn't a question, and Jake didn't feel like responding anyway. He just let the silence stretch, perfectly happy to let James stew, and then he heard the man laugh softly. "But… you haven't slept with her yet."

"I do have some self-control," he muttered.

"But that's wearing thin?" James asked, and he sounded a little calmer.

"It's not…" Jake groaned under his breath. "She wants… she asked me and—"

"Ah."

"Yeah."

James made a thoughtful sound before eventually going straight for the kill shot. "Well, are you going to?"

"Fuck this, I shouldn't have called you," Jake grumbled. "Tell Thalia— actually, never mind. Don't even mention—"

"Bloody hell, Jake," he interrupted, laughing quietly. "You've already insulted me, don't back down now."

"Stop screwing with me then and give me some actual fucking advice!"

"Fine," James said, letting out a sigh, and Jake was pretty sure he heard ice shifting in a glass. *A drink would have been smart before this.* "First, answer one question."

"What?"

"Do you love her?" James asked the question carefully. No mocking tone or anger beneath the words, which would have been easier to deal with.

Love was just such a big fucking word. He obviously cared about her, that wasn't even a question in his mind. And he already knew he'd put his life on the line and kill anyone that tried to hurt her… but the rest of his team cared about her, too, and they'd never hesitated to pull a trigger.

Wanting to tear her clothes off and fuck her brains out isn't love either, dipshit.

"Dammit, I—"

"Wait," James interrupted, *again*, and Jake almost laughed out loud at the insanity. "Before you answer, I want to be clear. It doesn't matter how long you've known her, or what's happened to either of you in your time together. I'm asking for your instinct. When you think about her, what do your instincts tell you? And why, of all the women you could pursue, did you choose her?"

"That's a lot to think about," he grumbled.

"It's a big question, but an important one before we continue the conversation." The clatter of ice came over the line, and Jake knew for sure that on the other side of the world, James was sitting down with a glass of some fancy liquor, waiting for him to figure out what the fuck was going on in his head.

Isn't this why you called him?

Jake dropped his head back against the metal siding of the workshop, tapping his skull again and again as he turned over the questions James asked him. Maybe if he hit his head enough times, an answer would shake out?

Not fucking likely.

Okay, forget love. What were his instincts? Thinking back to the first time he'd seen her file, Jake remembered being fascinated. Amazed. He'd seen a reflection of Thalia in Beth's story — which wasn't surprising considering their shared histories — but it wasn't even specific to the horrors. It was the strength to survive it. He'd respected her before he'd seen her for the first time. And then... she'd been all he could think about.

He'd wanted her even when he knew he shouldn't.

His instincts had told him to protect her, but if he was honest with himself, he'd always wanted more than that. There was just... something about her.

Something that no other woman could hold a candle to. Even thinking about being with someone other than Beth pissed him off.

So, according to James Hawkins, that was love?

Apparently.

"Fuck… I…" Jake scrubbed a hand over his face, debating, but he decided to trust his instincts, no matter how insane it sounded. "Yeah, I think I love her."

"You *think* you love her?"

"Screw you, James," he snapped, groaning. "Sometimes I really want to hit you, you know that?"

"Based on my experience with Kalen, that just makes us friends."

"Maybe I should call the Scot then," Jake muttered.

"You called me because my wife was taken by those bastards, and even though I was one of the bastards watching… we moved past it. We made it. I simply want to know if you're in this for more than just your hero complex."

Fucker. "Beth is not some goddamn conquest."

"So, you'll still be interested even when her life is no longer in danger, and she's doing well?" James pressed.

"That's exactly what I want for her, and if she'll let me, I'd like to be there to enjoy it with her." *Oh shit.* He'd started that sentence defending himself against James' bullshit, but as soon as he said it out loud… he realized it was the truth. The idea of a real life with Beth hadn't even popped into his head because there were still so many fucking obstacles in the way, but if he *could* have it? He'd take it in a second.

"Good. And you love her already, don't you?"

"Yeah... I do," he said, and this time he felt sure.

"Listen, our situations are different, Jake. I'm not going to pretend I know Beth or her particular issues well, and we honestly haven't had enough drinks together for me to have any idea of your particular kinks, but I can tell you that despite the way Thalia and I got together, I knew I loved her almost immediately... it just took me a long time to admit it to myself. But those first few weeks, months even, were all about convincing her I didn't just want part of her, and you have to do the same thing."

"What does that even mean?"

James sighed, taking another drink. "It means... you're going to see marks on her body that remind you of everything that's happened to her, and you'll want to kill someone over it — but those marks are a part of her, and so you have to learn to love them too. Every scar, every mark... every tattoo. She needs to know you want her exactly as she is, broken parts included."

"But I do," he argued.

"Convincing them is a lot harder than saying it," James replied, and his tone hinted at just how difficult that could have been for him and Thalia.

"Okay, how do I convince her?

"Show her that none of the marks scare you off. Don't avoid them. Kiss every inch of her. Be soft when she needs comfort, and... don't if or when she wants that."

"Yeah, I, uh— I'm not sure I want to talk to you about that."

"Understood. Just don't treat her like you have to be gentle with her because that will only piss her off. But pay attention, because whether they want to admit it or not, they *are* fragile in some ways, and sometimes your job is just to help hold her together until a bad moment passes."

"So, be perfect, and psychic, and everything will go smoothly," Jake mumbled sarcastically.

"Basically." James laughed, a much warmer and more honest laugh than any of the ones before. "It's not going to be easy, Jake. I didn't begin this conversation by telling you to keep your hands to yourself simply to be a prat. It was my honest advice, because there will never be a day that the Williams brothers don't cast a shadow somewhere on her life. But, as I've said before, you've never chosen the easy path, so I'm not surprised you fell for her. The strength it takes to survive… they're pretty amazing, aren't they?"

"Yeah," he breathed. "Unbelievable."

"Well, if you do have any questions on BDSM I—"

"I think I'm good," Jake interrupted.

"I was going to suggest you call Kalen and take a trip to Purgatory once you're settled in."

"Purgatory?"

"It's the facility he and Maggie operate, but there's no rush," James said. "Think of that as a next step if you end up moving in a similar direction as we did. First, you have to actually take the girl to bed and not disappoint her."

"I don't disappoint."

"Good to know!" James chuckled. "If that's everything, I'll wish you well then. Just a word of caution. Screw this up and I don't think Thalia will be extending any further invitations for you or the team to visit. Well, she may just leave your name off."

Hello, landmine.

"So, no pressure."

"Absolutely none," James replied, once again sounding like a fucking British aristocrat.

Jake had a lot of shit to think about, which was good. He needed to think things through before he crossed any more lines with Beth. And even though the conversation had started rough, the man had been helpful for all the reasons Jake had wanted to call him. Whether or not either of them agreed with each other's decisions, James was the only man on the planet he knew who could actually speak from experience.

Clearing his throat again, Jake stood up from the rusted bench and did his best to sound sincere. "Thanks, James."

"You're welcome. Feel free to call again if you have updates on Beth, or questions you think I can assist with," James replied, sounding friendly until all the warmth suddenly left his tone. "However, just to be clear, this will be the last time you insult my relationship with my wife. Understood?"

"Got it." Jake didn't get the chance to say anything else because James had already ended the call. It was probably some tactic to ensure he got the final word, but Jake didn't regret reminding the man of his history from time to time.

Plus, it erased any potential guilt for charging him the expenses of keeping Beth safe. His offer to help on the tech side of things was good, too. They needed a new lead, and if he could get the team something to sink their teeth into, then they'd all feel a little better.

Not that getting money and resources out of James Hawkins was going to make them forgive him. No, Charlie had been right when he said Jake had launched himself into a minefield.

There were so many ways things could go wrong, and any mistake with Beth would absolutely destroy his relationship with Thalia, and therefore James, and it would probably tear apart his team as well. But when he thought about a future where he'd fucked things up with her, none of those outcomes were even on his radar.

Beth was all that mattered.

And if it came down to a future with her or without her, there was no contest. He'd either be with her, or his life wouldn't be worth shit.

Maybe that's how he really knew it was love. The early stages, obviously, but every part of him was completely in agreement — Beth was his future.

Now, to get to that future, all he had to do was kill the bastards who were coming after her, hunt down the psychopath who'd dared to try and take her, somehow figure out how to tiptoe through the minefield of their growing sexual relationship, and keep his team from staging a coup and burying him in a shallow grave in the desert.

Easy.

Yep, no pressure at all.

It was just their entire future on the line.

THE END

About the Author

Jennifer Bene is a *USA Today* bestselling author of dangerously sexy and deviously dark romance. From BDSM, to Suspense, Dark Romance, and Thrillers—she writes it all. Always delivering a twisty, spine-tingling journey with the promise of a happily-ever-after.

Don't miss a release! Sign up for the newsletter to get new book alerts (and a free welcome book) at: http://jenniferbene.com/newsletter

---

You can find her online throughout social media with username @jbeneauthor and on her website: www.jenniferbene.com

Also By Jennifer Bene

Jasmine

Crazy Broken Love

Standalone BDSM Ménage Romance

The Invitation

Reunited

Dark Suspense / Horror

Burned: An Inferno World Novella

Scorched: A New Beginning

Noxious *(Anathema Book 1)*

Mephitic *(Anathema Book 2)*

Viperous *(Anathema Book 3)*

Appearances in the Black Light Series (BDSM Romance)

Black Light: Exposed *(Black Light Series Book 2)*

Black Light: Valentine Roulette *(Black Light Series Book 3)*

Black Light: Roulette Redux *(Black Light Series Book 7)*

Black Light: Celebrity Roulette *(Black Light Series Book 12)*

Black Light: Charmed *(Black Light Series Book 15)*

Black Light: Roulette War *(Black Light Series Book 16)*

Black Light: The Beginning *(Black Light Series Book 17.5)*

Black Light: Unbound *(Black Light Series Book 18)*

Black Light: Roulette Rematch *(Black Light Series Book 20)*

BOOKS RELEASED AS CASSANDRA FAYE

The Clarity Series (Dark Omegaverse Reverse Harem Romance)

Alpha's Clarity *(Clarity Series Book 1)*

Alpha's Promise *(Clarity Series Book 2)*

Alpha's Bond *(Clarity Series Book 3)*

Alpha's Trust *(Clarity Series Book 4)*

Daughters of Eltera Series (Dark Fantasy Romance)

Fae *(Daughters of Eltera Book 1)*

Tara *(Daughters of Eltera Book 2)*

Standalone Paranormal Romance

Hunted *(The Dirty Heroes Collection Book 13)*

One Crazy Bite

Dangerous Magic

Made in the USA
Las Vegas, NV
22 July 2022